# THE
# SOLOMON
# ORGANIZATION

*The Need*

*Sister, Sister*

*Immortals*

*Devil's Advocate*

*Blood Child*

*Perfect Little Angels*

*Surrogate Child*

*Playmates*

*Illusion*

*Reflection*

*Love Child*

*Sight Unseen*

*Teacher's Pet*

*Child's Play*

*Night Howl*

*Imp*

*Tender Loving Care*

*Someone's Watching*

*Brainchild*

*Pin*

*Weekend*

*Sisters*

# THE SOLOMON ORGANIZATION

## ANDREW NEIDERMAN

G. P. Putnam's Sons • New York

G. P. Putnam's Sons
*Publishers Since 1838*
200 Madison Avenue
New York, NY 10016

Library of Congress Cataloging-in-Publication Data
Neiderman, Andrew.
    The Solomon organization / Andrew Neiderman.
        p.    cm.
    ISBN 0-399-13806-4
    I. Title.
PS3564.E27S65    1993                    92-36566 CIP
813'.54—dc20

Printed in the United States of America
1   2   3   4   5   6   7   8   9   10

FOR MY COUSIN KEITH,
A GENTLE SOUL WHO TOUCHED US ALL

# Prologue

**M**eg Lester hurried back to her car in the Kwik Stop parking lot, her long, shapely legs gliding with quick determination. She placed the grocery bag on the floor of the passenger's side and eased into the glove-leather driver's seat of what Scott called their gently used Mercedes 580 SL. Her part-time work, which she had assumed would take her well into the late afternoon, had been aborted because her employer, Jonathan Sanders, had had to fly up to San Francisco. She'd been on her way to pick up her daughter Justine, when the sight of the Kwik Stop reminded her they needed milk. It would be easier to stop here, drop off the milk at the house, and then go fetch Justine, she thought.

Because today was a day for teachers' meetings and school was closed, Scott had agreed to take Justine with him to work. It was easy for him to have her at the car dealership. Old man Miller was crazy about Justine, and Scott had long periods of time between customers when he could amuse her.

So the instant Meg spotted Scott's car in the driveway of their two-story home in Westwood, she suspected Justine had gotten sick. She turned into the drive quickly, grabbed the grocery bag, got out of the car, and practically sprinted to the front door. When she stepped into the house, the silence that greeted her convinced her she was right. Maybe Justine had come down with one of those stomach viruses again, she concluded. She hurried through the hallway to the kitchen to put away the milk. As soon as she had, she turned to go upstairs when she noticed the powdery remnants and straws on the kitchen table. Her heart suddenly felt hollow.

She approached the table slowly and then touched the powder with the tip of her finger. She brought it to her tongue even though she really didn't need to substantiate what she had seen too many times before.

How could Scott do this? He'd promised he'd stop and he had Justine with him. Meg hurried to the stairway and marched up the steps, her heart pounding so hard, she could feel the thump reverberate in the back of her head. Just as she reached the top, she heard the laugh. It had the effect of an invisible wall, stopping her dead in her tracks. She listened and heard a moan. Her gaze went from the door to the bedroom she and Scott shared to Justine's bedroom door, which was slightly open.

For a moment Meg feared she wouldn't catch her breath again. She would literally asphyxiate here on the second-story landing of their home. Finally, she willed her legs to move her forward and she approached their bedroom door. She opened it in increments of no more than an inch at a time, until she could look in and see the back and buttocks of the naked woman straddling naked Scott. They were oblivious to any witness and continued. For a moment Meg was intrigued, more than shocked. It was as if her husband of nine years had been thrust into a porno movie.

The woman threw her head back and moaned. Scott's hands jetted up to her breasts, cupping and squeezing, the fingers tapping out an unheard erotic melody. The woman moaned louder and louder until she opened her eyes and caught the reflection of Meg in the mirror over the vanity table to the right of the bed. She froze.

"Oh shit," she cried.

Scott opened his eyes.

"What?" He looked at the woman's face and then turned to see Meg standing there. His mouth fell open stupidly and then his lips began to move without his uttering a sound.

"Justine!" Meg screamed and slammed the door shut. She ran to her daughter's room and found her on the floor by her bed doodling with a crayon and a coloring book. Justine looked up with surprise as Meg lunged at her. Her daughter was a tall five-year-old, but Meg didn't hesitate. With what seemed incredible strength, she scooped Justine off the floor and into her arms. Then she spun around and flew out the door to the stairs.

"Mommy!"

Meg's eyes were wide, her mouth pulled back in the corners. It was as if they were fleeing from a house on fire. In fact, Meg would not be able to recall how she had done it. Somehow, flying down those stairs with Justine in her arms, she didn't lose her balance. She burst out the front door and charged across the lawn, never once thinking it would be more logical to get into her car.

Instead, she ran along the sidewalk. Drivers going by looked with curiosity, but none stopped to inquire why a woman was running with a five-year-old child in her arms. There didn't appear to be anyone chasing her. Here in Los Angeles, just as in any major city, people rarely poked into each other's business, first out of fear, and second because of a coat of insensitivity that formed protectively to shield them from the dozens and dozens of tragedies that visited their streets daily.

"Mommy!" Justine finally screamed. She was being bounced so hard, her pigtails flew up over her head.

The moment Meg came to her senses, exhaustion set in. The muscles in her legs and back ached. It felt like a switchblade had been jabbed in between her ribs. She stopped and lowered Justine to the walk.

The child was crying now, sobbing silently, her little shoulders rising and falling.

"Oh, honey," Meg gasped. She knelt down and embraced her daughter. "I'm sorry, sweetheart. Mommy didn't mean to frighten you."

Justine wiped her eyes.

"Why are we running, Mommy? Where are we going?"

"Going?" Meg stood up and looked around. Where were they going? She thought for a moment and then seized Justine's hand. "Come along," she said.

She walked her to the corner and turned right. They went nearly another five blocks before stopping at Sharma Corman's house. Of all her friends, Sharma was the most competent and dependable. Sharma was the sort who knew the best doctor for each ailment, the best beautician, the best person to do nails, the best masseuse. She even knew the best plumber. And what was equally impressive was the fact she always had all the relevant information—addresses, phone numbers—at her fingertips.

Meg pressed the doorbell and waited, her chest still heaving, the aches and pains unrelenting. Marta, Sharma's Mexican maid, opened the door.

"Mrs. Lester, buenos días."

"I must see Mrs. Corman, Marta."

The maid saw the pain and tension in Meg's face and the

confusion and fear in Justine's. For a moment she was frozen, unable to act.

"Quickly, please, Marta."

"Right away, Mrs. Lester." She rushed back to get her. Meg stepped into the house. She tried to catch her breath and then knelt down to brush the creases out of Justine's dress. The child still looked quite terrified.

"It's all right, honey. It's all right."

"Meg!" Sharma said, coming quickly from her den. "Patricia and I were just talking on the telephone about you. We were . . . what's wrong, Meg?" she asked, now that she was close enough to take in Meg Lester's demeanor.

"Oh, Sharma," Meg said and immediately burst into tears.

Sharma Corman had been through it before. She knew.

"The bastard," she said and took Meg into her arms, while Justine gaped up in shock and fear at the scene unfolding before her.

# 1

Scott Lester felt like he was burning up. Everything was closing in on him. The sweat trickled down his temples and his shirt collar had become a hangman's noose, tightening more and more with every word spoken against him. He couldn't believe this was happening, even though he was actually here in the courtroom.

"We're asking, Your Honor," Meg's attorney had begun, "that Mrs. Lester be granted sole custody of Justine and that Mr. Lester's contact with the child be limited to supervised visits, at least for the remainder of these formative years."

The judge had nodded. Scott had felt his scowl and thought the expression on his face was as good as an agreement, even before all the evidence was revealed. Maybe he would have been better off with a female judge than a man who looked like everyone's grandfather.

"I thought we had become civilized when it came to divorces and children," Scott complained to his attorney, Michael Fein. "And that kids didn't have to be dragged through this garbage."

"That's true to a large extent with what we would call amicable divorces, but it doesn't mean the state relinquishes its right and responsibility to look after the welfare of minors. The state won't assign custody to a parent who is shown to be addicted to drugs and alcohol and irresponsible, one who can't provide the child with a safe and moral environment. Which is what your wife and her attorney are out to prove," he added dryly.

"That's bullshit. She's just out for revenge."

"Maybe so, but these witnesses testifying to your cocaine habit, your failure to be where you are supposed to be; witnesses telling the court you brought a minor into a bar to sit in the corner and wait while you drank and flirted with other women . . . these bar bills, these bills from liquor mart," his lawyer rattled on as he flipped through Meg's attorney's brief, "won't look like bullshit to the court. And that boss of yours didn't do us any good either, admitting to your tardiness, your failure to show, your problem with tried-and-true customers lately."

"I'm going to lose my job because of this," Scott whined. "She'll get me fired and then I won't be able to come up with child support or house payments or . . ."

"That's not her problem; it's yours."

"It's going to be hers, too, damn it. I can't believe she actually put a detective on me and sent him around interviewing my boss and practically everyone I know. She's not capable of doing all these things," Scott declared.

"She did it."

"She didn't do it . . . her pack of female sharks did it," he muttered and gestured at the women who sat right behind Meg.

They'd been at Meg's side through the whole ordeal: Patricia Longstreet, who even before this latest catastrophe, never missed an opportunity to put him down; Brooke Thomas, the prettiest of Meg's confidants who had been a model in New York before marrying a record producer and moving out to Los Angeles. Scott had made the mistake of hitting on her a few times. Now, she was one of Meg's witnesses, eager to describe that afternoon he showed up at her home to offer her a hit and a matinee.

"I literally had to push him out the door," she claimed in the prehearing testimony. "He was already high and he was driving!"

And then there was Sharma, the worst shark of all, whom he believed hated men in general and him particularly. If she could have castrated her first husband, she would have. She was the one who had told Meg all men are cavemen at heart. *Don't ever trust your husband.* How self-satisfied she looked sitting there listening to the testimony against him and watching Meg's lawyer construct the picture of him as an unfit father. Every time Sharma looked his way, she smiled triumphantly.

He sighed and sank deeper and deeper into his seat as the proceeding continued. Soon he would be under this table, he thought.

Scott had already consented to the division of assets, including the house. But the problem with the house was neither of them had the means to buy the other out. They had to wait for a buyer to come along, which might take awhile given the current slump in the real estate market. In the meantime, he had to move out, still keeping up his share of the mortgage and house payments. And, in addition, he now had to carry the rent for his new crummy apartment. After child support, he'd be lucky to have enough left over for a decent pair of new shoes.

But that wasn't enough to satisfy Meg. She was going to pound him into the ground and use Justine as the hammer. Despite his extramarital activities, he believed he loved Justine as much as Meg did. One thing should have nothing to do with the other. But Meg was determined to win sole custody. She would deny him all visitation rights if she could.

Hours later, Scott lowered his head like a flag of defeat and then suddenly turned to focus on the man sitting in the rear of the courtroom. It was as though he had felt the man's eyes on his neck. Aside from the courtroom officials, his attorney, Meg's attorney, Meg's friends, and the few witnesses Meg's attorney had brought, there was no one else present, no one but this man. None of Scott's so-called buddies had the time.

Scott couldn't account for the man's presence. He looked too old to be a law student observing. He could be another attorney, Scott thought. Someone who'd arrived early and was just sitting in to pass time.

But the man smiled at him and nodded as if they were friends. Did he know him?

Scott welcomed this distraction. Things weren't going his way. His attorney had never been optimistic from the start and even appeared reluctant to take his case.

"I would like to adjourn at this point," the judge declared, "and resume ten o'clock Monday morning."

No one offered any opposition. When the proceeding ended, Scott gazed at Meg, but she wouldn't look his way. The night before he had had a nightmare in which Meg was pushing him into a freshly dug grave. He was struggling to pull himself up, and she stomped on his hands and swung a shovel at his head. The first spoonful of dirt in his face woke him and he sat up sweating and gasping for breath. His heart was pounding so hard he had to put on the light and inspect his hands to see if he had any bruises. It was that vivid a dream.

How difficult it was now even to imagine being head over heels in love with her. She had become so hateful, so distasteful to him, that simply conjuring her image riled him, churned his stomach, and drove his blood pressure sky-high.

He and Meg had met at his business college in Albany, New York. At the time, Meg was working in the secretarial pool. She was from Jamestown, a small city located in the western part of the state. A more innocent and unassuming girl, he couldn't have found. To her, Albany was a major city. She had never been to New York or to Boston or Philadelphia, and California . . . that was like another planet.

But he loved her that way. He used to tell her she was like a "drink of fresh water." She had an honesty, a simplicity that made it easy for him to relax when they were together. There was no subterfuge, no conniving, nothing more beguiling than her soft blue eyes and light brown hair; nothing more tantalizing than the patches of freckles on the crowns of each of her cheeks, than her naturally ruby lips and the dimple in her chin; and there was nothing more sexually enticing than her long legs hidden under those full-length skirts and her surprisingly full bosom, a wonderful discovery the first time they made love. She had no need for Fredericks-of-Hollywood lingerie to titillate him when they slept together; she wore no heavy makeup when they went out. She was a natural girl, delightfully naive about her own gifts. It was like stumbling on an uncut diamond.

It had been his idea to live in Los Angeles. He had been there only once before, but he had been smitten by the glitter of sunlight on the hoods and trunks of Mercedes convertibles, the tall palm trees, the bright foliage, the rhythm of the city, the beaches and the music. Everywhere else people ate to live and worked to eat; here they lived to eat and worked to play, at least on the Westside where beautiful women dressed in expensive fashions and young hunks in tight jeans paraded down the clean sidewalks and streets as if they were already cast in a movie and were simply rehearsing their moves and lines.

The magic of L.A. seemed to be that everyone was in the movie business, no matter how simple their work. Beauticians strove to cut the hair of celebrities, store clerks packed groceries for Linda Hamilton, John Candy, or Steve Martin; real estate agents sold the former homes of Bette Davis, Clark Gable, or Tom Selleck. You didn't have to be a successful lawyer or doctor to exchange a few words with last year's Academy Award nominees; you just had to be here, waiting. Sooner or later, it would happen; they would come.

He had a list of celebrity clients himself and was on first-name basis with two of the biggest producers in Hollywood. He had sold each of them a couple of cars, as well as a few to their wives and girlfriends.

At first Meg was afraid of Los Angeles. It was too spread out; it made Albany look like a village. The weather was warm but the people were cool, she would say. She cried; she missed her family, she complained about the traffic, the smog, and the crime. But he didn't give in and soon she accommodated herself to their lifestyle in ways he never imagined she would.

If he hadn't brought her here, she wouldn't have changed, he thought. She might still be that uncut diamond and not a sophisticate who had discovered the need to be her own person. How you going to keep them down on the farm once they've seen Rodeo Drive?

Now he regretted introducing her to the women who he believed had poisoned her against him, even before she discovered his extracurricular activities. He wanted her to have friends who lived in Beverly Hills, Westwood, and Brentwood. But they had convinced her he was treating her as his slave, his alter ego. In the end they had convinced her to compete with him. He should have kept her locked up in some hick upstate New York town just as she'd once wanted.

Spilled milk, but he would cry over it now. She had the better lawyer; it looked like she was going to win custody of Justine; she lived in the house, and he had to provide support. And all because he had been caught with his pants down.

"What do we do now?" he asked his attorney.

"Nothing," he said.

"Maybe we should go back over some things."

"You can't change facts, Scott," he said. "We'll present our side the best we can under the circumstances."

"What does that mean?"

"Just what I said," Michael Fein replied dryly. "See you ten o'clock on Monday."

Even his own attorney wanted to get away from him as quickly as he could, Scott thought, watching the man hurry up the aisle.

As Scott started up the aisle, he saw that the gentleman in the rear of the courtroom had remained.

"Philip Dante," he said. Scott took his small but long-fingered hand tentatively into his and shook it. Philip Dante smiled. He was only about an inch or so shorter than Scott, who stood nearly six feet tall. Dante's dark blue pin-striped suit was custom fitted to his slim torso. He had a narrow waist and full, firm shoulders. He looked athletic and robust because of his crimson cheeks and lively gray eyes.

"I was passing through the courthouse and just had to stop in to see another poor fish get gutted," Philip Dante told him. "It's reassuring to know you haven't been randomly selected to suffer a singular fate."

"You're here for a divorce, too?"

"I was, and like you, I was crucified on a cross of exaggerations, accusations constructed by my wife's skillful and, I must confess, very talented attorney."

"Yeah," Scott said. "Despite what I was told, my wife's got a better lawyer. I think mine feels worse for her than he does for me."

"There's a bizarre attitude about children and mothers in this society—the courts are heavily weighted in the woman's favor. The truth is more children are ruined by their mothers than by their fathers."

"Absolutely right," Scott agreed. He liked this guy, liked the way he put feelings concretely into words.

"And a sharp lawyer can make Cinderella's stepmother look like Mother Teresa," Dante said.

"Tell me about it."

"You look like you could use a drink," Dante said. "There's a little pub I've discovered nearby, a retreat I went to during the recesses. Care to join me?"

"Sure," Scott said. "Why not? I don't think she has her detective on my tail anymore, not that it matters."

Dante laughed, a short, thin laugh through clenched teeth. He started out, Scott alongside.

It resembled a Dublin pub: small and cozy with what looked to be a regular bar crowd. No one there took much more than perfunctory interest in Philip Dante and Scott when they entered. They sat at a booth and talked, Scott more loquacious than usual because he found this stranger receptive and understanding, smiling and sneering at the right times. Also, feeling deserted by his friends, Scott had a great need to open up to someone sympathetic. He had no family here and Steve, his older brother back in New York, was like a stranger to him. They were so dissimilar, Steve always more settled, more responsible and reliable, the kind of man who seemed forty when he was only twenty. When Scott called to tell him about the divorce, Steve said he had expected it.

"Everyone who goes out there gets messed up in one way or another," he said with his typical New York superiority. "The hedonism takes its toll quickly. You've got no one to blame but yourself, Scott. I'm sorry for you. Meg was a gem."

The annoying thing was, Scott couldn't refute his brother. He and Meg had become just another statistic, perhaps a predictable one.

"I can't believe this is all happening to me," Scott said. "I feel like I'm sliding down a greased tunnel . . . nothing to grasp . . . nothing to stop it, know what I mean?"

"Exactly," Dante said.

"Two days ago, I called her. I wanted to get my computer. We have this temporary agreement set up that I have to call first."

"I had that, too. I couldn't come before nine in the morning or after six in the afternoon."

"Yeah, I have the same limits."

"Standard stuff. They all follow the same handbook," Dante said. Scott nodded.

"Anyway, when I get there, I found she had put all my stuff in the garage: clothes, papers, even my pistol. Slowly but surely, anything and everything that's related to me, that reminds her of me, she's getting out of the house. Soon my daughter will wonder if I ever existed," he added bitterly.

"I know," Philip said softly.

Scott looked up, encouraged to go on.

"I was thinking of getting a photograph of her attorney and blowing it up to make a dart board. Did you hear him in that courtroom? His face haunts me. I mean, it's as though she was his kid sister or something, for God's sake."

"He's just doing his job," Dante said with surprising tolerance and understanding. Scott's eyebrows rose. "If you don't respect your enemy, you defeat yourself."

"I'll remember that next time," Scott replied. "Not that there'll ever be a next time."

Dante laughed.

"You'll change your mind, buddy. Sometime down the road, you'll run into another goddess and be ready to throw yourself on the sacrificial altar."

"Not me," Scott vowed. "Never again." He sat back and closed his eyes. He hated himself for being so negative. He was only thirty-one and he felt as if life itself was a burden these days. The sun was never bright enough and the stars were never blazing anymore. It was as though some evil deity had thrown a filter over everything, turning white to gray and making everything else pale accordingly. He hated looking at himself in the mirror anymore. Staring back at him was this sad sack with bags under his sleepy, chestnut brown eyes, a complexion like a boiled potato, and dark brown hair that looked flat and dull. He had lost weight, picking and nibbling on T.V. dinners and fast food. Nothing tasted good anyway. Nothing pleased him. His attitude had affected everything, especially his work. When he caught the reflection of himself in the showroom windows, he saw a man who looked weighed down, overwhelmed, trampled. And he knew he couldn't be a depressing pessimist and sell expensive automobiles.

"You're a car salesman?" Dante asked him as if he could read his thoughts.

"Yeah. I've been with Miller Mercedes in Westwood as long as I've been in L.A. Me and the old man hit it off from the start. It was an unwritten understanding that as soon as the old man retired, his son Wayne would step into his shoes and I would become head of sales. I don't think there's much hope of that happening now."

"Don't count yourself completely out yet," Dante said, offering the first note of optimism.

"It doesn't look too good. The old man turned out to be a better witness for Meg than for me. I'm going to find myself on the grass in Santa Monica, sleeping beside other homeless people and lost souls."

Dante laughed.

"It's not funny," Scott said. He didn't like being the object of anyone's humor, and this was really too serious to be humorous. Dante's smile fizzled and his eyes became small, intense.

"No, it's not," he admitted. "I had the same black thoughts, but there's a way out of this."

"Sure. Suicide," Scott said and waved to the waitress. "Another dry Rob Roy please," he ordered. "You want another?"

"I'm fine," Philip said.

"What do you do, Phil?"

"I sell insurance, and like you, my job was in jeopardy. Insurance companies want their salesmen to be straight down the road conservative—rocks of Gibraltar, family men, responsible, reliable, the whole nine yards."

"What do you mean, your job was in jeopardy? It's not anymore?"

"Things couldn't be better for me," Dante said, smiling.

"I don't understand. I thought . . ."

"How old's your daughter?" Dante asked quickly.

"Five."

Dante nodded.

"A great age. They're just starting to learn things in school; they're full of questions and they dote on you. Every moment you're with them is more precious than the moment before. I bet nothing beats the feeling you have when you're holding her little hand and walking with her. I suppose you've taken her to Disneyland."

"And Knots Berry Farm and Universal. I was going to take her to Magic Mountain the weekend . . . the weekend all shit broke loose."

Dante shook his head.

The silence churned Scott's stomach. Visions of Justine looking up at him lovingly when he came home passed through his mind and were quickly followed by the memory of her eyes moving over the pages of her children's stories when she sat in his lap and he read to her.

The waitress served him his Rob Roy and he brought it to his lips immediately. Then he continued to stare absently at his random memories of Justine.

Dante began, slowly, softly, his voice building as he continued.

"Someday, another man is going to move into your house and sleep in your bed and kiss your child good night. In time, she'll think of him as her father. It's only natural."

Scott fought back the tears building in his eyes. He felt as if his throat would close and he would choke to death at the table.

"It isn't fair," he whined. "I'm not the only one at fault here."

"Oh?" Dante leaned in, obviously more interested in this.

"Sure. We had our minor spats like any two married people," Scott continued quietly. "Then she got in with a group of women . . . the wives of some of my customers . . . female sharks."

"And she changed, I bet," Dante said, "just like my wife."

"Yeah," Scott said, grabbing onto this rationalization. It provided justifications and excuses and hope. What difference did it make if he stretched the truth a bit? He was fighting for his life, for God's sake. "Yeah, she changed. Suddenly, she started comparing us to people in the neighborhood, like the Krammers who own a service station and have one of the biggest houses, drive expensive cars . . . Lillian Krammer was always calling Meg to tell her about something else she had bought . . . rubbing it in. 'Billy Krammer barely graduated high school,' Meg would say, 'and look how they live. A lot of good your business degree and the promises the Millers make do us.' Suddenly, what we once considered a great lifestyle was not good enough."

"Before she married you, was she this money-minded?" Dante asked.

"Hell no. I didn't pretend to be anyone I wasn't or tell her I had a bundle hidden away. We met at my school. She knew what to expect. But we had passion then and it seemed to block out any other concerns," he added sadly. "And Meg was certainly no gold digger."

"Whose idea was it that she go to work?" Dante pursued as if he had assumed the role of Scott's attorney and they were in court.

"Hers. Suddenly being a wife and mother was a . . . a form of slavery, demeaning. She started taking these courses over at UCLA, meeting younger, more aggressive women. I'd come home and find the house a mess."

"Your spats grew more intense," Dante said, anxious to get the story out.

"Exactly. She flitted from one thing to another—EST, Transcendental Meditation—she even flirted with The Church of Enlightenment, whatever the hell that is. Then she got this idea she was an inhibited artist and she was off taking art lessons and making trips up to Topanga Canyon to do nature scenes. But I put up with all of it, hoping she would come to her senses. She says she did all this because I ignored her," Scott said. "But that's her side of it."

"I understand. Completely," Dante replied.

Scott shook his head. "The way her attorney twisted things in that courtroom today, making me sound like a cell keeper."

"You only wanted her to fulfill her responsibilities," Dante offered.

Scott brightened.

"Yeah. That's it. I was working twelve, fourteen hours a day to make the kind of income we now required. The least she could do was see after the house and our daughter."

"So she went to work for . . . an architect?" Dante said. "Jonathan Sanders?"

"Yeah." Scott paused and stepped back into reality. "How'd you know that?"

Dante sat back.

"I confess to being a little more interested in your case. In so many ways, it's like mine."

"How do you mean?"

"Well . . ." Dante looked down. For the first time, Scott noticed how long the man's eyelashes were. Some women found that very sexy, he remembered. As Dante twirled his glass in his fingers, Scott noted the expensive-looking diamond pinky ring in a gold setting. It had a unique shape—triangular. "My wife Victoria caught me with another woman in almost the same way. She's a dental hygienist and she came home from work unexpectedly."

"Oh?"

"This architect your wife works for, Jonathan Sanders . . . handsome man. I've seen him."

"You have?"

Dante nodded.

"Ever suspect there may be hanky-panky between them?"

"No." Scott saw the smirk on Dante's face and reconsidered. "But maybe I should have. Maybe I could have brought that up in court. Maybe . . ."

"It's too late to bring that up before this judge now."

"I bet you're right," Scott said anyway. "I bet Sanders was hitting on her. Now that I think about it, she couldn't wait to go work for him and she always rushed off whenever he called."

"Yes," Dante said, nodding. "They're not as pure in heart as they make out to be in court, eh?"

"No."

"But you'll be the one who suffers the most, not her. That's the way the system works, even here in sophisticated California."

Scott felt the anger in his stomach fester. He realized how hard he was glaring at his vivid recollections of Meg and her sharks and snapped out of his reverie. Dante was smiling.

"So what happened with you?" Scott asked forcefully.

"Oh, me." He shook his head and looked down at the glass he was fingering in his hands. "You'd think I'd be safe . . . she had appointments, people's teeth to clean. Unfortunately, one particular day she had some cancellations."

"And came home early and found you next door humping the neighbor?"

"Yes. My son, Marvin . . . he's four . . . a great kid, sharp as can be and very outgoing. We're pals."

"You didn't take him with you when you went next door to do the neighbor, did you?"

"Oh, no. I left him alone in the house, which got her almost as angry as finding me with Maureen. That was the neighbor's name, Maureen."

"She married?"

"No. A divorcée. Beautiful, very sexy," Dante added, smiling licentiously.

"Yeah, I had a divorcée recently. They can be very, very sexy," Scott said.

"Exactly," Dante said, widening his smile. "After getting it regular so often, they're usually horny and, er . . . willing to do almost anything."

"Yeah, but it doesn't sound like the same situation to me," Scott said and downed the remainder of his Rob Roy. "Adultery is almost the national pastime. The court would still let you share in custody of your son."

"Well." Dante looked down again. "I couldn't take that chance. Not with the attorney my wife had. He brought up other things that would influence a judge, things that were distorted and exaggerated," he added, looking up.

"What do you mean, you couldn't take that chance?" Scott sat back. "How did you turn things around?"

"I was lucky. I ran into a friend who had also suffered through a divorce and custody battle. He told me about the Solomon Organization," Dante said softly.

"The what?"

Dante leaned toward him, very conscious of anyone hearing them speak.

"How much do you love your daughter?"

"It's stupid to even ask."

"I can't promise you they'll help you, but they'll give you a hearing."

"Who will?"

"I told you, the Solomon Organization. It's the court of final appeal for men like us, a private organization, funded by sympathetic, wealthy men."

"What court? Who are they?"

"A couple of lawyers, one's a judge, so they know how much the system's tilted in favor of the wife. There's also a doctor and a psychiatrist, and an educator, a very sensible and qualified group."

"Why do they call themselves the Solomon Organization?"

"Don't you know your Bible? Two women came to King Solomon, both declaring the child was theirs. He ordered the child cut in half and a half given to each, and one woman said, give the child to her.

"Solomon knew that woman was the true mother. She would rather another woman got the baby than the baby die.

"Such wisdom," Philip said, shaking his head in admiration. "And that's what they have—wisdom, the wisdom to know if something should be done and what should be done."

"And you think this . . . organization . . . can help me?"

Dante shrugged.

"Maybe. They'll consider your case, listen to your story, and decide. All I can tell you is they helped me."

"How?"

"My son . . . he lives with me and my mother, not with my wife."

Scott stared, hardly blinking. He realized he was holding his breath.

"Even though the court decided against you?"

"Well, the court never actually rendered a decision," Philip said. "But there was no question what it would have been if it had. Just as there's little question in your case." Dante leaned forward again, his face filled with excitement. "Why don't you make an appeal to the organization. I can set it up right now with a phone call." He looked at his watch. "Time's of the essence. They'll need to read the transcript up to now."

"How can they get that?"

"They have their ways. Well?"

Scott thought. Supervised visits whenever he wanted to see his own flesh and blood, and limited at that.

"Okay," he said quickly. "The way things are going, I'll try anything." Dante smiled.

"Wise decision. I'll be right back. Order me another drink, please, and one more for yourself," Dante said, rising.

Scott signaled the waitress and then sat back wondering exactly what it was he had agreed to do.

# 2

Meg Lester didn't join the chorus of laughter around her at the front window table in Antonio's Trattoria. Instead, she turned away to gaze at a man and woman strolling hand in hand along the sidewalk on San Vincente Boulevard in Brentwood. Occasionally, they would pause to look at something in one of the upscale stores, and whenever they did so, the man would move his arm around the woman's shoulders and draw her closer, embracing her as if he was terrified of losing her.

Scott and she were once like that, Meg thought. She would never have dreamed then that she'd be sitting here after the start of a brutalizing divorce proceeding, her marriage in ruins. She continued to watch the couple, ignoring the joviality around her.

Meg was tired of perfunctory laughter anyway, tired of participating in the cackle just so no one would feel uncomfortable, so no one would stop to offer her suggestions or voice her pity. She was tired of putting on an act. As far as she was concerned, what they said about Los Angeles was true: so many people were so immersed in illusions, so affected by the film and television world everywhere around them that they all became performers. All of them, including her, walked around imagining theme music in the background.

As if to demonstrate her thought, a very attractive, tall young woman with ebony hair streaming down over her shoulders paused on the grass mall in the center of the boulevard and posed: her right hand on her hip, her left hand combing through her hair. She wore a metallic blue, skin-tight exercise suit that made her small rear end glitter in the California sunshine. Practically every male driver spun around. Horns blared, brakes squealed. The woman tossed her hair back with a quick gesture and continued to cross the street, her long legs moving to the rhythm of her own soundtrack.

Meg sighed, realizing how much she longed to be young again, just starting, just discovering. She felt as if the events of the past few weeks had aged her years, and she certainly didn't feel like the heroine some of her girlfriends were making her out to be. What's more, she was growing tired of these so-called victory celebrations: wine and cheese parties, lunches and dinners with just the girls, two of whom here at the table were already on their second marriages. Whatever happened to the idea that a failed marriage was a tragedy, not something to be celebrated?

Sure, she hated Scott for what he had been doing and she hated who he had become, but there was a Scott with whom she had fallen in love and with whom she had had a child, a Scott in whom she had once placed all her trust, a man who was full of promise and affection, who thought the day began with her smile and ended when she kissed him goodnight and turned over in bed to go to sleep.

What about the memories of their courting—the funny little

things he used to do, the way he would pop up unannounced, pretending coincidence; what about that wonderful period when they lived on impulse and improvisation, when it was nothing for her to put aside all her plans and get into his car and with no luggage, nothing, rush off to spend a weekend at some cabin retreat near Lake George?

What should she really do with all those cards filled with romantic words . . . the cartons of pictures from their vacations, the special little gifts he surprised her with at dinners? Burn them as Sharma had suggested? She still hadn't brought their marriage certificate to the girls to stage their ceremonial bonfire. She claimed she couldn't find it. As much as she hated the Scott who now existed, she loved the one who had been. But it was painful to cling to the good memories. Sharma might not be wrong, she thought.

"Why are you so pensive, Meg?" Patricia Longstreet asked. "Are you feeling okay?"

Meg nodded quickly, but looked down, aware that everyone's eyes had been drawn to her.

"I'm just tired," she said. "Every morning I wake up hoping it's all been a dream, a nightmare. I was so stupid to ignore the signals, to let so many things slide by. Instead of confronting our problems head-on, I dove into every possible distraction I could find." She raised her head, her eyes burning with tears. "Just like a stupid ostrich."

"Don't worry, honey. As soon as this is over, you'll get over him," Sharma Corman said, sharply, "and faster than you think."

"Will I? I don't think I'll ever forget the man I married," Meg said.

"What do you mean, Meg?" Brooke Thomas asked.

"I didn't divorce the man I married," Meg said. "I divorced a complete stranger."

Everyone was quiet for a moment, digesting Meg's thought. Sharma found it disagreeable and smirked; Brooke maintained her angelic smile, and Patricia narrowed her eyes and softened her lips in the corners. She was a redhead with a cherry blossom complexion, small featured, the daintiest of the clan and the most intelligent, as far as Meg was concerned. Patricia worked part-time as a coverage reader for one of the better known movie producers.

"What are you planning to do when this is all over, Meg?" she asked.

"What do you mean, what is she planning to do? She's planning to do better," Sharma declared.

"I might go home," Meg said, staring down at her bowl of Angel hair and tomatoes. She had barely eaten.

"Home?" Sharma said, sitting forward. The tall brunette sat back with an arrogant air. She twisted her mouth and squinted as if in pain. "You don't mean . . . back to New York to that boondock town you were brought up in, do you?"

Meg shrugged.

"My sister wants me to come home," she said. She smiled. "Abby's four years older than I am and has been married happily for nearly ten years. They have three children. She thinks I'd be better off where I have family and lots of old friends."

"Well that's good for her," Sharma said, "but not for you."

"How do you know what's good for her?" Brooke snapped. All of a sudden there was a minor rebellion at the table in Anthony's Trattoria.

"That's running away!" Sharma Corman declared. "That's letting a man ruin your life. Don't go off with your tail between your legs. Show him you can make it without him."

"Sometimes that's easier said than done," Patricia Longstreet said softly. "We need them."

"We don't need them!" Sharma Corman insisted.

"Speak for yourself, Sharma," Brooke Thomas said. "I need them." She smiled licentiously, setting Sharma off on one of her favorite themes.

"Sure we have sexual needs; sure we want romance and we want to be loved, but if we let them think we need them more than they need us, they'll revert to the cavemen they are at heart. Every man wants to conquer every woman, Meg. That's his nature. My first husband Charlie couldn't keep his eyes from following every piece of ass in sight. You've got to keep the reins tight and make sure they know you're no fool.

"You're going to whip his ass from one end of this city to the other in that custody hearing. He should be the one who hightails it out of here, not you."

Lectures and lessons, philosophy and theory, Meg thought, all her girlfriends, everyone in the clan, seemed to be a veteran of one bad affair or another. Everyone had been burned. Somehow all male-female relationships had degenerated into them against us.

This wasn't what she had dreamed and imagined when Scott had proposed. Of course, much of it had to do with the things he had said. Looking back through wiser eyes, Meg sadly concluded Scott was a salesman even then; he'd always been a salesman.

"From now on," he had said, "I'm a 'we.' Me doesn't exit in my vocabulary. What pleases you, pleases me, and what makes you unhappy, makes me unhappy, Meg. We're going to eat together, sleep together, dream together. It's marriage with a capital M."

Those words haunted her. Taunted her was more like it. She wished that along with the judgments that would be handed down after the divorce proceeding, there was a power that would wipe her mind of all memories involving Scott. A blank slate, that's what she dreamed of.

She had to admit she was a different person from the impressionable young woman who had fallen in love with Scott Lester, but Los Angeles hadn't existed as a viable place to live until she had met him. The house, all they had, the car, the things she really enjoyed here, even these friends were all because of Scott in one way or another. Everything carried his stamp on it. That was why she harbored the belief that in the end she just had to move away.

"I mean," Sharma continued, "imagine coming home unexpectedly and finding your husband had brought a woman into your house! Into your bed! He should be nailed to a cross of fire."

Brooke and Patricia looked away for Meg's sake.

"I've got to get going," Meg said. "I have some things to do at the office and I don't want to be late picking up Justine." She dug into her purse.

"Forget it. We're treating," Sharma declared.

"You treated me the last time," Meg protested.

"That's all right. You're still in mourning," Patricia Longstreet said. She was the one of the three who had suffered the most through her divorce.

"Mourning? That's ridiculous," Sharma declared.

"No, it's not." Patricia held her ground for once and stood up to her overpowering friend. She turned back to Meg, her hazel eyes tender, sad.

"I know what you're feeling, Meg," she said. "It's really more like someone you loved died. You don't want to admit that, to say you loved him, not after what he's done to you, but you did and . . ." She smiled like a co-conspirator, "You might still love him."

"Don't tell her things like that," Sharma said.

"Shut up, Sharma," Brooke said. She wore a gentle smile on her face, too, but she looked like she was enjoying the emotional tension. For a moment, Meg had the feeling Brooke thought she was on the set of some soap opera. This is my life, Meg thought, my life, not some serialized afternoon slop.

Brooke's reaction encouraged Patricia to continue.

"If you want to go home, go home," Patricia said. "Even if it's just for a short while to catch your breath."

"I might just do that, Patricia. I don't know how long I can continue getting up in the morning and dress myself in this angry demeanor. I feel like I'm putting on a suit of armor every day. I don't laugh, I don't smile. I hate what I look like."

"And the more you hate yourself, the more you hate him for making you that way," Patricia concluded.

"If there's one thing she doesn't need now, it's self-pity," Sharma said, slowly regaining her control of the clan. "She's had a bad time, but whether she knows it now or not, she will be stronger and wiser because of it."

"You almost make it sound as if divorce is a good thing, Sharma," Meg responded. "Well, maybe it is necessary. I certainly felt it was for me, but Justine keeps asking about her father, and the house is cluttered with broken promises. To tell you the truth, I'm sick of it. Sick of hating him and sick of loving him, sick of detesting the sight of him and sick of wanting him."

The tears pressed against her lids, but she held them back.

"It's as if . . . as if marriage was one of God's big jokes. I'm sorry," she said, wiping her cheeks. "I've ruined everyone's good time. Thanks for lunch," she added and got up quickly.

"Meg!" Sharma cried.

"Let her go," Patricia said, firmly gripping Sharma's wrist.

Sharma tore her arm free and glared at her. Then she took a deep breath and as if she were releasing fire like a dragon, sighed, and said, "Men!"

As soon as Meg stepped out of the restaurant, she practically jogged down the sidewalk to her car. Away from her girlfriends, she stopped trying to hold back the tears. They streamed down and across her cheeks. She pressed the car alarm clicker on her key chain and the vehicle produced that dumb metallic gulp. This was a city full of alarms. Houses were secured in devices hooked to windows and doors; everywhere cars sounded off because someone tapped a bumper or leaned on a hood. Meg read where even children were being wired so if a stranger came near them, they could set off sirens. Why wasn't there an alarm for a failing marriage, a siren that went off as soon as your husband lost interest in you?

She plopped in the Mercedes soft leather seat and tried to calm herself down. A package of Scott's breath mints was still in the ash tray; some reminders he had written to himself remained in the pocket of the door, and behind the visor was his comb. Angrily, she opened the window and as she pulled away and started down the boulevard, she began to throw out whatever belonged to him. She resembled a sailor on a sinking ship, trying to lessen its weight by casting off whatever wasn't nailed down.

Her sobbing grew harder, longer. Sharma just had to bring it up; she just continually had to mention Meg finding Scott in bed with another woman. Meg was beginning to think Sharma got off on the story; she never failed to find a way to resurrect it.

But it was as if Sharma had written the textbook entitled, *How to Get an Unfaithful Husband*. She took her every step of the way, from the detective to the attorney to the accountant. Together with Brooke and Patricia, they became Meg's little support group, her cheering section: the team. She had needed them and they had come through for her, but like the man who hated the messenger bringing bad news, she had begun to resent them for being so right and for knowing the most intimate details.

Meg took a deep breath and stopped her sniveling when she realized that she had somehow driven to Jonathan Sanders's offices in Santa Monica. She couldn't remember the trip. Just lucky I didn't have an accident, she thought as she pulled into the parking lot. She got out of the car, locked and alarmed it, and then hurried into the two-story wedgwood blue house that had been converted into an architect's offices.

"Oh, Meg, we tried to find you," Vikki Carson, Jonathan's junior partner, said, turning from the front desk when Meg entered. "The school's been calling. Justine's not feeling well."

"Oh, no," Meg said.

"Jonathan said not to worry about the filing and the book-keeping. You can do it when you can."

"Thanks," Meg cried and ran out. If it wasn't one thing now, it was another. She was still being tossed about in a hurricane of personal trouble, a little boat adrift on an angry and unfriendly sea. Abby, she thought. I do want to come home.

She thought about Justine as she drove to her school. The child hadn't been eating well and had been slowly drifting into a deeper and deeper melancholy since the divorce proceedings had begun. The concept of two people tearing apart from each other and in the process destroying everything they had built together was a notion Justine couldn't fathom. Daddy wasn't coming home to sleep and to eat with them anymore. He never would. There was a vast gap in her life, an emptiness she couldn't fill.

Despite his extramarital activities, Scott had been a loving father, doting on Justine. Meg would be the first to admit that, although she found it disturbing that Scott respected and guarded his relationship with his daughter more than he had with his wife. Why wasn't *this* relationship as holy and as sacrosanct?

His lawyer had attempted to show Scott was a responsible

father. How absurd that seemed in light of some of the things Scott had done; how twisted and distorted it made their lives look. Her attorney told her that ninety percent of all of it was posturing and she should let it go into one ear and out the other; which was something more easily said than done because this was her and Justine's lives they were deciding.

Meg hurried into the school and down to the nurse's office. Unfortunately, she didn't need directions. She had been here twice before during the last two weeks.

"Oh, Mrs. Lester," the nurse said, rising from her desk. She glanced toward the room in which Justine was resting.

"What's wrong?"

"She has no fever, but she's complaining about those stomach cramps again," the nurse said. She was a dark-haired woman in her late forties with eyes that were like gaping holes to her thoughts. "She is a very depressed young lady," the nurse added, a little more caustically than Meg expected. "Have you considered some therapy?"

"Therapy?"

"Children of fresh divorces often undergo counseling," the nurse replied pedantically. "Unfortunately, it's like an epidemic around here," she added. Meg blanched.

"I assure you it wasn't something I wanted to happen."

"Oh, I didn't mean . . ."

"Can I have my daughter, please," Meg said. "I'd like to take her to a doctor and get some professional advice," she added. Who would ever imagine that shy little Meg Turner from Jamestown would become a raging, flaming woman of independence three thousand miles from where she was born and bred?

The nurse paled and then moved quickly to get Justine. Meg felt her heart pounding. Her five-year-old daughter stepped out of the room. Her light brown hair was disheveled, the sweet chestnut ribbon Meg had tied in it this morning was gone.

Justine's small, round sapphire eyes were bloodshot, the dried tears smeared down her soft cheeks.

"Hi, honey," Meg said. "You don't feel well again?"

Justine ground her tiny fists against her eyes and then, with her lips trembling, looked up at Meg and shook her head. Right now, Meg could see only herself in Justine. The child was a smaller reflection of her own misery and depression.

She knelt down to hug her and kiss her forehead and cheek. Then she brushed back her hair.

"You'll be all right, honey. Mommy will make you better."

"You have to just sign this form," the nurse said in her official tone. Meg stood up and seized the pen. She scribbled her signature on the paper and thrust it back.

"Thank you," Meg muttered. She took Justine's hand and marched her out of the nurse's office. Her daughter kept her head down. Meg caught their reflection in a showcase window. They looked like they were fleeing.

Look what he's done, she thought; look what he's done to Justine and me. Any thoughts of mercy and forgiveness that had passed through her mind these past few weeks popped like soap bubbles and dissipated quickly. She looked forward to continuing the custody hearing on Monday and driving a stake into Scott's black heart.

"THIS IS BERNARD LYLE," Philip Dante said and stepped aside so Scott could see the short, stocky man standing behind him in the doorway of Scott's claustrophobic studio apartment.

"Hello," Scott said, not hiding his perplexity. Why had Philip brought someone? This trip and meeting were supposed to be clandestine. Could this guy be another candidate for the Solomon Organization? What was Dante doing, gathering them up all over the city? Scott raised his thick, brown eyebrows, questioning. Philip smiled.

"Bernard is an escort."

"Pardon me?"

"You'll have to put up with their protocol. They have their procedures down to a science and vigorously insist on following the guidelines to the T," Philip explained.

"Really?" Scott looked at Bernard Lyle again.

"Absolutely, Mr. Lester," the muscular little man said, stepping forward out of the shadows. Even in his suit and tie, he looked like a miniature version of the Hulk. He didn't crack a smile. Under his patch of reddish-brown hair, he had an alabaster complexion, the face of a statue, every line distinct and deep, his eyes cavernous in the yellow tinted light above Scott's apartment door.

Scott wasn't about to invite them in. He was too ashamed of the depth to which he had fallen: from a three-bedroom, several hundred thousand dollar home in Westwood to this one-by-four furnished by K-Mart. Anyway, their attention was momentarily shifted to the sound of howling laughter. Somewhere toward the center of the complex, one of the tenants was having a party. Inconsiderate, as Scott found many of them were, this tenant had his windows open, the music pouring over the project and invading everyone else's space.

Scott hated it here. It was one of those inexpensive beehive constructions indigenous to Los Angeles. Someone could rent monthly, no lease required. Consequently, it attracted the most transient types—dreamers who had enough money to chance six or seven months in the City of Angels in an attempt to achieve fame and fortune. Many were neophyte actors or actresses, writers and artists currently employed as waiters and waitresses, shopping market clerks and secretary-receptionists. Definitely not his crowd, but it was all he could afford at the moment.

"Ready?" Philip asked.

"As I'll ever be," Scott replied. He stepped out and closed

the apartment door. When he turned to be sure it was locked, he felt Bernard Lyle's hands begin on his shoulders and start to move down his back and sides. He realized the escort was frisking him.

"What the hell's going on?" he asked, spinning around.

"Precautions," Lyle said, continuing his search. Scott looked at Philip, who shrugged.

"Standard preliminary procedure," he said. "Humor them," he added sotto voce.

"What are they afraid of?" Scott asked. Protocol or no protocol, he disliked being searched. He had suffered enough indignities and wasn't about to endure any more. Philip closed and opened his eyes, urging Scott to be patient. Then he turned to Lyle as soon as he stepped away from Scott.

"Satisfied?"

"For now," the stern man replied. He fixed his green eyes on Scott's face and studied him with an intensity that made Scott uncomfortable. He felt as if the man was a walking X-ray machine and he had just been scanned for weapons or explosives, as well as a tape recorder. It made him hesitant. Bernard Lyle sensed it.

"Let's go," he said without further delay. He turned and started down the walkway toward the parking lot, not waiting to see if they were alongside him. But Scott lingered. Under the overcast night sky, the shadows cast by the spotlights and pole lamps swallowed Bernard Lyle as he walked ahead.

"Where did you find him?" Scott whispered. "House of Wax?"

Philip laughed.

"I warned you they're a bit dramatic," he said. "But don't laugh at them. They take themselves very seriously."

Scott shook his head, his hands on his hips. "I don't know why I let you talk me into this."

"You've run out of options, buddy," Philip replied. "Unless, of course, you've decided to accept the inevitable outcome and become a stranger to your own child." Scott's hesitation quickly dissipated. He nodded and started after Bernard Lyle.

When they reached the parking lot, Scott blew a soft whistle. A white, stretch Mercedes limousine awaited. The tinted windows kept what little light there was out of the interior of the vehicle. When Bernard Lyle stepped into the car, it looked as if he had dove into a tunnel and disappeared.

A black driver held the door open for him. Scott gazed into his egg-white eyes for a moment. The tall man was expressionless, the indifferent servant. Scott followed Bernard Lyle into the limousine. Philip got in beside him and the door was closed, but so softly and so tightly, Scott felt he had entered a tomb. The aroma within brought to mind the fragrance of dozens of roses in a funeral parlor, a seemingly apt image.

Bernard Lyle sat on the plush leather seat across from them, still not smiling, still not shifting his gaze from Scott's face. His heartbeat began to quicken. This was a mistake; he was making a mistake, he thought vaguely. But he felt it was already too late the moment he sat down and the limousine door was closed.

The chauffeur got in and they drove out of the lot, slipping into the city traffic so unobtrusively, it was as though they didn't exist. This was the epilogue to the nightmare that had begun the afternoon Meg came home unexpectedly.

They made their way to the freeway and headed downtown. The lights of the skyscrapers were hazy in the marine fog that had settled itself around the city. Cars whizzed by on both sides of them, continuous streams of lights and metal. When something slowed down the traffic, they all hovered behind each other, creating a glowing line, tentacles of some metallic octopus that belched exhaust and had an engine for a heart.

When they reached the Harbor Freeway, they pulled off the

exit and went to the side of the road. Bernard Lyle reached into his pocket to produce a black blindfold. He handed it to Scott.

"What's this?" Scott asked without taking it.

"Just another standard procedure," Philip said. "They'd rather their exact location was kept unknown until they decide on your case. I'm sure you can understand."

"You're kidding?" Scott said. "You want me to put this on?" Bernard continued to hold it out, unflinching. "Jesus, talk about dramatics," Scott said, taking it. He put it over his eyes and sat back.

"Now what do you do, drive me around for hours so I won't be able to tell where I'm being taken?"

Philip laughed. Scott heard Bernard tap on the window and the limousine continued.

"Where the hell are we going?" Scott asked nervously. "I feel like I fell into some spy movie."

"Relax, Scott," Philip said. "We're almost there. Believe me," he added with disdain in his voice, "there's not much to look at anyway down here."

After a few more minutes, Scott felt the limousine slow down abruptly and make a sharp right. He felt the front of the car dip and then he heard a garage door squeak as it opened. He sensed they had gone below the street into the underground parking lot of some building. The limousine came to an abrupt stop and Scott started to remove the blindfold when Bernard Lyle seized his wrist firmly.

"Keep the blindfold on until we tell you to take it off, Mr. Lester," Bernard ordered.

Scott was helped out of the vehicle and led to a nearby elevator. They guided him in and then he felt the lift. Moments later, he was led out. Doors were opened and he was walking over what felt like rather plush carpet. Finally, Bernard Lyle lifted the blindfold off and Scott faced a door simply labeled,

*Conference Room.* He gazed to his left and saw he was in the corridor of some office that had maroon carpeting. Back on a wall in the lobby he had been guided through, he saw a picture of a steel bridge.

"Keep your eyes forward, Mr. Lester," Bernard snapped. Then he knocked on the conference room door. He didn't wait for a reply. He opened the door and they entered.

Seated so firmly in a semicircle and barely moving, the five men resembled a three-dimensional fresco. The only light came from a pole lamp that had been placed behind them, but the illumination was directed toward Scott and Philip like a small spotlight. It made it difficult for Scott to see their faces, although he did see that they were all dressed in conservative suits and ties. Bernard Lyle moved quickly to take a position in the right corner, crossing his hands in front of him, his feet a shoulder's breadth apart. Talk about being overly dramatic, Scott thought.

"Please, have a seat, Mr. Lester," the man at the center said. Scott glanced at the two dark wood chairs set facing the committee, and then looked at Philip who nodded. They sat down.

Scott gazed around the room and saw it was dark paneled with the walls bare except for a large, round clock. The blinds on the two large windows were down and shut tight. The room had no personality, no identity. It was simply functional space, all business.

"We'll get right to the point, Mr. Lester. All of our members have read the transcripts of the proceeding to date; we've gone over your divorce agreement and we've perused the briefs of your wife's attorney and yours. We have a few more questions, but we won't keep you long."

"That's all right," Scott said. He sat back and folded his hands against his stomach. Now that he was here, he was rather intrigued. Who were these guys?

He took his time, spoke clearly, and answered all their questions. They had obviously gone over the details closely, picking up words, expressions, even the most seemingly inconsequential facts.

After about twenty minutes of answering questions, the man to Scott's right turned a page in the folder before him. The triangular diamond pinky ring on the thick, wrinkled finger caught the rays and glittered. Scott recognized it as the same ring worn by Philip Dante. Someone cleared his throat. Scott glanced at Philip, who nodded and smiled with confidence and encouragement.

"In the event you are awarded custody of your daughter, how will you manage?" the man with the pinky ring asked.

"I don't see any problem. I've got a lot of leeway with hours at my job. I intend to hire a full-time housekeeper."

"Your finances wouldn't suggest that possibility, Mr. Lester," the man in the center said.

"Well, I expect to do well with the sale of the house. I've got a little money put away in places Meg couldn't get to, even with her crackerjack accountant on my tail," he said proudly.

Everyone was silent for a moment. Bernard Lyle stepped forward out of the shadows. His face looked aglow, his eyes luminous. Scott glanced at Philip, who winked.

"What about alcohol and drugs?" the man on the far left snapped. He tapped the pages of the court transcript.

"That was all distorted way out of proportion," Scott replied quickly. "I drank a little to take off the edge, but . . ."

"And drugs?" the man in the center snapped.

"I admit I took a few hits once in a while. Things were quite depressing at home with Meg off doing her own thing half the time." He sat back. "Of course, I'd be different if I had custody of my kid, more responsible," he quickly assured them.

"I'm interested in this reference to a violent incident," the man on the left said. "Your wife claims . . ."

"I swear to God, I never hit her like she says I did," Scott volunteered. "All that crap about coming home drunk and striking her . . . she was at me as soon as I walked in the door. I'll admit that one time I pushed her out of my way and she fell and hurt her shoulder. That was it. I regretted it immediately, but she insisted on running off to the doctor."

"To build her case," Philip Dante said. Scott turned, surprised at Philip's unexpected assistance. "She was already seeing her attorney."

"Yeah," Scott said, even though he had no evidence that Meg had acquired legal services before she had caught him with Mrs. Tannebaum. He seized the theme Dante had established, however, and ran with it. "This last incident was not the so-called straw that broke the camel's back. She was plotting and planning against me for some time. I was practically . . . entrapped."

The committee was silent again, each silence seemingly deeper and longer to Scott. He looked up at the ceiling. Somewhere in the building, a pipe shuddered as water rushed through it.

"I want to know more about this architect your wife worked for," the young man in the center said suddenly. He leaned forward and Scott was surprised to see he was a man easily in his late sixties or even early seventies, though he still had a healthy head of hair, albeit thin and starch white. What was more striking were his sharp, hard features: a chiseled jaw, with gray eyes so still and deeply set they looked like they were sinking back into his skull.

But he had such a young voice and in the shadows . . . it was as if he had aged in moments right before Scott's eyes. The others leaned into the light now, too, and each face was an added surprise. The man on the far left didn't look as old as his hands suggested. He looked more like a man in his forties, and the man on the far right looked no older than Scott.

Philip cleared his throat. Scott looked at him and nodded. This was just what they had discussed.

"He was banging her, I'm sure. In fact, I think she started seeing him months ago, even before she had gone to work for him. My lawyer said I couldn't counterclaim adultery in the custody hearing because I didn't have one hard piece of evidence. They were never seen together in restaurants or anything like that. No smoking pistol in her hand, like there was in mine, but I knew it was going on. She always denied it, of course."

"Tell me," the man in the center said, "how do you really feel about all this?"

"How do I feel? How do I feel," Scott muttered. He raised his head.

"She's living in the house," he snapped, his thoughts just bursting into words. "With all the payments I have to make, I barely have enough to keep up this crummy apartment I've got, but that's not what eats at my craw," he said, pounding his chest so hard that Philip Dante actually winced.

"No. What eats at my heart," he said, recalling Philip's exact words, "what eats at my soul is that another man is eventually going to move into my house, sleep in my bed, kiss my child good night. In time, she'll think of him as her father. It's only natural."

Scott felt the tears building in his eyes. Deep inside, he meant every word, even though he had stated it so dramatically for the effect it would have on this committee, whoever the hell they were. Philip looked pleased.

"Gentlemen," the man in the center mercifully declared, "I think we've heard enough and we're all familiar with the facts of the case."

"I don't have any money," Scott said. It seemed appropriate to mention it at the time.

"We don't want any money from you, Mr. Lester," he replied as if the suggestion was ridiculous. "If we decide in your favor,

we simply want you to be a good father, a reliable and responsible parent."

"That's all we want from you," the young man on the far
right said. "That's all we can ask of any man." He sounded
disappointed, like someone who wished he could ask for more,
much more.

"But how do you guys work? I mean, do you have some
influence with the courts? What's the story?"

"We have influence with everyone related to the situation,"
the man in the center said.

"But . . ."

"Thank you," Philip said and urged Scott to his feet. He took
Scott's arm and nodded toward the door.

"Oh," Scott said, confused. He walked with Philip. At the
door, he turned. There were more questions on his lips. Surely
they had more to say, more to tell him, but at this point, even
their hands had been pulled back into the shadows.

"Stop worrying," Philip said when they stepped out. "You
were great in there, fucking great. That last bit about your
daughter . . ."

"What bit? I meant every word. It's killing me that I won't
see my own kid whenever I want," he said bitterly.

"You will. Believe me."

"I don't understand," Scott said, looking back at the closed
door. "What do I do now?"

"Nothing. You wait, but it won't be long. It wasn't long for
me," Philip added. He handed Scott the blindfold again.
"Sorry," he said. "Until we leave the building and the immediate area."

Scott took it reluctantly and put it on. Philip threaded his
arm through his and started him forward.

"What about the Hulk? Isn't he coming along to be sure I
don't peek?"

"He only escorts us here. No need for him to escort us home. Relax. We'll stop for a drink. You look like you need one and from now on, no one's gonna hold it against you and try to make you look like an unfit father."

Scott smiled. His heart was pounding.

"But when will we know what they have in mind? I mean, who are these guys and how do they intend . . ."

"Will you relax." Scott heard Philip open the outer doors and then he directed him into the hallway to the bank of elevators. "You came here because it was your final court of appeal, right?" Philip said, holding the elevator doors open for him. He guided Scott in.

"I mean you had no other choice. She fixed it that way. She tried to castrate you. I'm confident the committee will arrive at that conclusion."

Scott heard the doors closed.

Scott took a deep breath and stood back while the elevator dropped them quickly. With the blindfold on, he felt as if he were being lowered into a dark pit.

Finally, after five more minutes of wearing it in the car, Philip lifted it off and Scott saw they were turning off Fourth Street and heading back to the freeway.

In more ways then one, he had no idea where he had been.

# 3

cott closed the file on his desk and inserted it into his desk drawer. Sadly, that was the most substantial thing he had done all day. He checked the time and then gazed absentmindedly out the showroom window at late Saturday afternoon traffic flowing up and down Westwood Boulevard. Saturdays were usually a lot busier and a lot more exciting for him, even after a night out on the town.

After his meeting with the Solomon Organization, he and Philip Dante had stopped for a drink. He certainly needed it; the whole experience had been bizarre. Now that he thought about it, it even seemed quite ridiculous. He felt foolish for going along. To top it off, Dante spent most of the time talking about life and disability insurance, trying to convince him that his needs were changing. Scott wondered if this wasn't all part of some elaborate scam to sell people policies. In the end, he was glad to get home, even to the solitary confinement of his claustrophobic apartment.

He spent the rest of the evening dozing on and off on his

sofa watching television until two in the morning. He couldn't drum up enough enthusiasm to venture out. Pursuing women or having a good time seemed incongruous at the moment. He felt like someone in a period of mourning who had to restrain from pleasure until a decent amount of time had passed. None of his so-called buddies called anyway, just like none of them had come to stand by him in the courtroom. Even Carl Stevens, his closest friend in Los Angeles, was suddenly occupied with family matters.

Family matters . . . Scott smirked. Carl was the one who had brought him to the Blue Moon in Santa Monica where he got his cocaine and engaged in a few of his extramarital affairs. But everyone was treating him like a pariah now, as if associating with him was bad luck.

Maybe it was, Scott thought sorrowfully. Now that he sat here behind his desk thinking about what he had once had and how good things had been, he felt like a man who had just come out of a terrific tailspin, dumbfounded as to how it had all happened. It just had. One day awhile back, he woke up feeling sorry for himself, feeling he had fallen into a rut. He thought he was climbing out of it by putting a little added spice into his life, but all he had done was deepen the groove.

Depressed, he sat there mesmerized by the traffic. He was in such a daze, he didn't hear Mr. Miller step up to his desk.

The sixty-seven-year-old man resembled a retired pro half-back and looked ten years younger than he was. He had a ruddy complexion and a full head of silver white hair that was like a neon sign announcing vibrant health. He still attended his gym religiously and paid tribute to the narcissistic god of deltoids, biceps, and pectorals. A man full of strength and verve, he detested weakness, especially emotional and moral weakness. Scott respected Stanley Miller, and at least in the beginning, he appreciated his fatherly advice.

Scott's own father had died before Scott had reached his tenth birthday, and his brother Steve had tried to take on some paternal responsibility in his place. Maybe that was why his brother always seemed so much older.

"What happened with Cy Baum this morning?" Stanley Miller demanded. Scott snapped out of his trance.

"What? Oh, he said he might keep his car another year."

Miller grimaced.

"He's been trading in every three years like clockwork, Scott. Didn't you point out the modifications in his model? If the ash tray changed, he'd trade his car in, for Christ sakes."

Scott shrugged.

"I told him, but he seemed to talk himself out of it the longer he was here looking."

Miller shook his head.

"The Scott Lester I first hired would never have let him get away," he said. "How much longer's it going to be before you get your life in order so you can give me a hundred percent again, Scott?"

"Hey, Mr. Miller . . ." Scott raised his arms. "She's put me through hell."

"Put yourself there," Sidney Miller replied. "I wouldn't talk to you like this if I didn't consider you my second son, Scott, but I must tell you I'm disappointed. You were my golden-haired boy, straight-down-the-road Americana: ambitious, good-looking, married to a pretty woman who cared about you, a beautiful child . . . everything going your way, and then you go and think with your dick."

"I . . ."

"Look, maybe I shouldn't put my two cents in. My wife says it's none of my business what you do with your personal life, but it is if your personal life hurts the business. I'm putting you on notice, Scott. Get your act together."

He shook his head and walked back toward his office. Scott

saw Wayne watching from his office door. By looking away quickly, Stanley Miller's son demonstrated either his unwillingness or his inability to run any interference when it came to his father. Scott was on his own. He felt the gloom sink in deeper and settle itself like a pound of lead in his stomach.

He felt this might be literally true when he went to stand, for it took more effort to bring himself to his feet, and his arms trembled as he pushed himself up. He looked toward Wayne's office again, but Wayne had closed his door and was already on the telephone. Maybe talking to a prospective new sales manager, Scott thought sadly. First, he was losing his real family, and now he was losing his surrogate father and brother.

He lowered and then raised his eyes quickly when a familiar limousine pulled up in front of the dealership. The back door opened and Philip Dante stepped out dressed in a fashionably cut charcoal gray pin-striped suit and tie. He started toward the front entrance and then stopped and gestured emphatically for Scott to come out.

Scott looked toward Mr. Miller's office. He didn't see him, so he started out. He had only fifteen minutes left anyway, he thought, and no one was breaking down the door to buy a new car today.

"What's happening?" Scott asked after he stepped into the late afternoon sunshine. He put on his sunglasses quickly to block the glint off the hood of the shiny, luxurious automobile.

"Celebration time," Philip said. "Come on."

"Celebration?" Scott looked back again and this time saw Mr. Miller standing in his doorway looking out at them. His face was etched in a scowl.

"The committee," Philip said, approaching. "They've made a decision in your favor. You impressed them, buddy." Philip came closer. "In fact, you did better than I did. It took them longer to make a decision on my behalf."

"What happens now?" Scott asked.

"They'll rectify the situation."

"How?"

"Whatever method they choose is best. You don't have to think about it. That's the beauty of the Solomon Organization. The organization takes responsibility from here on in and you just enjoy it."

"I don't know," Scott said. He looked back at Mr. Miller. "Maybe I'd better rethink everything. I gotta know more about these guys. This is all happening so fast, I don't know where I am or what I'm doing. Maybe . . ."

"Maybe you've been beaten and trampled so much lately, you don't know how to greet good news and good luck," Philip interjected with a smile. He put his arm around Scott's shoulders and brought his lips close to his ear to whisper, "I've got our celebration all planned and taken care of; it's waiting inside the limo."

"Huh?"

Philip pressed his right palm down on Scott's head so he would bow and peer through the opened rear door. Seated within were two rather buxom, good-looking young women. One was a dark brunette and the other was a platinum blonde, both wearing silk blouses and showing a lot of cleavage. They both smiled.

"Where did you find them?"

"Trade secret. You like?"

"What's not to like?"

"Good. You get to choose," Philip said. "It's your party. In fact, if you want, you can have both."

"Really?" Scott smiled.

"Yeah, really. I've got this great house to party in, loads of champagne and caviar . . ."

"This is their limousine, right?" Scott asked, stepping

back. The chauffeur just sat staring ahead. "They know about this?"

"Uh huh. It's just an added benefit. They sympathize with you and want you cheered up," Philip added. "A real nice bunch of guys, you know what I mean?" He winked conspiratorially.

"This is crazy," Scott said, but the depression was being drawn out of his body so quickly he couldn't stop it. It made him feel loose and young.

"We're going to have a damn good time, eh?" Philip said, holding his arm out. "After you, Mr. Lester."

Scott was sure Sidney Miller was still watching them so he didn't turn around. The old man wasn't going to like this, but the old man wasn't going through a potential nervous breakdown. Scott edged toward the limousine.

"Hi," both girls said.

"Get in," Philip coached.

Scott took a deep breath like someone about to dive under water, and stepped through the open door. The two women moved apart to make a space for him right between them. Philip Dante got in and closed the door. He sat across from them.

"Hello," Scott said, looking from one to the other. They both had beautiful eyes and great teeth. The scents they wore were not cheap. These weren't run-of-the-mill prostitutes, he thought. They snuggled up.

"He's not bad," the brunette said and giggled.

"Better than the last one," the blonde agreed.

Scott felt the heat that was in his face quickly move to his loins as both girls placed hands on his thighs.

"Let's have our first toast in the car," Philip said, taking a bottle of champagne out of the cabinet and then handing everyone a glass. The limousine began to pull away from Miller's Mercedes, Sales and Service. The black chauffeur did not look back. His face was expressionless; he looked bored and unimpressed, Scott thought, like a man who had seen this time and time again.

Philip poured the bubbling pink liquid into glasses and then filled his own.

"To the rescue of Scott Lester," he said, raising his glass. The girls giggled. Philip winked. "And to the Solomon Organization," he added. Then they all drank, Scott the last to bring his glass to his lips, his hand trembling slightly until the sparkling liquid flowed down his throat and washed away any apprehension that lingered.

MEG LESTER SLUMPED down on the sofa and pressed the neck of the telephone receiver closer to her cheek. She was prolonging the conversation, clinging to her sister's voice as if there was something magnetic about it. The truth was she longed for her companionship more than she cared to admit. When she and Scott had first come to Los Angeles, he would always get so upset every time she mentioned her homesickness or how much she missed family. Going back would be admitting failure, and Scott had too much an ego to do anything like that.

Gradually, but surely their lives had improved materially. Scott landed this prestigious and affluent position with the Westwood Mercedes dealership. Not only was he making good money selling expensive automobiles, he was associating with high rollers, who gave him good financial advice from time to time, not the least the encouragement to purchase a house when the real estate market was most favorable to buyers. Almost immediately after they closed escrow, the property accelerated in value. For a while, especially in the beginning, it looked like California was really the land of gold.

Occasionally, she would stop and wonder: *Is this really what I want? Are we really happy?* Whenever she ever brought up any of these deeper concerns, Scott or her new friends would immediately chastise her for getting "too heavy," "thinking too hard," "being a party pooper."

But one Sunday afternoon after she and Scott had driven down to Huntington Beach and found a relatively deserted section on which to sunbathe and picnic, she had expressed these concerns more forcefully and confessed that sometimes she felt they were caught up in the pursuit of happiness to the extent that they had forgotten what it was they were after.

"What is it we want?" she asked softly. "More money? A bigger house?"

"I don't know," Scott said, visibly annoyed that she hadn't put these concerns to rest. "All I know is because we came here, we have more money and a bigger house. And besides, could we be sitting out on a beach in March back East?"

"Not a beach, but maybe we'd take a hike up a mountain like we did that one afternoon in Saratoga, remember? All we had for lunch then was a loaf of bread, a package of cheese, and a thermos full of ice tea."

"Poor but happy, eh?" he said with ridiculing laughter in his voice.

"Something like that," she replied undaunted. He shook his head.

"That's not what I remember. I remember wondering about how I was going to make mortgage payments, car payments, charge-card payments, and still save money for our kids' educations. I remember long, dreary winters staring out at leafless trees. I remember gray shadows over everything.

"I'm not ashamed I feel good here. So I'm a hedonist. Hey, you only go around once," he argued. "Stop worrying so much. Relax and be happy."

Finally, she'd taken his words to heart, and look where she was—alone in their big, California home, waiting to put the finishing touches on their divorce.

"I hope it's all over on Monday," she told Abby. "I couldn't take more than another day of this. I feel like I'm stark naked in that courtroom; everything, including the kind of toothpaste we use, is admissible evidence."

"Come home, Meg," Abby pleaded. "As soon as you can, come home. Do you want me to come out there to get you and Justine?"

"I don't need you to do that, Abby. Thanks." She sighed. "I will come home. I can't promise you I'll stay, but you're right. I need to see everyone again." She laughed. "I'm even looking forward to Aunt Erna's sour beet soup and sugarless almond cookies."

"Uncle Charley's going in the hospital for prostrate surgery," Abby said.

"Oh, no. Is it serious?"

"He has a tumor. We'll see," Abby said cautiously. Suddenly Meg felt terribly self-centered, concentrating solely on her own problems. Everyone had problems and needed comfort and support. The old Meg would have asked after the family first and talked about herself second.

"I always liked Uncle Charley. Will you call me as soon as you hear anything?"

"Of course. How's Justine today?"

"She's better. I got her to eat something, but I'll probably have to do what that bitch of a school nurse suggested—get her into therapy. At least she won't feel self-conscious about it—a few of her friends are seeing child psychologists for one reason or another. It's almost a mark of affluence out here," she added bitterly.

"Why would you even think of staying there after going through something like this?" Abby said.

"I don't know. I'm so confused and upset, I couldn't make a sensible decision about what to have for dinner right now. We'll talk when this is over."

"And you're here."

"Yes, and I'm there. Thanks, Abby. Thanks for being my big sister again."

"I never stopped," Abby said. "I just couldn't get through much before. Too much Gucci static."

Meg laughed.

"I'll call you tomorrow," Meg said.

"Good. Go to sleep early. See, I remembered the difference in time. I haven't called you at six-thirty in the morning your time for ages."

Meg laughed again. It felt so good to do so. It seemed ages since she had.

"Love you," she said.

"Me too," Abby replied. Her voice cracked. Meg cradled the receiver quickly and took a deep breath. Her chest ached, but she was tired of crying, tired of tears and tired of feeling sorry for herself.

*Get stronger, Meg Lester,* she coaxed. *Get stronger.* You have a child who needs to be emotionally and psychologically mended. For a while, maybe for the rest of your life, you're going to have to be mother and father.

She sat up quickly and took a deep breath. Then she went upstairs to check on Justine. She found she had fallen asleep, but she had kicked off her blanket with her tossing and turning. Meg fixed the blanket neatly around her daughter and then kissed her forehead and brushed the strands of hair back. She stood there for a moment looking down at her, lost in her love.

A slight tinkling sound drew her attention to the door. It sounded like the metal louvers in the den downstairs being rattled. She listened again, but now she heard nothing but the pounding of her own heart.

It wasn't easy learning to live alone again, she thought. There were so many new and revived fears. Despite Sharma's fix on female independence, Meg had to admit she liked depending on a man, liked feeling his strength and knowing he was there if she needed him. Not that Scott was much good around the house, she thought. Most of the time if an appliance went bad or there was some problem with the plumbing, it was she who had to see that it was fixed.

But noises and shadows, strange tinkles in the night . . . that was different.

Maybe he had gotten stoned or drunk and had violated their agreement as to when he would come here, she thought and went out to the top of the stairway to listen.

"Scott?"

She waited. Nothing.

Scott had left his nine-millimeter pistol here and she had put it in the garage along with his other things during one of her periods of rage. That was stupid, she thought. Not that she would know what to do with it; she never even had held it before.

*Meg Lester*, she told herself, *don't let your imagination run wild, and whatever you do, don't become some terrified little girl again.* Sharma will have you banished from the female sex. She laughed to herself and stepped down the stairs firmly. She would read, watch a little television, and go to sleep. Every night that passed, every morning that came brought her another inch or so away from the horror that was and closer to the peace of mind that awaited. She had to believe that; that had to be her sustaining faith.

She turned at the bottom of the stairs, deciding to get herself a cup of warm milk. It would soothe her stomach, calm her nerves, and help her get drowsy. Old-fashioned remedies, but we cling to them in times like these; it's like turning back and embracing Momma by following something she said or did, she thought and concluded that tragedy and disappointment turned us into children again.

For the moment, she didn't mind being a child. She liked the feeling, liked recalling how safe and warm it was in her mother's arms while she rocked her and hummed softly, chasing away her childhood fears. Hopefully, she would be able to give Justine the same sense of security, even after all this.

Her head down, a sweet angelic smile on her face, her arms folded under her bosom, Meg walked through the hallway, not even gazing to her right or left and thus never seeing the looming shadow that metamorphosed into a man. He stepped forward in the den doorway and struck her sharply on the back of her skull with the head of that ceramic cupid for which she had overpaid just three, short months ago when shopping had been a way to relieve some of the frustration.

She never uttered a sound after being struck. It was as if someone had dropped a curtain of lead between her and her thoughts. She folded quickly and then seemed to float, turning and twisting like a body caught up in a raging stream before finally settling to the bottom. A steady trickle of blood began to draw a jagged line across the back of her scalp. It dripped to the beige, Berber carpet, the material quickly absorbing and accepting the precious fluid.

Bernard Lyle hovered over her for a moment, his shadow draping her like a shroud. Then he dropped the cupid at her side and kicked it over so that its cherubic face was turned toward hers—his little joke. He did not turn to flee. Instead, he casually strolled down to the kitchen himself, as if out to complete Meg's mission. He opened the refrigerator, found something cold to drink that pleased him, poured himself a glass, and then retreated to the living room to wait.

There was still much to do.

SCOTT GROANED and turned over. Not realizing he was already at the edge of the sofa, he fell on his face on the carpet and for a few, long moments, kept his eyes shut. The whole world was spinning. He expected to pass out again. But he didn't lose consciousness even though the sharp headache made him wish he had. He felt around his temples, expecting to touch a pair of iron pincers or something.

He sat up and took a deep breath. Then he kept his eyes open and let himself grow used to the darkness. The surroundings were familiar, but it was confusing. *Where the fuck am I?*

When the realization set in, a cold chill whipped across his chest and seemed to settle like a fist of ice around his heart. He was home . . . in the house in Westwood, but how the hell did he get here and where was Meg?

He struggled to his feet and then flopped back on the sofa. Not only did he have trouble navigating; he had trouble merely standing. He could have passed out again; he wasn't sure. When he opened his eyes once more, it seemed as if some time had gone by. He took another deep breath and reached over to turn on the lamp beside him. The light exploded, striking his face so sharply he grimaced and squeezed his eyes closed protectively. He had to take it in small increments, opening those lids a millimeter at a time. Finally, he was able to look around again and take stock.

He was in the living room and maybe, as he had suspected, the world was topsy-turvy because the easy chair across the way was on its side and that antique side table Meg had spent a small fortune on was down beside it, one of the bony legs snapped. Magazines and books were strewn about and what looked like Meg's precious Leek leaf was cracked into two pieces.

He shook his head. What the hell happened here? When did it happen? He struggled to recall his most recent memory and visualized the two women Philip Dante had brought along in the limousine. Later, in one of the bedrooms of that beautiful house, they had sandwiched him between their nude bodies.

Everyone had been laughing. The blonde fed him champagne like a mother feeding her infant formula. He sucked on the neck of the bottle. They'd gone to someone's home somewhere in Pacific Palisades. He remembered that much. He remembered laughing and laughing, gagging on the champagne, and then . . .

He woke up here. Huh? Was this some sick joke Philip Dante had pulled? Dropping him off in Westwood to show her she couldn't push him around?

He brought himself to a standing position again and steadied himself with the arm of the sofa. Deep breaths, he told himself. Keep taking deep breaths. It seemed to help; he garnered strength and was able to walk. He went to the door of the living room and gazed out, listening. Where was Meg? She sure as hell wouldn't be happy to know he was here, he thought and turned to his right.

At first her sprawled, twisted body seemed like an illusion, part of a dream. She was in such an awkward position, her skirt up above her knees, her rear end turned toward him. One arm was extended and then twisted above her head and the other was back, her palm up, the fingers curled.

"Meg?"

Silence came back at him with the impact of a sledge hammer. He knew before he drew closer to her that she wasn't going to respond.

"Meg?"

He knelt down, the motion making everything in his back scream like rusted hinges. His knees threatened to buckle and send him cascading over her twisted torso. His gaze went to the dried blood on her neck. He followed the line up through her hair and saw it disappear under the strands. A dark stain on the carpet stretched under her chin, and beside her, the little cupid smiled, a blood stain on its own forehead.

"Oh, shit. Meg!" He shook her, but she didn't moan and her eyes didn't open. She felt cold to him.

He drew his hand back as if he had been jolted with electricity and struggled to stand. For a moment he clung to the wall and gaped down at her, still unbelieving. Then, he thought about Justine.

Mustering new strength, he hurried down the hall, seized the bottom of the bannister and pulled himself up the stairs like a man ascending a steep hill, tugging and groaning all the way until he had reached the top. He shot forward toward Justine's bedroom. The door was wide open.

He stopped in the doorway and clung to the jamb. Her bed was empty, the blanket pulled back, the pillow still creased where she had lain her head. A quick perusal of the room told him she was not there, not in the bathroom, not hiding in a corner or behind a dresser... nowhere. Our bedroom, he thought, and hurried to that one, only to find she wasn't there, either. The bed was untouched. She's hiding somewhere in the house, he thought, terrified.

"Justine! Sweetheart! Justine!" He charged about frantically, his calls growing more and more desperate. He put on every light in the house, upstairs and then downstairs, but still there was no sign of her. He paused beside Meg again, trying to think, trying to be sensible.

How could this be happening? What was going on? Dante, he thought. Dante would know. He went to the telephone, but it wasn't until he lifted the receiver that he realized, he didn't know this man's number; he didn't have it in his pocket address book, either. He didn't even know the man's address. Scott had never asked and Dante had never mentioned it.

Information, he thought, and punched it out quickly.

"City please," the mechanical voice responded.

"Los Angeles, Dante, Philip."

"How are you spelling that sir?"

"Dante, Dante. D . . . a . . . n . . . t . . . e."

"Thank you." There was pause. "I'm sorry sir. I don't have a Philip Dante."

"What do you have?"

"A lot of Dantes sir. Do you have an address?"

"No."

"I'm afraid I can't . . ."

"All right, thanks," he said, hanging up quickly. He sat there thinking. The only other name he knew was Bernard Lyle's, the unpleasant escort. Bernard Lyle. Yes. He dialed information again and asked for Lyle, but he got the same result. No Bernard Lyle listed.

"What the hell's going on?" he demanded frantically. "Is he unlisted?"

"No, sir."

He hung up again and began to pace. He had been in such a frenzy, so angry and confused that he forgot to ask Dante the most obvious questions: where do you live? Who do you work for?

Should he phone the police? He had to phone the police, of course. But what was he going to tell them? Christ, he was with a couple of broads having a hell of a time and the next thing he knew he was here and Meg was sprawled out and his daughter was missing. Panic set in. He charged toward the front door and actually stepped out of the house and started down the driveway before he stopped and realized they would only come for him anyway. It was better that he be the one who called them. That would be in his favor. He reentered the house, but the telephone rang before he could get to it.

He stood there for a few moments, undecided. Then he realized it was just possible Dante was calling him. There was a good explanation as to why they had left him here, and they had Justine, safe. Sure, that had to be it. He seized the receiver.

"Hello."

Silence for a moment.

"Scott? Is that you?"

He didn't reply.

"I know it's you, Scott, you bastard. You'd better say something." It was Sharma Corman. He froze; he couldn't speak. "Where's Meg? Put Meg on the phone this instant!"

He hung up, dread dropping over him like a black sheet, enveloping him in gloom and doom. They'd be all over him now, scratching and mauling him—the sharks, tearing him apart with a vengeance. The moment he called the police, it would begin. He had to find out what was happening and absolve himself of any blame before it started. But was he without blame? After all, he had gone with that man and appealed to that group of male vigilantes.

He went to the kitchen and got himself a glass of water. Then he sat at the table, waiting, desperately trying to remember what had happened between the time the blonde said, "I go first," and his waking up in the living room. But nothing came to mind, nothing . . . not a clue.

They were going to rectify the situation. Wasn't that what Dante had told him? But how the hell did this rectify the situation? Unless, of course, they had decided that neither Meg nor he were fit to have custody of Justine. What did that mean? Where was his daughter?

He envisioned her being woken and carried out of the house, terrified and hysterical, screaming for Meg, screaming for him. It brought tears to his eyes. What have I done? he thought. My God, what have I done? He got up and returned to Meg's body.

"I'm sorry, Meg. Honest, I'm sorry," he whined. "All of this got out of hand and I just lost it. I . . . ."

He thought he saw her fingers twitch.

"Meg?"

He knelt down beside her and did what he hadn't done before: he felt for a pulse.

There it was, faint but definitely there. Ecstatic, he hurried back to the phone and dialed 911.

"My wife . . . she's been attacked. And my daughter's missing!" he cried.

"What's the address, sir?"

He rattled it off.

"What condition is your wife in?"

"She's unconscious. She's been struck in the head."

"An ambulance will be on its way. Stay put, sir. A patrol car is in your vicinity."

"Thank you. Please, tell them to hurry."

He returned to Meg's side. Her pulse hadn't changed and she made no sounds. Thinking he had to do something else, he went and got a cold, wet cloth and put it over her forehead. Then he fetched a pillow from the sofa and lifted her head gently to put the pillow underneath.

He could hear the sirens in the distance. The stronger they sounded, the more hopeful he became. They found him sitting there, clinging to Meg's hand, rocking back and forth and muttering apologies.

# 4

To Scott it seemed he had been sitting in the interrogation room for hours, just sitting there staring down at his hands, turning his fingers this way and that, studying the lines in his palms, inspecting the crevices in his skin like some alien who had just inhabited this body and was intrigued with the smallest details. He didn't know whether he had sunk into his own world or whether this room was just soundproof, for he wasn't aware of anything going on around him in the police station.

After Meg had been loaded into the ambulance, they had put him into the police car. He protested when he realized they weren't taking him to the hospital, but they didn't pay much attention. Instead, they brought him directly to this room and left him, promising someone would come in to see him soon.

Now, sitting beneath the bright, glaring tubular neon lights, he felt exceedingly warm. His lips were so dry he scratched his tongue every time he ran it over them. Yet, he didn't sweat. It was as if the perspiration was oozing into him. He envisioned drops of scalding water dripping into his stomach, searing his organs. He took a deep breath and waited, feeling more and more like a prisoner sitting in a cell adjacent to the gas chamber.

Aside from a small, narrow, high window across from him, there was nothing remarkable about the room, except that it had the scent of disinfectant. He imagined after every interrogation, a custodian appeared and washed down the floor, table, and chairs contaminated by the dregs of society dragged here.

The click of the door snapped him into a stiff posture and he looked up expectantly.

Two men entered, one tall, easily six feet three, all legs and long arms. Must have been a good basketball player, Scott thought. He had thin, light brown hair so fine it looked like the breeze from someone walking by would lift it out of place. The tall man smiled, but his dark brown eyes were fixed on Scott like a cat preparing to spring on its prey. He had his jacket off, his gun visible, strapped under his arm. Scott thought he was a man in his late forties, definitely pushing fifty. His partner, a much shorter and stouter man, maybe five feet eight, didn't smile. He looked ten years or so younger, but meaner. There wasn't even the pretense of politeness in his face. He appeared to have only disdain for Scott.

"How you doin', Mr. Lester?" the tall man asked.

"Why did you just leave me sitting here without any information?" Scott replied quickly. "How's my wife?" he demanded.

The tall man didn't break his smile, but the short man, smirked.

"It will be a while yet before they call us, Mr. Lester. You know how it is . . . they got to run all sorts of tests, X-rays, blood work . . ."

"She's still alive, if that's what you mean," the shorter man said.

"What about my daughter? Any news as to her whereabouts?" he asked anxiously.

"We were hoping you could tell us," the shorter man said.

Scott sat forward again and nodded gently.

"I know how this looks," he said.

"How does it look, Mr. Lester?" the tall policeman asked. He stared a moment and then smiled and said, "I'm Lieutenant Parker and this is Detective Fotowski. We call him Foto, for short."

Lt. Parker pulled out a chair and sat across from Scott. Fotowski remained standing, glaring, his arms folded across his barrel chest. He had wide shoulders and a thick neck, the upper body of a college wrestler with the necessary competitive and aggressive gleam in his eyes.

"It looks like I did it," Scott said. "We're in the middle of this nasty divorce proceeding, battling for custody of our daughter."

"Did you do it?" Lt. Parker asked. He rested his forearms on the table and clasped his hands. There was nothing else on the table, but the top was crisscrossed with scratches, some carved deeply. The ranting of the frustrated and the trapped, the guilty and the innocent, Scott thought and imagined suspects, not unlike himself, grinding pens, fingernails, even teeth, into the wood while they waited.

"No," Scott said, shaking his head vigorously. "I did not do it."

"We lifted a pretty clear set of prints off that statue," Lt. Parker said softly. "Are they going to match yours? It was clearly the weapon used," he added.

"I don't see why. I didn't touch it; I can't remember ever touching it. Meg bought it recently. Paid a lot of money for it, I thought. I wasn't crazy about it."

"Crazy enough to hit her with it, though," Fotowski said calmly.

"No. Absolutely not."

"We'll see."

"You want to tell us exactly how you came to find her unconscious on the floor?" Lt. Parker said.

"I think I'd better wait until my attorney arrives," Scott replied. Fotowski's eyes were burning through him. "Before I say anything else, that is."

"If you're innocent, what are you worried about?" Fotowski snapped.

"I've seen enough movies and television. I know how people get . . . get confused, say the wrong things."

"There's nothing to confuse, no wrong things to say if you have nothing to hide."

"You have no objection to giving us a set of your fingerprints, do you, Mr. Lester?" Lt. Parker asked quickly.

"What? No, I don't suppose . . ."

"Fine. Why don't we just do that while we're waiting, and, in the meantime, if you think of something you want to say, we'll be glad to listen. I don't see why we have to bring him out there to take his prints, Foto, do you? Just bring the pad in here."

Fotowski didn't reply. He threw another look of contempt at Scott and then left. Lt. Parker sat back.

"Divorce," he said shaking his head, "it's never easy, no matter what they say."

"Were you divorced?" Scott asked quickly. He assumed if the policeman had gone through something similar, he would have some compassion.

"No, but my younger sister was last year. Pretty rough. Her husband was a son of a bitch, lazy, drank up what little money they had, mean to the kids . . . the whole nine yards. When she dragged his ass into court," he said, sitting forward again, "he was one unhappy bastard. No telling what he would have done to her if I weren't around."

"It wasn't like that for me," Scott said quickly. "I mean, I wouldn't hurt Meg."

Lt. Parker shrugged.

"People hurt each other in many different ways. For some, it's no big deal to slip from one way to another. First, you're irresponsible and inconsiderate, then you're downright cruel. Finally, frustrated yourself, you swing out, shocked by what you've done, what you're capable of doing. I've seen it many times. The only thing that will make you feel better is confessing."

"I didn't hit my wife with that statue," Scott said firmly. The tall policeman nodded, professing a deeper understanding. He's humoring me, Scott thought. He thinks I've lost it.

Fotowski reappeared with the fingerprint ink and paper. He slapped it down beside Scott and proceeded to make a copy of his prints. Then he handed him a wet towel. Lt. Parker and Fotowski exchanged glances and then Lt. Parker stood up.

"We'll be right outside, Mr. Lester," he said. "As soon as your attorney arrives . . ."

"I want to know about my wife."

"I'm going to call the hospital right now," Lt. Parker assured him. Scott watched them leave and then continued to clean off his fingertips.

It was nearly a half hour more before Michael Fein, Scott's attorney, showed up. The man always looks distracted, Scott thought when his lawyer entered. He always gives me the feeling I'm interrupting something more important.

"Hello, Michael."

The five-feet-ten-inch chubby, dark brown haired man avoided looking at Scott. He sat down quickly and placed his briefcase on the table. Then he looked up and shook his head, his mouth drawn back in the corners.

"What the fuck happened? What did you do?"

"I didn't do this, Michael."

"Why were you in the house so late? I thought we had agreed . . ."

"Someone brought me there."

"Excuse me?" He lifted his bushy eyebrows, his face softening until he almost smiled. It was his way of demonstrating how silly he thought Scott sounded. He had often done that when they had discussed Scott's strategy for the custody hearing.

"I was at a party . . . champagne, caviar, girls . . . the next thing I know, I'm waking up in the living room. I thought it was someone's idea of a joke—dumping me in the house like that, but . . ."

"But you got up and found Meg with her head smashed in."

"Yeah," Scott said. "Exactly."

Fein shook his head. He didn't open his briefcase. Scott wondered if he carried it just so people would know he was an attorney.

"I spoke with the investigating police officers before I came in here, Scott. They've got a quick read on the fingerprints. Yours match the prints on the statue," he said dryly. Then he took a deep breath and sat back, his soft, very feminine lips turned in and that annoying dimple in his right cheek forming.

"That can't be," Scott said. "It's a mistake."

"Did you pick up the statue?"

"No. Absolutely not. My first thoughts after seeing Meg went to Justine."

"What about Justine, Scott? Where is she?"

"I don't know." His attorney looked skeptical. "You've got to believe me, Michael. This is all a frame-up. I . . ."

"Look, Scott," Fein said, "I'm really not a criminal lawyer. I'm not prepared to represent you on this. I handle divorces, usually routine family matters. I've never even argued for a client in traffic court."

"What are you saying?"

"You need someone else now? This is all different."

"You think I did this, don't you? Well, why did I stay there? Why did I call the police?"

"Scott, it wouldn't be in your best interest to confide in me any more. I've already taken the liberty of calling someone for you, a firm that specializes in criminal cases, especially felonies: Orseck, Greenberg and Wilson. They're sending someone over."

"Christ," Scott said. He looked down. It seemed as if the floor was rising or his legs were shriveling. Any moment he'd smash his face into the scuffed brown tile.

"I'm sorry, but I'm doing what's in your best interest."

"Bullshit," Scott snapped. "I'm not stupid. You're running away from me."

"Scott . . . if you want me to give you advice, it's simply to tell the truth."

"I am, damn you!"

Fein nodded and started to rise when the door opened and Lt. Parker came in.

"Got the hospital report," he said. "Your wife remains in a deep coma. The blow has created pressure on the brain that has to be relieved in surgery. The operation is critical. For now she's on life support."

"Jesus."

Scott looked from the policeman to his divorce attorney. They looked of one face: contempt.

"Mr. Lester's new attorney should be here any moment," Michael said.

"Okay. You told him about the prints?"

Michael Fein nodded. "I did."

"We're booking him. Mr. Lester," he said turning to Scott, "you're under arrest for what right now is attempted murder. You have the right to remain silent . . ."

Scott heard the sound of laughter through the opened door. Somewhere else in the station someone was happy or amused. The joviality stimulated his memory, and for a moment, the image of Philip Dante appeared. He was dripping champagne over the bare breasts of the platinum blonde. Everyone was laughing.

"Go on," Philip coaxed him. "Lick it off."

". . . might be held against you in a court of law. Do you understand, Mr. Lester?" Lt. Parker concluded.

"Huh? Oh. Yes."

"Right this way, Mr. Lester," Parker said, stepping back.

Scott turned to his divorce attorney.

"Michael?"

"Someone will be here to help you any moment, Scott." He shook his head and walked out quickly.

"Mr. Lester?"

Scott stood up, unsure his legs would sustain the weight of his torso.

"You know," Lt. Parker said as Scott moved toward him, "the district attorney might consider kidnapping charges, too. Your daughter is still missing."

Scott felt the trembling start just above his knees and rumble up through his stomach and into his chest. He closed his eyes and then walked out into the clamor created by other arrests, other police business: suspects professing their innocence, prisoners screaming for their rights, patrolmen and staff exchanging small talk. No one seemed to notice him. He was already part of the woodwork, another citizen of hell.

JUSTINE FELT MOVEMENT beneath her and opened her eyes. The blanket smelled new, but it wasn't a pleasant scent, not like the talcum powder aroma of her own linen. Mommy always made everything smell nice and familiar. Justine longed for those fragrances of home, the scents that filled her with security and contentment: bouquets of flowers, little soaps of all shapes and colors in her dresser drawers, Mommy's skin creams and perfumes.

The automobile hit a rise in the highway and bounced slightly. It was dark outside, but the illumination cast by other cars rushing in the opposite direction revealed the patrician features of the nurse seated at Justine's feet. The woman stared ahead, unmoving, her attention fixed on the highway unraveling in front of them.

The nurse's uniform was starched spotless. When three cars went by in a row, Justine was able to see more of the woman. Her complexion was almost as pale as her clothes. Her eyes seemed to hold some of the flashing light and radiate for a second or two. She had dark hair, cut very short, the very rear and sides of her head shaven so close it reminded Justine of Sammy Altman, the boy in her class who developed ringworm in his scalp and had to have his head shaved.

There was no music in the car, no radio, tape, or disc player playing like Mommy and Daddy always had going when they drove anywhere. This was a very big car, too. It was the biggest car she had ever been in, and there was a window between the front of the car and the rear. When the light next invaded the automobile, Justine turned to look toward the front to see if Mommy or Daddy were sitting there.

They weren't. The man who sat with his back to them on the passenger side was a stranger. He, too, remained as still as a statue. The interior of the car was so quiet, Justine was afraid to raise her voice, afraid to ask any questions.

She remembered now. One moment she had been asleep in her bed, and the next moment she had felt a pin prick on her shoulder. She had woken up, but her room was so dark, it had been hard to see anything. She had started to call for her mother and father. At first, a voice had begged her to be quiet; it had been a man's voice, not one she recognized. She had been quiet for a few seconds, but then she had become frightened again and had started to call for her mother. Then a female voice—harsher, sterner—had snapped at her, demanding she be still.

A lamp had been turned on, but for some reason everything had begun to look out of focus. A woman in white was taking some of her clothing out of the dresser drawer and stuffing it quickly into her small suitcase. Justine had tried to sit up, had willed herself to lift her torso, but nothing happened. Turning groggily to her right, she'd confronted an unfamiliar smile.

"Easy," the man had said. "Just relax and you will be fine."

She was so tired again; she couldn't keep her eyes open any longer, and then . . .

She was here, in this big car. Where were they going? Where was Mommy? She took a deep breath and started to sit up. The nurse turned slowly.

"Where's my mommy?" Justine cried.

The stranger in the front turned and slid the window open. "She's conscious already?"

"Looks that way, doesn't it?" the nurse replied sharply.

"You didn't give her enough. I told you. She's big for her age."

"I don't like giving too much of it," the nurse said.

"She's awake," the man said as if the obvious needed to be stated.

"That's okay. I'm the nurse, aren't I? This aspect is my responsibility."

Justine didn't understand any of the argument. The banter intrigued her, even fascinated her, but she was just as lost as before.

"I want my mommy," she said.

"Now you're a big girl, Justine. Old enough to understand," the nurse said. When she turned to her, she just turned her head. It looked like the nurse was a mechanical thing, her head completely independent of the rest of her. "Your mother is not here and she can't hear you anymore, so there's no use crying. Just lay your head back on the pillow and sleep until we get there."

"Where are we going?" she asked.

"To your new mommy and your new daddy," the nurse said.

"Shut up," the man in the front said. "You want to be a horse's ass about whose responsibility is whose . . . Orientation is not your responsibility," he said firmly.

"Do you want the child screaming all the way? Would that be better?"

"No. What would be better is giving her enough of the stuff so this doesn't happen. This is the third time it has," he reminded her.

The nurse sat back, her shoulders turning inward. To Justine it looked as if the woman was closing up, folding into herself.

"I wanna go home," Justine whined. "I wanna go home."

No one paid any attention. Justine began to sob, softly at first and then harder and harder until her entire body shook. The nurse turned around again, only this time, her right hand flew up, soaring through the darkness. She slapped Justine sharply on the cheek. The smack came so fast and was such a surprise, Justine choked on a cry and swallowed the sounds. Her body still heaved, but silently now. She was terrified.

"Keep quiet," the nurse ordered.

"Great," the man in the front said. "That's just fine. Orientation will have a wonderful time with her now."

The nurse sat back again.

Justine closed her eyes real tight. Mommy told her that whenever she had a bad dream or a bad thought, that was what she was to do.

*If you press down hard enough and shoo away the nasty*

*thoughts, they will disappear. Close your eyes, honey, and count to ten. Then think about something nice, make yourself think about your dolls or something you love to eat. Go on. Count.*

"One, two . . ."

What did the nurse mean by "your new mommy and daddy?" How can I have a new Mommy and Daddy? Was this because Mommy and Daddy were having a bad fight and weren't going to live in the same house anymore? I don't want a new Mommy and Daddy, even if . . . even if they fight. Maybe, if I told these people . . .

"I don't want a new Mommy and Daddy," she said. The nurse didn't turn, didn't act as if she had heard. Justine repeated: "I don't want a new Mommy and Daddy." Slowly, the nurse turned again. In the flash of light from a passing tractor trailer, the nurse's face was clearly revealed.

Her face was so pocked and scarred, her skin looked like wax that had melted and rehardened. There were ridges and grooves and tiny crevices everywhere, even on her chin. And she had no eyebrows! What's more, her lips were almost the same pale shade as her skin. Justine recalled turning the knob on the television set and tuning in one of the pay cable channels that was showing a horror movie. The sight of the creature was just as terrifying as the face of this woman. On the television, the woman had just been burned in a fire.

The nurse's eyes held the light, just as before, and glowed.

"Sure you do, honey," she said softly. When she pulled the sides of her mouth back to smile, the rest of her face folded and crinkled as if it were made of cellophane. Her teeth were bone white. "Mommies and Daddies have to be together, otherwise they're not good Mommies and Daddies and you don't live in a happy little world."

"Hey," the man in the front said.

"Mommies that fight with Daddies make children sick inside

and when children are sick inside, they grow up to be bad Mommies and Daddies themselves. The sickness is always with them."

"Will you shut the hell up," the man commanded.

"My mommy and daddy were bad like yours, too, and I had to go live with a good Mommy and Daddy. But, I'm glad I did."

"Orientation is not going to like this," the man warned. "They're not going to like this one bit."

"It takes time," the nurse said undaunted. "At first, you're afraid. I was just as afraid as you are now, but after a while, when you're with a good Mommy and Daddy, that fear leaves you and you're happy. And the sickness won't be in you anymore. Isn't that nice?"

Justine simply stared through the darkness at the ashen visage that loomed over her.

"Finished? Are you finished?" the man demanded.

"Yes, I think we're finished. I think we'll be good now, won't we, dear?" she asked, raining down a smile.

Justine took a deep breath and then with all the strength she could muster, she shrieked.

"MOMMY!"

The nurse moved quickly to her little black bag. In moments she was pulling down the blanket. She leaned on Justine, pinning her arm against her side, and then she stuck her with a needle again. All through it, Justine screeched until her lungs felt hot and her ribs ached. When the nurse was finished, she tucked the blanket around Justine so tightly it became a straight jacket entrapping her. She tried kicking, but the nurse was practically sitting on her feet now.

Soon she grew dizzy and then everything was hazy. Her eyelids became heavier and heavier until she couldn't keep them open.

"Just count," she heard her mother say.

"One," she whispered. "Two . . ."

And then everything was black and just as Mommy had promised, the bad thoughts and images were replaced by nice thoughts, nice pictures: her dolls, Daddy and Mommy laughing, her birthday cake, blowing out the candles . . .

SCOTT SAT WITH HIS BACK against the cold wall in the holding cell. Drenched in depression, he didn't seem to mind the gloomy atmosphere, the stench of urine, and the filthy-looking drunk across from him snoring through every orifice in his body, the gross sound reverberating with such volume, Scott felt it vibrate his spine. Fingerprinted again, photographed with a number, and made to empty his pockets, he felt demeaned, denuded of any semblance of self-respect. In the macho eyes of the policemen around him, he was less than an insect, a wife beater, a child snatcher.

He closed his eyes, wishing he could drift into unconsciousness and wake up as he had after his gall bladder operation three years ago to find that it was all over. Why not? he mused. Why not anesthetize people like himself, innocent people charged with a crime and forced to parade through the maze of the criminal justice system? His attorney would be like a surgeon, performing the necessary operation to free him of the cancer of the accusation. And then, when it was over, he could regain consciousness, be handed his personal effects, and released.

We could have judicial insurance just like we have medical insurance, he thought, continuing the fantasy. So that after it was all over, he would simply submit the bill to his insurance company and even the financial burden would be relieved. The justice department, the district attorney's office in particular, would have to foot the bill for a headline story in the *Los Angeles*

*Times* and some radio stations that said, *Scott Lester Found Innocent of All Charges.*

Lost in this fantasy, he didn't hear the policeman call his name until he did so for the third time.

"Lester, you deaf or what?"

He sat up.

"Your attorney is here," he said and opened the cell door. "Let's go."

"My attorney? What about the anesthesiologist?"

"Huh?"

"Nothing," Scott said, standing up. He took a deep breath and walked out. The guard closed the door and indicated he should continue down the corridor. They came to a bland wooden door at the end and the guard turned the knob.

"Mr. Lester," he announced and stepped back so Scott could enter. He did so slowly. Every time he had entered a room lately, it resulted in some more unhappiness.

But this time, seated at the conference table was a rather attractive dark-haired woman with the brightest hazel eyes he had ever seen. She wore her hair cut and curled just shoulder high. She had petite facial features with a chin that made a soft turn up into high cheek bones. Her firm bosom lifted against the light blue Chanel silk suit jacket when she sat back. Under the jacket she wore a pearl silk blouse, the two top buttons undone.

"Please sit down, Mr. Lester," she said, indicating the chair across from her. "I'm Faye Elliot, from Orseck, Greenberg and Wilson."

"You're my lawyer?" he asked, surprised they had sent him a female attorney.

"Yes," she replied. "Do you have a problem with that?" she followed, those hazel eyes sharpening as they narrowed.

"I don't know," Scott said sitting down. "I've had lots of problems lately."

Faye Elliot nodded.

"That's for sure," she said. "I've spoken with Michael Fein, so I know the history of your relationship with your wife and the current divorce preceding and battle for custody of your child."

"Justine," Scott said. "Her name's Justine. Meg picked it out, but I always liked it."

"It's a very nice name," Faye said quickly. She was firm, stiffly seated, all business. "Now I assume you understand the charges that have been made against you. They're going for attempted murder. I've already had a quick discussion with the assistant district attorney. I think if the whereabouts of Justine can be determined, we can deal."

"Deal?"

"Get them to reduce the charges. You'll plead guilty and . . ."

"Just a minute. Hold it," he said, sitting forward. "I'm not guilty of anything. I mean, I didn't attack Meg and I did not kidnap Justine."

"Mr. Lester, here's what they have: motive—your wife has filed for divorce and you're losing the fight for joint custody of your daughter. In fact, it looks very likely that you will be severely restricted when it comes to her; opportunity—you were found at the scene of the crime, even though you were clearly not supposed to be on the premises at that hour and there is evidence that a struggle ensued; weapon—confirmed; this little statue was used to bludgeon your wife; finally and conclusively, your prints are clearly on it."

"I didn't do it," he insisted. "I found her. I called the police. If I did it, why would I call the police and stay there, huh?"

Unflinching, her eyes straight, her lips firm, she leaned toward him.

"Precisely for what you are doing now—using it to establish your innocence. That's what the district attorney will say," she said, sitting back. He stared at her.

"All right, Mr. Lester . . ."

"Scott. If you're going to be my attorney, at least call me by my first name," he said. "I feel like I'm in an IRS audit instead of a conference with my attorney."

She blinked. He had finally broken through that facade of efficiency and officiality.

"I'm sorry," she said. "I'm just trying to be realistic. At times like this, it doesn't pay to dabble in illusion, pretend things are better than they are just to spare feelings."

"You very experienced?" he asked.

"Not very," she confessed. She hesitated and then admitted, "You're my first violent crime."

"What? Oh, I get it," he said, "they sent you because everyone thinks this is a fait accompli, huh? A lost cause. That's why you're marching me through it so quickly."

"Mr. Lester, that . . ."

"Scott. Call me Scott, damn it." She blanched. "Look," he said more calmly, "I know how it looks. I don't need you to spell it out, but I swear to God, I didn't do it. I may be an asshole to do some of the stupid things I've done, but I'm not a vicious, violent individual. Hell, the last time I've been in a physical confrontation of any sort was the sixth grade and the other boy, Rube Martin, kicked my head in." He took a deep breath. "Please, give me the benefit of some doubt. If you don't, who the hell will?" he pleaded.

Her face softened, first her lips relaxing and then her eyes warming. She flipped open a legal pad and opened a pen.

"All right, Scott, what were you doing at the house?"

He thought a moment.

"I don't know," he said.

"Excuse me?" She finally smiled.

"I was left there . . . dumped."

"Dumped?"

"I was unconscious at the time... stoned," he added, his voice dropping.

"I see. Who dumped you?"

"A friend, or at least someone I thought was a friend. His name is Philip Dante." She wrote it down.

"How long have you known Mr. Dante?"

"Not long. Days," he said.

"Where did you meet him?"

"In court. I turned around and he was sitting in the back observing the preceding. Afterward, we talked and went for a drink."

"How did you get into this situation... dumped?" she asked, sitting back and folding her arms under her bosom.

"I went to a party with Philip Dante. It was kind of rowdy. Lots to drink... champagne, girls. I must have passed out. Next thing I know, I wake up in the house."

"You went to a party with a man you had just met, drank yourself into unconsciousness..."

"Well, there was some coke, too," he confessed.

"Mr. Lester... Scott, admitting you were under the influence of drugs doesn't let you off the hook. Under the law, people are still accountable—"

"I didn't hurt Meg," he insisted.

"The prosecution will prove the other possibility; they will convince a jury. Even if I was willing to put forward this line of defense, I would be irresponsible to let you believe it could be argued successfully in a courtroom with grown-ups."

He flinched. She looked down at her notes.

"You told the investigating officers, Lieutenant Parker and Detective Fotowski, that you never touched the statue of cupid. How do you explain your fingerprints being on it?"

"I don't know," he said, shaking his head. "Maybe I did touch it once."

"You shouldn't have been so definite in saying you didn't," she complained.

"Yeah, well the next time this happens to me, I'll clamp my lips together from the moment I'm picked up until my attorney arrives. I'm innocent. I didn't think of doing things to protect myself until it was too late," he moaned.

She took a deep breath. The lines in her neck were so smooth, he thought. How could he sit here admiring her looks? he wondered. Maybe he was crazy.

"All right," she said after a moment. "What about this Philip Dante? Can we get a hold of him and have him testify that he brought you to the house?"

"I don't know."

"What's his phone number?" she asked, leaning over, "and address?"

"I don't know," he said. She looked up. "I tried calling him as soon as I discovered what had happened at the house, but the information operator didn't have a listing, not even for an unlisted number."

She shook her head. "Can you hear yourself? Do you understand what you are saying? Can you begin to imagine how a jury presented with the evidence will react?"

"I didn't hit my wife with that statue," he insisted. He hated the whiny sound in his voice.

"Can you find this Mr. Dante? Do you know where he works?"

"He's an insurance salesman," Scott said, grabbing onto that fact desperately.

"Okay. What else do you remember about him?"

"He was involved in a nasty divorce and custody hearing, too," Scott said quickly and continued to rummage through his mind, tearing the shadows away from his memories. "He has a son . . . little boy named Marvin and his wife's name is Maureen. No, not Maureen, that's the woman his wife caught him with . . . Victoria. Yeah, that's it," he said happily. "She works for a dentist."

"You know a lot about him without knowing his address and phone number," Faye Elliot said.

"Yeah, well, he told me his situation."

"Uh huh. That information is helpful, Scott, but it would still require the services of a private investigator to locate the man, and that's expensive."

"I don't care. It's more expensive for me to be wrongfully accused and convicted. I'll mortgage myself to the hilt, sell everything of value I own." He leaned toward her. "Money should not be of any concern at this moment, don't you agree?"

"Yes," she said. "If you have it or can get it."

"I'll get it. Can you get me out of here?"

"There's a bail hearing in the morning. We'll try," she replied.

"I've got to sleep in that hole," he said with a sigh. His tone made the comment sound like a complaint.

Faye didn't look sympathetic. "I'm innocent. Really." He sat back calmly. "Who else but an innocent man would protest his innocence in the face of such an overwhelming case against him?" he asked.

Faye Elliot smiled, this time a wide, warm one.

"If we can find this man and he can testify to bringing you to the house and dumping you there as some sort of sick joke . . ."

"Yes?" Scott leaned forward.

"And the coroner determines that the time of the attack on your wife was much earlier . . ."

"A huh."

"We can establish some reasonable doubt. Does your wife have any other enemies you know?"

"I'm not her enemy," he said. "I was an unfaithful husband. I screwed around, hooked myself into a cocaine habit, but I wasn't her enemy. I was angry about her trying to cut me off from Justine. I'll admit that, but I wouldn't try to kill the mother of my child."

He didn't want the tears to fill his eyes; he hated revealing his weakness in front of a woman he had never met before; he hated the groveling and the pleading; he despised himself as he now was, but somehow, he knew he had to cling to enough self-respect to care and to do battle for his survival.

"I'm sorry," Faye Elliot said. Her femininity appeared to rise to the surface. "Does she have any enemies?"

"None I know." He hesitated. Should he tell her? He wasn't afraid of betraying the Solomon Organization; that was the furthest from his mind. He was afraid he would lose the morsel of sympathy he had evoked from Faye Elliot. She would see him as a plotter, a co-conspirator. Even if he had no knowledge of what they were going to do, he was still an accomplice. If he could just locate Dante and do what his attorney suggested . . . create reasonable doubt.

"And you have no idea, no thoughts or suggestions as to where Justine might be?"

"No. Wherever she is," he said softly, straining to get out the words, "she must be terrified." He shook his head, a single tear escaping. He hoped she didn't see it fall. "Maybe I am guilty," he muttered.

"Pardon?"

"Guilty of creating the situation that enabled all this to happen." He took a deep breath and sat up. "But I didn't try to kill my wife or kidnap my daughter."

"Okay," she said, folding her notebook. "Try to get some sleep. I want you to look as good as you can for that bail hearing tomorrow."

She stood up and tapped on the door. The guard opened it.

"Good night," she said and left. He heard her heels clicking down the hall.

"Let's go," the guard said, eying Scott's departing attorney with a leer. "Not bad," he added. "I'm tempted to commit a crime."

His laughter wrapped itself around Scott as they started back to his dingy cell. It was as if a giant spider had woven a web. He could only wait for the sting. Just like the trapped fly, he knew it was coming. His passion for life was so great, he could even tolerate the stinking, dark hole to which he was returned.

# 5

Justine opened her eyes and was surprised to find herself in the prettiest, brightest bedroom she had ever seen. She sat up slowly, almost afraid to take a breath. The two windows across from her were draped in cherry pink and white curtains. The walls were covered with the Loony Tunes paper that depicted all her favorite cartoon characters.

Whoever had put her here had first visited her dreams and made a shopping list of all her desires and wishes. To the right of the windows was a doll house big enough for her to crawl into filled with miniature furniture. There was even a miniature television set with real miniature dials that worked. On the wall to her left were a half-dozen shelves loaded with the largest collection of stuffed animals she had ever seen. Every single one that she owned and every single one that she ever dreamed of owning was there, all smiling down at her, just waiting to be cuddled and loved. Below the shelves was a gigantic toy chest with Bugs Bunny etched out on the front. His toothy smile promised the chest contained more delightful surprises.

She gazed at the bed she was in. It was her very own bed with its white posts and pictures of Mickey and Minnie Mouse on the headboard. These were the same fluffy pillows and this was her pink and white down comforter. She pressed the soft material to her face. The linen even had a similar pleasant scent. Was she home? How could she be home? She didn't have all these things at home.

A cuckoo clock on the top shelf and in the middle of the stuffed animals opened its door and the bird jetted out to cluck the hours. It looked like Big Bird from Sesame Street. She couldn't help but giggle when the bird jerked back in and the doors closed. Then, as if on cue, a music box on the small desk began to play. Atop it, a beautiful ballerina started to pirouette. Justine watched in fascination until the door to this room was opened and a very pleasant looking elderly lady entered carrying a tray on which there was a glass of orange juice and a bowel of hot cereal. She stepped lightly over the thick white shag rug, lifting and dropping her feet as if she were afraid she would step on eggs.

She had her silver blue hair pinned up in a bun and wore wide rim, gray metal framed glasses. Her cheeks were rosy and she had a warm, soft smile. She was dressed in a bright blue house coat with big pockets. The dress went down to her ankles, which were covered with thick, flesh-colored socks. Her shiny black shoes had wide, thick soles. She was somewhat chubby with soft, heavy arms, wide hips, and a matronly bosom.

"Good morning, honey," she sang. "This morning, since it's your first morning with Grandma, I've brought you your breakfast. Here," she said, placing the tray carefully on Justine's lap. "Just hold it a moment until I get your little bed table out from under the bed. That's a good girl."

When she bent down to get the table, Justine saw she had a pretty aqua pearl comb in her hair.

"Just lift the tray now. That's a good girl; that's Grandma's good girl," she said and slipped the table over Justine's legs. She helped Justine place the tray on the table.

"What do we have?" she asked Justine and then pointed to the glass of juice. "We have freshly squeezed orange juice to give you vitamin C." She pinched Justine's cheek gently. "And we have a good healthy cereal to give you more vitamins and iron and calcium to make sure you have good teeth. Grandma always brings the bestest things to her grandchildren," she added and widened her smile to reveal a gold tooth. "Now are you going to eat for Grandma?"

Justine was still too overwhelmed to speak. She could barely nod her head, but it was enough to make Grandma clap her hands together and squeal with delight.

"That's my girl; that's my good girl," she said and handed Justine the glass of juice. She drank it slowly, her eyes never leaving the jolly old lady who stood beside the bed gloating. "You've got to be hungry," she said. "Everyone's hungry when they come to Grandma's."

Justine blinked and thought. She knew that Daddy's mommy was dead and gone to Heaven, along with his daddy. She knew Mommy's daddy went to Heaven and Nanny Turner was back East where Aunt Abby lived. Where did she get this new Grandma?

"Come on now, dear. Eat your cereal while it's still warm. It will feel good in your tummy," Grandma said.

Justine put down the emptied juice glass and lifted the cereal spoon. Grandma nodded, still beaming as Justine began to eat the cereal. It wasn't bad and it wasn't too hot like hot cereal often was when Mommy made it.

"Grandma is so happy you've come. It was very lonely here without little feet and little hands. I like to hear the laughter of my grandchildren. Oh," she said, clapping her hands together again, "we're going to have such a good time."

Justine swallowed some cereal and paused.

"Where's my mommy?" she asked.

"Oh, you mustn't ask Grandma anything. You must wait until Doctor Goodfellow comes to see you. Doctor Goodfellow is a very wise man, who knows all the answers to all the questions. All my grandchildren love Doctor Goodfellow. He makes them feel safe and secure like a warm bath.

"After breakfast, I'm going to help you take a warm bath and then we'll dress you in your nice new clothes," Grandma said and walked over to the closet. "See," she said, sliding the door open. Justine gazed at the garments, many still showing their tags. "Everything's new and pretty." Grandma reached in and plucked out a pink taffeta dress with a white lace collar and sleeves that had white lace cuffs. "How about this one first?"

"I want Mommy," Justine said after a moment. "Where is she?"

"Oh, dear, dear. You're not going to cry or anything, are you?" Grandma said and made a terrified face. "It's no good for Grandma and you don't want Grandma to get sick, do you?" The kind-looking old lady pressed her palm over her heart and closed her eyes. Then she opened them quickly.

Justine shook her head.

"That's a good girl. That's Grandma's girl. Finish your cereal while I run your bath. We have bubble-bath drops so you can sit in the foam. Don't you like that?"

Justine nodded; she did.

"Little girls should always smell sweet and be clean and that means your hair, too. I'll wash it and chase away any dirt. Then you will be all set to talk to Doctor Goodfellow."

"And he'll tell me where Mommy is?"

"Of course," Grandma said. She clapped her hands together again. "I'm so glad you've come," she sang. "We're going to have such a good time until you have to go away. We'll make cookies, all shapes and sizes. Did you ever make cookies?"

Justine shook her head. Mommy was always promising to do something like that, but she never had.

"Then won't that be fun?"

Justine nodded.

"What a good girl. But then again, all Grandma's little girls are good girls or else . . . they'd never come to Grandma's."

Justine watched as Grandma went into the bathroom and started to run the water, singing as she worked. What a nice voice she had. What a nice place this was. She was sure that in such a nice place with such a nice old lady, Mommy couldn't be too far away. Everything was going to be all right. She kept eating; the cereal was so good and she couldn't wait to crawl into that doll house.

SCOTT FELT LIKE a piece of meat, a slab tattooed with a number and hung on a hook. The bailiff read out the numbers and the slabs were sent along until they ended up in front of the judge, who barely looked up from the papers he shuffled around on his desk. He was a small man with a bushy salt-and-pepper mustache and a military-style haircut. Whenever he did look up, he shifted his big eyes from side to side as if checking the corners of the room for assassins. There was something comical about him; he reminded Scott of Groucho Marx.

But there was nothing comical about the situation, Scott thought. This was his arraignment. Faye Elliot already told him the prosecution wanted him held without bail. She would have to argue and convince that odd-looking man to give him his freedom.

He couldn't believe all the noise around him. This was nothing like the courtroom scenes depicted on television. Not even "L.A. Law" was this realistic, he thought sadly. Why hadn't he been warned what to expect? How could he maintain any dignity being grouped in with drug dealers, prostitutes, burglars, car thieves, and armed robbers. There was no one of his ilk here, no white-collar criminals, no one in a jacket and tie.

He gazed around dejectedly. He was going to suffocate, turn blue and die before he had a chance to prove his innocence. He imagined that if one of these accused died on the spot, no one would notice. The proceeding would continue and sentence would be pronounced over his corpse. They might even deliver the body to the penitentiary. No one really looked at him. They might not notice his demise.

He vaguely heard his name read. The charges against him seemed so ridiculous they had to be talking about someone else. How he longed for a drink or a line of coke, something to lift him out of this sewer. I'm going to be flushed down the toilet, he thought. Any moment they're going to stuff my head into the pipe.

Faye nudged him. She wanted him to stand up straight and look the judge in the eye.

"Not guilty, Your Honor," he said as firmly and as clearly as he could. He wanted to add, "of course."

"Mr. Selzer," the judge said, turning to the young prosecutor. Scott thought the lawyer looked like one of those yuppie types who drove up in their leased BMWs and came in to consider a Mercedes . . . until they heard the numbers. Every one of them was a waste of time.

"Your Honor," the young prosecutor began, "the state feels that as long as Mrs. Lester's daughter is still missing, it would be in the best interest of both her and her daughter for Mr. Lester to be held over to trial. We are asking that bail be withheld and he be returned to the county jail until such time as the whereabouts of Justine Lester can be determined."

"That's absolutely ridiculous, Your Honor!" Faye Elliot exclaimed. The judge looked up, his eyebrows rising. Did she say the secret word? Scott wondered. Were they on Groucho's "You Bet Your Life?" "Mr. Lester has an absolutely spotless record; he doesn't even have a speeding ticket on his license. He is employed in a highly reputable firm. He owns a home, maintains a mortgage, has financial obligations and business commitments."

"He has attacked his wife and kidnapped his daughter," the prosecutor retorted.

"Allegedly. This is not the trial," Faye said.

"Your Honor, this would not be the first time a parent has run off with a child just before or just after a custody decision has been made against that parent. The state wishes to ensure . . ."

"This isn't a custody hearing," Faye Elliot cried. "My client is being accused of attempted murder!"

"At last, a factual statement," the judge declared. "Mr. Selzer, Ms. Elliot has a point."

"But . . ."

"Bail will be set. Name a figure, Mr. Selzer."

"Your Honor . . ."

"Name a figure or I'll set it."

"One million dollars!"

"Your Honor," Faye began, but the judge held up his hand.

"Bail is set at two hundred thousand dollars. Trial date has been set for October 4. Next, please."

"Is that it?" Scott asked.

"You have to come up with twenty thousand dollars."

"Twenty . . ."

"You'll put up your house and a bail bondsman will put up the money, unless you have that money set aside somewhere."

"Sure," Scott said. "In the backyard." She didn't appreciate his sense of humor. There was reprimand in those big hazel eyes. "Sorry," he muttered.

"The most important thing, as far as you are concerned now," she lectured, "is for you to find this Philip Dante." She scribbled an address on her legal pad and then ripped out the page. "This is the name and address of a private detective my firm has used on occasion. I haven't ever met him, but I was told he is the most reasonable yet effective investigator in town."

Scott took the paper and gazed at what she had written. Great handwriting, he thought.

"Henry Dyce?"

She nodded and closed her briefcase.

"He's in West L.A.," Scott said. "I know this area; it's residential."

"He works out of his apartment. Low overhead. He's supposed to be good," she added. "An ex-L.A. detective."

"Why ex?"

"He's not a team player, which is all right for a private investigator. Look," she said, indicating they should start to exit the courtroom, "I've already spoken to Mr. Dyce. He knows you're coming to see him. Get there right away and keep me closely informed as to progress."

"Am I allowed to go to the hospital to see my wife?" Scott asked. The question gave her pause.

"You can do most anything, but you can't leave the state. On second thought, visiting your wife might be a good idea. Call me before you go up to the hospital," she said. "I don't mean to sound conniving, but it can't hurt for you to show concern about your wife. I want to know exactly when and how often you go."

"I am concerned about my wife," he said abruptly. "And my daughter. Until I'm vindicated, the police won't look elsewhere and she won't be found." He sighed deeply. "One of these days," he added, "you're going to believe I'm innocent."

"I'm going to put up the best defense I can, Scott." She smiled. "But it wouldn't hurt my efforts if you turned out to be innocent."

"Thanks."

"You know where to reach me," she said. Honey, he thought, I don't know if anyone ever reaches you.

As soon as the arrangements were made for his bail, Scott phoned the hospital to ask about Meg. He was connected to patient information.

"Mrs. Lester's condition is unchanged," an indifferent, mechanical voice replied to his inquiry. He didn't say thank you; he hung up and went to see Henry Dyce.

The private investigator lived just off South Barrington Avenue. Scott knew the area because he had once picked up a UCLA graduate student at a sports bar and taken her home. She lived only a block east of Henry Dyce.

It was one of those gray days some Los Angeles residents enjoyed, but not Scott. Despite the length of time he and Meg had been in Southern California, Scott was not bored with one day of sunshine after another. He fed off the brightness the way a vampire fed off blood. Gray days, rain, even partly cloudy days, affected his moods. In the early days out here, he used to love calling his friends back east and grinding the weather reports into their very souls.

"It's nine in the morning and I'm out on my patio having coffee," he would tell them in mid-January. They called him every name under the sun, but he bathed in the envy. No one would be envious of him now, he thought sadly and parked his car after checking and rechecking the No Parking signs. Los Angeles had the best parking enforcement in the world. It seemed like there was a traffic cop or meter maid for every block.

Henry Dyce's building looked at least forty years old: a three-story, white stucco that was gray stained from years of smog and grime, smoky windows with faded wooden casements, and a pathetic flower bed in the courtyard with vaguely trimmed hedges along the walls. The iron gate in front was bent away from its hinges so that the lock was a virtual vestigial organ. There was no need to buzz a resident to get into the lot, but Scott found Henry's name and number and pressed the button anyway to tell the man he had arrived. A resident or visitor had to walk through the courtyard to the front entrance.

When it was first built and for a time afterward, this place must have been quaint and sweet, Scott imagined as he made his way. Dyce lived on the third floor; there was no elevator. At least he might have a view, Scott thought and marched up the steps.

He stopped at Dyce's door and knocked. There was no response, so he knocked again, harder this time. After a moment, the door was opened and Scott was surprised to be greeted by a stout, six-feet-two-inch black man who looked like he might once have been as handsome as Sidney Poitier. Now fatigue filled the bags under his eyes and his hairline receded a few inches from his forehead. He was grimy-looking and unshaven, his two- or three-day beard as rough as granite with thick patches on his chin and just under his lower lip. He was dressed in a stained T-shirt and very worn beltless jeans. He stood shoeless in dark wool socks. Scott thought he easily had size twelve or thirteen feet.

The door of Dyce's condo opened directly on the living room, which was unfortunate, for any visitor was immediately greeted by the worn furniture and mess—clothes and magazines strewn about the sofa, coffee cups, glasses and crusted dishes left on the tables for days, newspapers opened and spread on the faded and stained brown carpet, and light caramel drapes that looked like they had never been taken down and washed since the day

they had been put up, maybe forty years ago. They hung list-
lessly, shapeless, and added that pathetic touch to simple slov-
enliness.

Dyce saw the look on Scott's face.

"The maid ain't been here," Dyce said. "For two or three
years," he added and smiled. At least he has great teeth, Scott
thought and extended his hand.

"Scott Lester."

Dyce swallowed up Scott's fingers in what looked like a swol-
len palm and fingers. They weren't; the man just had huge
hands and forearms.

"Come on in. It's all right. You been inoculated?"

"Against what?"

"Well, no man's every gotten pregnant in here." Dyce cleared
off one of the deep cushion chairs and gestured. "I'm just havin'
some coffee."

"No, thanks," Scott said quickly. He might go to jail for
something he didn't do, but he wasn't going to catch any diseases
beforehand, he thought. Dyce smiled again.

"I'm a bachelor," he said as if that justified being a slob.

"Me, too. Now, that is. Is this what I have to look forward
to?" he asked gazing around. Dyce laughed.

"How long were you married?" he called from the kitchen.

"Nearly ten years."

"No shit," Dyce replied. He returned, mug in hand. "I was
married a year and a half. She couldn't stand a policeman's
life. A real party girl, could drink and dance 'til dawn and then
some. I used to beg her to go home just so I could catch a few
winks before going on duty. Coulda got me killed, livin' like
that."

Scott nodded. Other people's lives and troubles had little
interest to him right now. Dyce felt it.

"So give me some background here."

"How much did Faye Elliot tell you?"

"Diddly," Dyce said, sitting on the sofa without moving the magazines and newspapers out of his way. "Just that you needed someone found; it was crucial to your defense. Defense against what?"

"Charge of attempted murder. They think I kidnapped my daughter, too."

"Attempted murder? Your wife?"

"Yes."

"How old's your daughter?"

"Five. I can't believe she left all this out," Scott said.

"She was quick, like talking to me was beneath her."

"That's her," Scott said. "But I got the feeling today in court that she's good at what she does, and like they say, you don't have to fall in love with your doctor; let him just cure you."

Dyce grunted.

"Who do I gotta find?"

Scott described Philip Dante and the situation as quickly as he could. While he spoke, Dyce peered at him periodically over the rim of the coffee cup. The man has policeman's eyes, Scott thought. He felt the questions, the analysis, and study. Dyce listened without speaking.

"You do a lot of this sort of work?" Scott followed.

"I get a bone thrown to me from time to time. Enough to keep me in black-eyed peas."

Scott nodded. Considering how critical it was, why did Faye Elliot send him to this man? Perhaps she didn't know how down and out he really was, Scott thought.

"But, I always get my man," Dyce added. "Don't let this fool ya," he said, indicating the disheveled apartment. "Chevy on the outside, Mercedes on the inside."

Scott smiled.

"That's what I sell . . . Mercedes."

"No shit. All right," Dyce said, sitting forward. "I'm a hundred-a-day plus expenses, which is dirt cheap nowadays." Scott nodded. "I don't get your man it's because he don't exist. That's a promise."

"All right."

"What I want you to do now," Dyce said, reaching under the sofa to come up with a pad and pen, "is sit back and start remembering this Dante from the first moment you set eyes on him. I want every detail about him, no matter how small or stupid it seems to you, understand? I want to know his looks, how he talks, how he walks, any special gesture, clothes, identifying body marks, and every tidbit about his life he revealed. Go back over the things he said, as close to word for word as you can get. Don't worry about boring me. Understand?"

Scott nodded. For the time being, he thought, he would leave out any mention of the Solomon Organization. If they found Philip Dante, he felt positive, the man would reveal Justine's whereabouts. He still had hope he could get out of this without complicating his defense.

"Okay," Dyce said, sitting forward. "Relax, sit back. Go ahead, close your eyes and remember."

Scott began to selectively recall the events that had occurred over the past few days. As he did so, he had the eerie feeling he was telling a story about someone else.

"I was in court; the day's proceedings were just about over when I turned around and saw this well-dressed man sitting in the rear of the courtroom . . ."

JUSTINE LOOKED UP from the amazing doll that said, "Mommy, I'm hungry. Can I go for a walk? I love my new dress and new shoes. It's time for my nap." All Justine had to do was push the little button on the doll's back, and each time it came up with another question or statement.

Justine was sitting on the floor in front of the doll house.

She was dressed in the new taffeta dress and wore shiny new shoes and white socks. She even had new panties and a new undershirt. Grandma had washed her hair, dried, and styled it like a professional hair dresser. It never felt as soft or lay as gently against her shoulders, neck, and back. Then Grandma helped her get dressed and told her she could play with anything she liked. She took her tray and promised she would return. When Justine asked for her mommy again, Grandma promised Doctor Goodfellow would be coming to see her shortly. Now he was apparently here.

Doctor Goodfellow was a gray-haired man with friendly blue eyes that made him look younger than he was. When he smiled, as he was now, his eyes became even brighter blue. He wasn't short, but he wasn't very tall, either. He was very slim with dainty-looking shoulders and soft-looking hands. He wore a dark blue suit and tie. When he drew close enough, Justine caught a whiff of his sweet cologne. He knelt down beside her and took her hand gently into his. He wore a beautiful triangular diamond ring on the pinky and, for a moment, she was hypnotized with the gleam in the stone.

"Good morning, Justine," Doctor Goodfellow said. "I'm Doctor Goodfellow. How are you getting along? Do you like all your new things?"

She nodded. When Doctor Goodfellow spoke to her, he looked right into her eyes so intently she couldn't look away.

"Here," he said, taking her smoothly into his arms and then standing. "Let's sit down on your bed and have our first good talk, okay?"

The skin on Doctor Goodfellow's face was so smooth, it looked like he never had to shave. He had small features with lips that became pencil thin when he closed his mouth. When he did that, a small dimple appeared on his right cheek. Justine felt like putting the tip of her finger in it.

He set her down gently on the bed and then sat down beside

her. When he crossed his legs, she saw that he had small feet. Everything about him was diminutive. He looked like a man with a young boy's body, and especially, a young boy's smile. But he had a man's voice—deep and yet melodious with such a happy tone she expected he would start to sing to her any moment.

"I'm here to help you," he began, "to make sure you're happy and you have all the things you need and want."

"I want my mommy," Justine said immediately.

"Well that's what I'm here to talk about first," he said quietly. "You're a big girl so you already know that people have to go away forever and ever sometimes. You know where they go?"

Justine shook her head because she wasn't sure what Doctor Goodfellow meant.

"They go to Heaven to live with God. You know about that, don't you?" She nodded. "Usually they don't go until they're very old. Like your daddy's mommy and daddy and your mommy's daddy, remember?"

Justine nodded. Her little heart began to beat faster for reasons she didn't understand. Her body was reacting to thoughts and ideas that were threatening to be spoken and were yet unheard.

"Well, sometimes, accidents happen and people have to go to Heaven before they're old. You know about that too, right?"

She shook her head. She didn't want to hear this; this was not heading for something nice.

"They do, Justine. They get hurt badly. Oh, maybe in car accidents or plane accidents. Once, a man I knew was walking on the street in a big city," Doctor Goodfellow said. He smiled, leading Justine to think he was going to tell her a nice story. "When way up high in a building he was passing, a woman accidentally pushed a flower pot over the ledge of her window. It fell and fell and hit my friend right on top of his head, and you know what . . ."

Justine shook her head, her mouth slightly open.

"My friend had to go right to Heaven. He didn't even have time to say goodbye to anyone."

That wasn't a very happy story, she thought.

"And the same thing happened to your mommy. It wasn't a flower pot falling out of a window that hit her. Something else hit her and she went right to Heaven," Doctor Goodfellow said, lifting his arm slowly and then pointing the tips of his fingers at the ceiling.

"I want my mommy," Justine said softly.

"Of course you do. Every little girl should have a Mommy. And a Daddy. But you don't have a Daddy anymore, either, do you? You remember . . . he left you and your mommy, right?"

Justine didn't nod, but she remembered.

"I want you to come with me next door where I have a television set and a sofa for you to sit on. I'm going to show you a little movie. Would you like that?"

Justine wasn't sure. She bit down on her lower lip.

"You will like it," Doctor Goodfellow promised. "Come on," he said, standing up and holding out his hand. Justine hesitated. "Oh, I forgot," Doctor Goodfellow said, smiling. He dug into his jacket pocket. "I have something delicious for you to eat while you're watching the movie on television. Here," he said, offering Justine a big, round red lollypop. "Red's your favorite flavor, right?"

She nodded and slowly took the lolly.

"Here," Doctor Goodfellow said. "Let me unwrap it for you." He did so and gave it back to her. "You can eat it now," he said. She put it into her mouth and began to suck. He extended his hand again, and this time she reached out and took it. Then she got up to walk with him out of the room.

The hallway was dark. There was just a little light coming

through a window way down in front of them. Doctor Goodfellow led her to a door nearby and they entered what looked
like a waiting room in the doctor's office. There was a leather
sofa, a leather chair, a table, and against the wall, a television
set. Under it was a video deck.

"You can sit right there in the center of the sofa, Justine,"
Doctor Goodfellow said. "Go on." He released her hand and
she climbed on the sofa, sat down, and looked up as he fiddled
with the video deck. The television set went on and then Doctor
Goodfellow sat down beside her.

Suddenly, Doctor Goodfellow was on television, too.

"Hello, Justine," he said and waited as if he expected her to
reply. He smiled. Justine looked at Doctor Goodfellow beside
her and saw he was smiling the same way he was smiling on
television. "I'm glad you're here to see my movie," he began
on television. "This is a movie about a little girl like you whose
Mommy had to go right to Heaven, just like your mommy had
to go. And just like you she was very sad and very frightened
at first.

"Her name is Gabrielle," Doctor Goodfellow said and then
turned to reveal a little girl sitting in the very office Justine was
now seated in. Gabrielle was about her age, too, only she had
light blonde hair. She looked small and afraid, just as Doctor
Goodfellow had said.

"This is Gabrielle's story, which will be your story, too.
Ready. Here it is."

The screen cut to a residential street in a city. First, there
was only the traffic and strangers walking up and down. Then,
the camera sought out Gabrielle and a woman walking quickly
up the sidewalk. Doctor Goodfellow, the narrator now, began.

"Gabrielle lived with her mommy in a big city. They lived
in an apartment, though, not a house."

Gabrielle and the pretty woman alongside her turned into
an apartment courtyard and headed for the front door.

"Because Gabrielle's Daddy had left them, Gabrielle's Mommy had to see to all Gabrielle's needs, and that was very hard for Gabrielle's Mommy. She had to work, take care of the house, and look after Gabrielle."

The camera panned the apartment building and then tightened on a window about six floors up. As it closed, Gabrielle's face became clearer in the window. She was looking out wistfully.

"Gabrielle couldn't do many of the things other children her age could do because her mommy was too tired to take her. Her friends had Daddies to take them to the park or to movies, or just to watch them play. Their mommies could take them, too, because their mommies weren't working, working, working."

The camera tilted down to the front of the apartment where Doctor Goodfellow stood smiling.

"Little girls," he said, "should grow up in homes that have both Mommies and Daddies. One day, poor Gabrielle lost even her mommy."

A view of a busy city street appeared.

"Her mommy," Doctor Goodfellow said, "was hurrying home because she was afraid Gabrielle would arrive from school before she would get there and then be all alone. She hurried and hurried and didn't watch where she was going and she walked right out on the street while cars were rushing by.

"One of those cars hit Gabrielle's Mommy and sent her right to Heaven."

The camera tilted up toward the sky. Then Doctor Goodfellow appeared full face.

"And poor Gabrielle was all alone."

The screen went blank and then suddenly there was Grandma bringing in a tray, just the way she had brought a tray to Justine in the morning. She was smiling and happy.

"But Gabrielle wasn't alone," Doctor Goodfellow narrated

over the picture of Grandma. "For she had Grandma and Grandma was there to look after her until her new mommy and daddy arrived."

A car was seen driving up. After it stopped, a handsome couple emerged. The man was tall and dark with a gleaming smile and the woman was very pretty with pretty blonde hair that lay softly over her shoulders. They were seen entering a room and then the camera panned to pick up Gabrielle, all dressed up, her hair as nicely brushed and styled as Justine's now was. The handsome couple went directly to her and in moments, it seemed, the pretty woman was holding her and kissing her.

"Little girls need Mommies and Daddies who love each other and will make a warm and happy home for them," Doctor Goodfellow said as the couple left, Gabrielle between them, holding hands.

Then followed a montage of happy scenes: Gabrielle with her new parents entering Disney World; Gabrielle with her new parents having a picnic in some pretty park; Gabrielle laughing with her new parents who played paddle ball with her on the lawn of their beautiful home, and finally, Gabrielle at the table ready to blow out the candles of her birthday cake. She did and the voices of her new parents were heard singing, "Happy birthday to you, Happy birthday to you, Happy birthday, dear Gabrielle, Happy birthday to you."

The movie ended with Gabrielle hugging her new mommy and then turning to be scooped up into her new daddy's arms.

"Wasn't that a nice movie?" Doctor Goodfellow asked. Justine nodded. She watched him get up and turn off the television set.

"I bet you'd like to have a nice new Mommy and Daddy, too, wouldn't you?"

Justine shook her head.

"I want to go home," she said.

Doctor Goodfellow's smile wilted. He dug his hand into his pocket and brought out a tape recorder.

"Come here," he urged and held out his hand. "Come on," he said more firmly. Justine took his hand and he led her to the window. He opened it and they looked out over the lawn toward the street. "Call your daddy," he ordered. "Go ahead. Say, Daddy, where are you? Say it," he commanded and brought the tape recorder closer. She started to cry, but he shook her hand. "Say it. Daddy, where are you?"

"Daddy, where are you?" she said.

"Good. Now say, when are you coming for me? Go ahead. When are you coming for me, Daddy?"

"When are you coming for me, Daddy?"

Doctor Goodfellow smiled.

"Good girl," he said, "but look. No Daddy. Your old daddy is not coming ever. But don't worry. You will go home, but to a new and nicer home, a home where the Mommy and Daddy don't argue and fight and hate each other to bits, a home where you can be happy forever and grow into a good Mommy yourself."

She watched him go to his desk to push a button on the side. A moment later, Grandma appeared. She and Doctor Goodfellow exchanged looks and then Grandma smiled.

"How's my little girl?" she cried and hugged Justine.

"I want my mommy," Justine said.

"Guess what's waiting for you in your room," Grandma responded.

"Mommy?"

"No, silly pumpkin. Come see," Grandma said, holding out her hand. "Come on," she urged.

Justine took Grandma's hand and followed her out to the corridor. At the door of Justine's room, Grandma paused and smiled down at her.

"Bet you can't guess what's in there," she teased. "Can you?"

Justine shook her head.

"That's all right. You don't have to guess." Grandma opened the door and Justine gazed in.

There, sitting in the middle of the floor, his little tail going back and forth, was the cutest little black and white puppy she had ever seen.

"Whose puppy is that?" Justine asked in a whisper.

"Why, he's yours, dear. To take with you to your new home. Your new mommy and daddy sent him."

Justine gazed at the puppy again. He stood up and began to wiggle his way toward her.

"You have to give him a name, too. He has no name," Grandma said. "What will you call him?"

Justine shrugged and knelt down to take the puppy into her arms. He started licking her, reaching her neck and cheeks. She giggled.

"I'll leave you here to play with him," Grandma said, "and to think about what his name should be. Okay?"

Justine nodded.

"Wasn't it nice of your new mommy and daddy to give you the puppy?" Grandma asked at the door.

Justine stared at her a moment. She thought about the handsome man and the pretty woman in the television movie, and she thought about Gabrielle's laughter when Gabrielle was with them.

Then she nodded and Grandma smiled and left her to ponder what she would call her most wonderful gift.

# 6

"May I use your telephone?" Scott asked Henry Dyce after he finished telling the private detective about Philip Dante.

Dyce stretched his long arms to reach down behind the sofa and came up with the phone. He crumbled a piece of newspaper and wiped off the base.

"Some tuna fish must've leaked out my sandwich while I was talkin'," Dyce said. He stood up to make a place for Scott. "Make yourself to home. I'm getting dressed."

"Thanks." Scott brushed off the sofa and sat down. His first call was to Miller's Mercedes.

"Hi, Mrs. Grossman, it's Scott. Mr. Miller free?" he asked quickly, imagining the look on the fifty-eight-year-old dour secretary's face. Mrs. Grossman was one of those employees who had been with a firm so long she believed she was part owner. Even Mr. Miller treated her like a partner. More importantly, he didn't resent her correcting and rebuking him from time to time.

"I'll see," she replied curtly. After a long moment, Sidney Miller picked up the phone.

"Hello, Scott. Where are you?"

"I'm taking care of some important business, Mr. Miller."

"You're not in jail?"

"No, Mr. Miller. I'm out on bail."

"How's Meg?"

"Her condition is unchanged. I'm on my way up to the hospital now."

"I see. Well, Scott, it looks like you've gotten yourself deeper and deeper into this mess."

"I know it looks bad, Mr. Miller, but I wanted to call to assure you of my complete innocence." His boss made no comment. "Once the facts are brought out at my trial . . ."

"Yes, we've been discussing that, Scott," Mr. Miller said. "In fact, Scott, I'd advise you to rethink your entire picture and especially your relationship with us."

"Mr. Miller. Things are going to get back to normal. I promise."

"I don't think that's an option any longer, Scott. I'm sorry, son. I really am. I know you need money, so I'm sending you a month's severance pay."

"But Mr. Miller, if I lose my job . . . it's another thing they'll hold against me. Please, don't do this now," Scott pleaded.

There was a long moment of silence.

"All right, we'll wait to make anything official. Let's just say you're on a leave of absence for the time being."

"Thank you," Scott said. He wiped off the sweat that had broken out on his brow.

"I'll pray for you, Scott. I really will. And, of course, we're all praying for poor Meg and Justine," Mr. Miller said.

Scott's throat felt as if someone with an iron grip was squeezing it closed. He managed a thank-you and a good-bye and hung up.

Dyce, wearing a reasonably nice pair of slacks and a pressed shirt, stood in the bedroom doorway, watching him.

"Lost your job?" he asked. Scott nodded. "You're worse than a man with the plague now. Nobody's gonna wanna be near you or know you. I seen it a thousand times."

"Thanks for the encouragement."

"Just tellin' it like it is. No sense avoidin' reality," Dyce said as he tucked in his shirt.

"You sound like Miss Iceberg."

"Who?"

"My attorney. Which reminds me. She asked me to call her whenever I went up to the hospital." He took out her card and began to dial the number. "She wants to record my loving-husband visits."

"Lawyers and doctors, they know the angles," Dyce said. He strapped on a model 10, Smith and Wesson 38.

"Yes, Miss Elliot, please," Scott said into the receiver. He eyed Dyce, impressed with how quickly he metamorphosed into an impressive-looking detective once the gun and the nice clothing were hung on that big frame. "Tell her Scott Lester is calling," he said. "No, that's all right. You don't have to interrupt. Will you just tell her it's three-thirty and I'm heading up to the hospital to see how my wife is doing. Thank you."

"Okay," Dyce said when Scott hung up the phone. "You got a third ear?"

"Huh?"

"Answering service or machine?"

"Answering service."

"Give me the number," Dyce said. He flipped out a small note pad to write down the number Scott gave to him. "Okay, check in periodically. I'll call in if I come up with anything substantial."

"Where are you going to start?" Scott asked intrigued.

"Friend of mine works for a big insurance company in town

and can poke around everybody's backyard with his computer. I got a couple of friends in the police department, too. Hell, Mr. Lester, that's what you're paying for . . . my friends." Dyce laughed and the two of them left the apartment.

Scott was shocked to see that the automobile Dyce got into actually started. It was a beat-to-hell late sixties Chevy Impala with a coat hanger for a radio antennae. The imitation faded brown leather upholstery was cracked and torn and the left rear window had what looked like a bullet hole in it.

"That wreck passes smog inspection?" Scott asked when Dyce rolled down his window.

"Smog inspection?" Dyce smiled. "Another friend in the right place," he said and drove off.

I'm placing my life and maybe my daughter's life in that man's hands, Scott realized. Every decision, every turn he made seemed to take him deeper and deeper into the muck. Maybe he should just lay down and surrender, let the system and whoever decided to punish him have their way, he thought. Right now he was losing his wife, his daughter, and his job. What more could they do to him? he wondered. Yet as he started off to see Meg, he was confident that somehow they would find additional torments.

One waited for him at the hospital. Meg was still in intensive care after the operation. Members of her immediate family were permitted a ten-minute visit every hour. There was a separate waiting room for ICU visitors, but when he stepped through the doorway, he froze, feeling he had just blundered in front of a firing squad.

They all looked up with various degrees of enmity and loathing, Sharma's scowl even more hateful and vicious than Meg's sister Abby's. In fact, maybe because he wanted it so much, he thought he detected a vague note of pity in Abby's eyes.

"Hi, Abby," he said, choosing to ignore the others. "Anything new?"

Abby shook her head. Abby was shorter and more matronly looking than Meg. She had a fuller bosom and larger features, taking after their father more than their mother. She had darker hair, but the same cerulean eyes. Her darker complexion hid any of the freckles that were a family characteristic. In the early days, he and Abby got along, even liked each other a lot, but after he and Meg moved to California, the strain of distance took its toll. Abby's visits became more and more infrequent, each one driving a wider wedge between them. He knew, for one thing, Abby wasn't happy with the modern day transformation in male-female relationships and the way Meg was embracing it. Abby held what was becoming a more and more of an old-fashioned belief that the husband was totally responsible for the wife's happiness or unhappiness. Therefore, she blamed him for any misfortune that befell the family and especially befell Meg.

Scott thought she looked out of place seated in the midst of Meg's shark friends anyway. Her hair style was too simple and certainly not the creation of a Fabio or a Niko or some other high-priced designer of coiffeurs. Her face was naked compared to the faces surrounding her with their elaborate and expensive makeup; her wardrobe lacked the glitz of the designer styles the others wore, and the only jewelry she donned was her Timex and wedding ring. Abby looked like a stranger in a strange land. Which was surely the way she now felt, he concluded.

"You have a lot of nerve showing here," Sharma snapped. It was more like she spit the words.

"She still happens to be my wife," Scott replied. "Look," he said, gazing from one end of the hateful montage to the other, "I don't care what you all think about me. The truth is I did not hurt Meg and I don't know where Justine is." He held up his hand, pinching his thumb and forefinger close to each other. "I'm just this far from going completely to pieces."

"What a pity," Sharma said.

"Sharma," Brooke chastised. He saw she wanted to end any possible confrontation. "We're in the hospital."

"I don't care. His dramatics aren't going to get him one iota of sympathy from me," Sharma flared. She looked up at Scott scornfully. "I called Meg that night and you answered the phone. I knew it was you even though you wouldn't respond. You simply hung up, but I've already told the police and the district attorney I will so testify in court," she said smiling.

"You're enjoying this, aren't you, you sick bitch."

"Just the part where I twist the knife into your balls," she retorted.

"Sharma!" Patricia cried.

Scott shook his head and stepped back.

"Could I speak to you alone, Abby? Please."

"Tell him to go fuck himself," Sharma advised.

Abby got up and joined him in the corridor.

"How can you sit there with those . . . creatures?" he began.

"You once thought these people were very special, Scott," she reminded him. "I remember Meg telling me how you chastised her for being an Eastern snob when she resisted socializing with some of them."

He closed and opened his eyes, something he always did when he couldn't escape responsibility for an act or a word. It was as if he thought he could blink and erase the unpleasantness.

"Abby, I didn't do it. I swear to God, I didn't."

"Whether I believe you or not is not important, Scott."

"It is to me," he said.

"How come? Six months ago you couldn't care less about what I thought or didn't think."

"That was six months ago." She nodded but kept her arms tightly folded around her body and remained stiff, a statue in ice. He let out the deep breath he was holding. "Did you get to speak to any of the doctors?"

"The pressure was relieved, but she hasn't regained consciousness. She could be in a coma for a long time. There's just no way of telling."

He nodded.

"I want to go in to see her, talk to her," he said.

"She's in a coma," Abby reminded him with some bitterness.

"She'll hear me," Scott said. He took another deep breath. It was so hard to breathe in here, he thought, stifling.

"What about Justine?" Abby asked. Scott shook his head.

"As long as the police believe I'm their only suspect, they won't look where they should," he said.

"And where is that?" Abby asked quickly.

"I don't know, Abby."

"If you didn't do this, who did?"

"I'm not sure."

"You have an idea?"

"There's something I'm checking out. It's too early to say yet. But before this is over, you'll see that I'm innocent."

"I hope so, Scott. It was bad enough you broke her heart with your extramarital business and your . . ."

"I know," he said. "Please."

Abby stared at him a moment, her eyes warming, her shoulders relaxing.

"I think I was the last to speak with her," she said, her voice cracking.

"What? When?"

"The night it happened."

"What time was that?" he inquired.

"Eleven-thirty my time."

"Eight-thirty, Pacific. That's very important, Abby. Did she say anything, tell you she heard anything in the house . . ."

"No. She sounded very tired, very lonely. She just wanted it all over. I know she was downstairs when we spoke because she said she was going to go up to check on Justine."

"Did you tell this to the police?" Abby shook her head. "You should, Abby. Where are you staying?" She didn't have to reply. "No, not with Sharma. Christ."

"She was the one who called me, Scott. You didn't. She's been very thoughtful and forceful; she had me picked up at the airport and made things easier. She got me a meeting with all Meg's doctors right away . . . made sure Meg has the best doctors. Thank God she was there to do it. You weren't," she added. It was like driving the final nail into a coffin.

Scott sighed.

"You better call the police, Abby and tell them about your phone call," he said and went to ICU.

"I'M GOING TO CALL him Little Bit," Justine announced proudly when Grandma returned. She was sitting on the floor in front of the dog house with Little Bit asleep in her lap, the puppy's snoot over her knee.

"Little Bit? What a funny name. Why are you calling him that?"

"Because he's just a little bit of a dog," Justine said. Grandma's eyes widened with approval. She was very impressed and said so.

"Oh, what a good idea. You're a smart little girl, maybe the smartest little girl Grandma's ever had visit. Oh, I know you're going to be happy and love your new home and your new family."

"I don't want a new family," Justine said. "I want to take Little Bit home to Mommy."

"But Mommy isn't home anymore, dear. Dr. Goodfellow showed you. She's in Heaven now and she's looking down at us and hoping you will be happy and well cared for again. Now you don't want to make your old mommy sad, do you? You know what happens when the people in Heaven are made sad?"

Justine shook her head.

"They moan and they groan and then they cry thousands and thousands of tears. That's why it thunders and lightnings and why sometimes it rains so hard we have floods."

Justine stared up at Grandma. What she was saying made sense. For the first time, Justine noticed Grandma had come in carrying something under her arm—a big book.

"Look what I have here," Grandma said when she saw Justine's eyes focus on the album. She held it out. "It's a picture album, full of pictures of your new mommy and daddy and your new home. Want to see it?"

Justine struggled with the opposing forces at work inside her. Curiosity, fascination with pictures, drew her to want to look in the book, but instinctively, she felt that as soon as she succumbed she would be closing the door a little more on any possible return to Mommy. Mommy was really gone, forever, just like Daddy.

Grandma sat on the bed and patted the space beside her. Then she opened the album on her lap. Justine hesitated.

"Oh, what a nice-looking man and woman," Grandma said. "And what a pretty house. There's a big yard for Little Bit to play in and is that . . . yes, it is. They already have swings and a seesaw and even a little merry-go-round. See."

Justine rose as slowly and as carefully as she could so as not to wake the dog. He whimpered, opened his eyes, but closed them again once Justine sat down on the bed next to Grandma and settled him comfortably in her lap once more. She stroked him gently and peered over Grandma's roller-pin arms to look at the pictures.

The man and the woman looked younger than her mommy and daddy. She didn't think they were better looking, but they were good looking. The woman had the same shade of light brown hair as Mommy did. In the first picture, the picture with them standing together and hugging each other, the woman was wearing a long, flowing skirt that looked like one of Mommy's skirts. The breeze made her hair float off her shoulders. Her eyes were bright and her smile soft, loving, very attractive. The man was looking at her and trying to look at the camera, but it was as if he couldn't take his eyes off her. They couldn't have looked more loving.

As if she heard Justine's thoughts, Grandma mentioned this. "Don't they look like they love each other a lot?" she asked. Justine nodded. "They do. They never fight or have bad arguments and they won't get divorced and live apart from each other so that you and other children they will have will have to travel from one to the other.

"You know what happens to children when their parents live in separate homes?" Justine shook her head. "They get confused, terribly confused, because they don't know who they're supposed to love more. The Mommy wants them to love her more, so she complains about the Daddy all the time when they're with her, and the Daddy does the same thing when they're with him. How do you think that makes the children feel?"

Justine didn't know what to say. She continued to stroke Little Bit.

"It makes them feel horrible because they don't want to hate their mommies or hate their daddies just because the Mommies hate the Daddies and the Daddies hate the Mommies. They wish they lived in a home like this one," Grandma said, turning back to the album. "See the pretty house with the little picket fence, the colorful flowers, the nice trees and hedges, and the nice sidewalk. I used to play hop scotch on a side walk like that when I was a little girl.

Grandma looked up and at Justine, a big smile on her face, her eyes wide and bright. "You know what hop scotch is?" Justine shook her head. "Maybe I'll be able to show you before you go. Would you like that?" Justine nodded. Grandma turned back to the album.

"And here," she continued, moving her puffy forefinger with its thick, yellow fingernail down the page, "see the backyard, all the play things." She turned the page. "Oh my, what's this?" she cried, pointing to a picture in the top corner. "Do you see what I see? It's in the backyard already."

Justine gazed down and opened her mouth, amazed.

There was a little dog house.

"And you know what you will do when you get there? You will paint *Little Bit* right above the door so he will know it's his new home, too. Wouldn't you like to do that?"

Reluctantly, at first, but now with more desire, Justine nodded she would.

"Let's look at your new room. Oh my!" Grandma exclaimed. "It looks just like this room only it's much bigger and there are many more toys. Look at your little desk, and is this what I think it is?" she asked, pointing to the corner of one picture. "What does it look like to you?"

"A television set," Justine said.

"Your own television. You can play all your own television games and watch your own shows whenever you want. Isn't this nice?"

Justine nodded; it was nice. It was . . . wonderful.

"I'm going to leave the album with you so you can look at it whenever you want," Grandma said, closing the cover. "In a little while, I'll come back with Little Bit's puppy food and you will feed him for the first time, okay?" Justine nodded, excited. "And then you know what we'll do? We'll go in the backyard here and let Little Bit do his pee pee and do do and you can run and play with him until he gets tired."

"Is he going to sleep here tonight?"

"Oh, yes. We'll put some old newspaper down so he can piddle if he has to, okay?" she whispered. Justine nodded. "Good. In the morning, Doctor Goodfellow will come to see you to get you ready for your trip with Little Bit."

"My trip?"

"To your new home," Grandma said, clapping her hands together. "All right," she said, standing. "I'll be right back with Little Bit's puppy food." She went to the door and looked back. "What a lucky little girl you are," she said, smiling. "I wish all my little girls could be as lucky as you, but so many of them are stuck in horrible homes with parents who fight and make them miserable.

"But," she said smiling again, "little by little, inch by inch, we're changing that," she said and left.

Justine stared after her for a moment and then looked down at her puppy. Was there a dog anywhere with as cute a pair of ears? She loved the way he wiggled his nose and whimpered, even as he slept. Carefully, she placed him beside her on the bed and turned back to the album that lay closed on her other side. She looked at it for a long moment, and then finally, despite her guilty feelings, she put it in her lap and opened it up to look at the pictures of what Grandma had correctly told her was to be her new home.

In every picture of them, the new Mommy and Daddy did look happy. The Mommy always wore pretty, bright clothing and smiled widely, looking up out of the picture as if she were looking at Justine. It was the same with the Daddy. His smile and his eyes were directed at her. She could almost hear their laughter. She hadn't heard her own Mommy and Daddy laugh together for a long, long time.

There were other pictures of the house: the cozy little kitchen with its yellow flowery wall paper, the living room with its circular sofa and fireplace, over which were Christmas stockings filled with candy canes and little presents, and the new Mommy and Daddy's big bedroom with a painting of a little girl and a dog much like Little Bit playing in a green field. It did look like a wonderful place to live.

And if Mommy was really in Heaven forever and ever, and Daddy was never going to come back . . .

Little Bit opened his eyes and struggled to his feet, wobbling on the bed.

"Look, Little Bit," she said, embracing him and placing him in her lap, "look at your nice new house."

SCOTT STARED DOWN at Meg. The blow to her head and the subsequent operation had done something to the area around her eyes, creating very dark circles, as dark as death. When you're this close to being a corpse, he thought, you start taking on the characteristics. His gaze followed the I.V. tubes to the bags of drugs and saline solution. She was plugged into so many different things, she looked like a switchboard. He returned to her face. It was expressionless, not a face in repose, not a face dreaming, not even a face suffering a nightmare or reliving the horror of what had happened; it was bland, her lips just a little bit loose in the corners. She's in limbo, he thought, floating in that corridor between life and death.

He sucked in his breath and stepped closer. As he did so, he was aware of the nurse watching his every move. They knew who he was and what he was accused of doing. Did they expect him to try to kill her here, too? They did, and the realization that they were looking at him as potentially lethal sickened him. Strangers no longer gazed at him with indifference. When his back was turned, they were whispering, and while they looked at him, their eyes were full of accusation and fear.

He started to put his hands on the side railing, but stopped, anticipating it would bring even more attention. Instead, he lowered his head and stepped a few inches closer.

"Meg," he said in a loud whisper. "I'm here. I'm sorry for what happened to you. You've got to believe me that I didn't want this to happen, never wanted it. I've screwed up our lives;

I know, but I never dreamed that this could happen to you or to me. I was stupid. I should have expected the worst. I have no excuse except my own weakness.

"I want you to get better, Meg. I need you to get better, not for my sake, but for Justine's. I'm going to find her again. I promise you that. And bring her home to you. So you see, you've got to recuperate. Justine needs you. I realize that now. She needs you more than she needs me.

"I'm so screwed up I'd only ruin things for her anyway. Get better, Meg. Please."

He didn't realize how long he was standing there with the tears streaming down his face until the nurse touched his arm.

"Mr. Lester, you'll have to leave now. I'm sorry."

"What? Oh. Yes. Has there been any sign, any change, any indication of change?"

"Nothing substantial yet, Mr. Lester. But we're hopeful," she added.

He nodded and started to turn away. Then he stopped and gazed at her once more.

"Scott," she had asked once, "what would you do if I died?" It was during the early years together. They had been curled up on the sofa, Meg lying against him, as they watched a re-run of "Love Is a Many Splendored Thing" on the old movie channel.

"I'd die, too," he said. "Oh, my body would be alive, but all the things that matter inside would be dead."

She liked that and, boy, did they make love that night.

What happened to that love, that feeling? He killed it with his self-indulgence, his pursuit of pleasure, which he had mistaken for happiness.

What good was all this knowledge now? he wondered. He'd be better off if he were the one in the hospital bed. In a true sense he was; he was right there beside her, only he had been

hit over the head some time ago. Drugs flowed into his blood-
stream, too.

He looked around at the other critical patients hooked up to
life-saving equipment and medicines.

"I've been in ICU so long, I feel at home," he muttered.

"What's that, Mr. Lester?" the nurse asked.

"Nothing," he said. "Thank you." He wiped the tears from
his cheeks and strolled out, afraid that if he looked back he'd
turn into a pillar of salt.

Abby was in the hall speaking softly to Sylvia Rubin, the
widow who lived next door to him and Meg in Westwood. They
were never very close neighbors, but on a few occasions, Mrs.
Rubin had done them the favor of looking after Justine when
neither he nor Meg could be home in time to greet her from
school. But Sylvia Rubin wasn't the sort of elderly woman who
did domestic chores of any kind. She had been left a sizeable
estate and was a very active person, vigorously involved in the
arts and a member of one committee after another to restore
theaters and maintain acting companies. She helped organize
and run charity affairs and often had her picture on the society
pages or in the Beverly Hills magazine. Scott knew she was
never particularly fond of him, so he didn't expect any sympathy
or support. The look of condemnation on her face when she
and Abby turned to him confirmed it. He shook his head.

"Nothing different," he said. "Hello, Sylvia."

"Scott. I'm sorry about all this," she said and pressed her lips
together firmly.

"Thank you."

"I've always liked Meg. I just had to stop by to see how she
was," she explained, more to Abby than to him. Abby nodded
and smiled. "At least there is one good thing about her still
being unconscious," she added and glared at him. "She doesn't
know Justine's still missing." She turned back to Abby. "She

just dotes on that child. She's a wonderful mother." She turned back to him. She was a stately woman, always elegant and refined. He couldn't remember ever catching her out of character. Even that one time he saw her in a bathrobe early in the morning, she looked like she could step onto the pages of *Maturity Today* to advertise some product for senior citizens. She could be a stand-in for Angela Landsbury on *Murder, She Wrote*, he had thought.

"Do you know your daughter's whereabouts, Scott?" she demanded with surprising authority. One part of him wanted to tell her to mind her own business, but a greater part of him was intimidated.

"Honest, Sylvia, I don't. I'm not responsible for what happened here." If he had to deny it to one more person . . .

His denial didn't impress her; she didn't change expression.

"I saw the limousine," she said.

"What?" He looked up sharply.

"I've already told the police. They came around to speak with me . . . a Lieutenant Parker and a Detective Fotowski. They said your attorney would find out what I said, so you might as well know now. I saw the limousine. I wasn't spying on your home or anything," she added. "I just happened to have returned from a committee meeting late and saw it in your driveway."

"What time?" Scott asked quickly.

"Eleven-thirty. Maybe a little later. I gave them a good description of the car, Scott. I'm familiar with limousines," she added, nodding at Abby.

"It was a Mercedes, silver gray, right?" he asked.

"Yes, it was."

"What else did you see? Did you see the license plate?" She didn't respond. "Did you see me?"

"No," she said.

"Did you see anyone?" She didn't say anything. "I don't mean to interrogate you like this, but . . ."

"I didn't linger to snoop," she said and then added, "but maybe I should have."

"Believe me, I wish you had," Scott said. "This is good," he continued. "This is good." Both women looked surprised. "At least they'll know I wasn't lying about being brought to the house. Once we find Philip Dante, that is."

"Who's Philip Dante?" Abby asked.

"It's too complicated to explain it all to you right now, Abby, but believe me, what Sylvia reported is going to help me prove my innocence. Thank you. I'll stay in touch," he told her. "And if you need me . . ."

"Where will you be?" Abby asked. He thought a moment.

"In the house," he said suddenly. "Yes. I'm going home." He strutted away. "I'm going home," he chanted. As he passed the waiting room doorway, he caught a glimpse of Sharma lighting a cigarette.

"Smoke yourself to death, you Amazon," he cursed under his breath. She spun around as if she could hear him and smiled coldly. And suddenly he thought, it must've been women like you who gave rise to the Solomon Organization.

He went directly to his suffocating apartment and packed. Then he drove to his house. When he pulled into the driveway, he had the eerie feeling that all that had happened had just been a nightmare to teach him a lesson. Actually, it was more like a prayer than a feeling. After he opened the front door, he stood there with his eyes closed, listening for Meg's footsteps or Justine's cry of joy at his arrival. He was greeted only by deadly silence, a morbid hush reinforced by the sight of the roped-off area and chalk drawing where Meg's body had been found. He stared at it a moment and then looked at the living room. Everything had been left as it was—furniture turned over, table leg broken, things strewn about. He didn't want to go in there, either. Maybe it was a mistake to come here, he thought. It was his desperate attempt to restore his life, a foolish symbolic gesture. Christ, they might even find a way to hold this against him. He should have asked his attorney's advice first. Without unpacking, he went to the phone and called to tell her.

"Not a wise move," she confirmed. "You should have remained where you were."

"But I have a right to be here. This is still my home and with Meg in the hospital, the agreement we had doesn't matter," he whined.

"That's true, but the police might think you're there to conceal something."

"I don't care what they think."

"You'd better start caring. I'm advising you to return to your apartment. You can do what you want, of course; but if you don't listen to what I tell you, it makes no sense to pay me," she added rather caustically.

Miss Personality, he thought.

"All right," he said. "I'll just get some of my things out of the garage."

"How's your wife?" she asked in a softer tone.

"No change. Oh, but our next-door neighbor was there and guess what. She told the police she saw the limousine here, the one that Dante brought me in, and she told them it was around eleven-thirty."

"Won't help us unless we get Dante to testify," she said, punching a hole in his small balloon of hope quickly.

"I know, but I thought with her collaborating . . ."

"Once we get Dante," she repeated. "Go home, Scott."

"I am home," he said sharply.

"You walked out of that home a while ago, Scott, and as Thomas Wolfe wrote, 'You Can't Go Home Again.' Call me as soon as you hear anything from Dyce. Gotta run."

After he cradled the receiver, he gazed around. He was like a chicken with its head cut off running madly about . . . to his crummy apartment, to home, and then back to his hole in the wall. But he had to at least go through the house once, just once, he thought and started up the stairs.

He stood in the doorway of the master bedroom staring at the bed and thinking about himself and Meg making love, especially during the first weeks here. The house was exciting then; everything about it was fresh and wonderful, it made their marriage and their love feel brand new.

He didn't shed a tear until he stood in his daughter's bedroom doorway and stared at the bed, left just the way it was when whoever it was came and took her. The blanket was folded back, the pillow still creased.

He couldn't stand gazing at her toys and stuffed animals, her little desk and vanity table any longer. He went downstairs quickly and then into the garage, surprised by the mess. Someone had rifled through the cartons, pulling out his things and casting them aside. Shirts, books, ties, everything was strewn about.

"My gun," he muttered and checked through the cartons himself, but he didn't find it. Did Meg come looking for it when she heard some noises? Maybe she had put it back in the night table in the bedroom. He rushed back into the house and up the stairs to pull open the night table drawer. It wasn't there. He made a mental note to mention it to Dyce. Then he took a few articles of clothing, some more of his personal effects and left.

Later, when he checked with his answering service, he found he already had a message from Dyce. The man, despite his appearance, was efficient.

"Mr. Dyce called to say that his friend has searched thoroughly with his computer and has found no one named Philip Dante working for any insurance company in Los Angeles, or even the immediate area. He'll be calling you later."

"Anything else?" Scott asked, his heart feeling like it was bobbing in his chest cavity.

There was a message from a customer who obviously had been away and had no knowledge of what had transpired. He wanted to come in to see a car tomorrow.

"Thank you," Scott said when the service operator told him that was it. He opened a cabinet and took out a bottle of Scotch. He poured himself three fingers and gulped most of it. Then he stared down at the counter, his eyes fixed on the bread knife. Slowly, he took it and carried it into the living room with him and his Scotch. He sat there sipping his drink and thinking.

*Where was Dante? Who the hell was he?*

He gazed at the knife and then turned his left wrist over and brought the edge to it. He was still sitting there holding the knife against his wrist when the sun went down, sitting there and staring at the blade, shocked by the realization that suicide was indeed a viable option for a man as trapped and destroyed as he was.

# 7

It was the telephone that saved him. When it came right down to it, it wasn't a fear of the hereafter; it wasn't a fear of committing a sin. He had hypnotized himself with the golden promise of ending his misery, of escaping the condemnation and the derision that seemed inevitable. But most of all, he had mesmerized himself by dangling the bright hope that he would escape the pain that came from thinking about Justine and from realizing that something he had begun for selfish reasons had resulted in so much terror and agony for her. Who could live and be happy with that knowledge?

He felt himself being drawn, urged, and prompted. Slowly, his fingers tightened around the handle of the knife, and he felt the sharp edge begin to slice through the thin layer of skin that protected his artery. His other hand moved like an independent creature, a part of his body in revolt.

Slitting your wrist is messy, he vaguely thought, but only for the people who came afterward to clean up. What did he care about them?

He closed his eyes. There was so much he wanted to say; so much he wanted to do.

And then the phone rang, the grating noise cutting its way through the dark, pulsating walls of his misery and bringing along with it light, life. He opened his eyes, surprised he had actually cut himself. He threw down the knife as he grasped for the telephone, a drowning man lunging for the life preserver.

"Hello."

"Mr. Lester, Henry Dyce. Did you get my earlier message concerning Mr. Dante?"

"Yes," he said dryly. "He talked so much about insurance and knew so much about different policies, he convinced me he was really an insurance salesman."

"Well, I just come from another one of my friends, the one who works for the police department. This Dante, whoever the hell he is, has no criminal record, not even a fucking parking ticket."

"That doesn't surprise me," Scott said.

"A huh. I checked out part of your story," Dyce said. "I went to see your boss, or should I say your former boss."

"Mr. Miller?"

"Yeah and he confirms that a limousine picked you up just before you were supposed to leave for the day. I even got a description of this Philip Dante that matches the description you gave me."

"And my next-door neighbor saw the limousine at the house eleven-thirty that night. She told me so at the hospital this afternoon."

"So the limousine picked you up and dropped you at the house; that doesn't prove you're innocent. You're going to need Dante. However, it looks like this guy gave you a phony name, a phony identity. Now the question is, why would he do that? Assuming you're telling the truth about the rest of it, that is," Dyce added.

"I'm telling the truth," Scott replied, his voice full of fatigue and defeat.

"I see. Well, I could check out various haunts, restaurants, bars, what-not, and work up a coupla more days of income for myself, but . . ."

"I told you the truth, but I haven't told you the whole truth, Mr. Dyce, nor have I told my attorney."

"I'm listening."

"I was hoping I wouldn't have to because it's only going to complicate things and make me look like even more of a bastard," Scott continued.

"No, I'd say you look about as bastard a bastard as you're gonna look."

"Not quite." Scott looked at his watch. "Let me see if I can connect with my attorney," he said, "and arrange for the three of us to meet."

"Okay. I have a hole in my social calendar and will be home all evening."

Scott called Faye Elliot's law agency, even though he knew the offices had been closed for the day. Their answering service responded, and he explained how it was of paramount importance that he speak with Faye Elliot as soon as possible. The service operator promised she would convey his message. Ten minutes later, Faye Elliot called.

"I've got to see you as soon as possible," he began.

"Can't it wait until the morning?"

"I haven't told you everything and Henry Dyce has run up against a brick wall. There is no Philip Dante. That is to say, the man who I knew had apparently made up that name, so we can't find him."

There was one of those now famous long silences.

"Scott, look," she followed, "we can still talk to the district attorney and work out a settlement here."

"Please. Once you hear my story, you'll understand why this

man would give me a false name. I'm sure now that they've got my daughter."

"Who's they?" she asked impatiently.

"Where can we meet?"

Now there was an even longer pause, filled with bad vibrations. His attorney was simply annoyed, he thought. He was interfering with her love life or something.

"I have a dinner appointment I can't break. If you insist this can't wait until morning . . ."

"Every hour that passes now takes Justine farther and farther away from us."

"Then why didn't you tell the truth right from the start?" she snapped.

"I thought . . . I was hoping that once we found Dante, I would get the problems solved. That was naive and stupid of me. I see that now, but before it gets to be too late . . ."

"It's probably days past too late," she replied. "All right. Meet me in my office at nine P.M."

"I'm bringing Dyce," he said.

"It's your money," she replied and hung up.

"Thank God you're on my side," he said to the dead receiver. He called Dyce and arranged to pick him up at eight-thirty. Now that he was about to reveal his role in this bizarre series of events, he felt lighter, felt some relief. It was as if he had just gone to confession and the guilt was already lifted from his shoulders.

More importantly, he was going to get them. They had nearly killed his wife and they had stolen his daughter, setting it up so he looked guilty. He was going to find Justine and expose them at the same time. Permitting himself to be hopeful stimulated his appetite. He realized he hadn't eaten anything since the morning. He threw on his jacket and left the apartment, deciding to walk up to Hamburger Hamlet.

The moment he made the turn out of the apartment complex and started up the sidewalk, he sensed he was being followed. He hadn't heard footsteps; he just had the feeling someone was standing behind him, looking over his shoulder. He acted as nonchalantly as he could at the corner, waiting for the light to change. Just after it did, he turned to look back and saw a man get into a car that pulled up alongside the walk. But the car remained there. Scott crossed the street and continued toward the restaurant. When he turned left to walk on the other side, the car started away from the curb and slowly came toward him. As soon as he stepped into the restaurant doorway, he turned around and waited. The car cruised by slowly and he saw the two detectives: Lt. Parker and Dt. Fotowski.

They think I'm going to lead them to my daughter, he thought. The stupid bastards.

But then again, given the information they had and the story he had told, why shouldn't they suspect him and follow him? They were doing what they could to protect Justine. Maybe soon, he thought hopefully, maybe soon we'll be on the same side.

He took a table in the darkest corner, as far away from other people as he could get. He ate quickly, chewing his food mindlessly, indifferent to the chatter and laughter around him. Somehow, because his life was so miserable, he expected everyone else's to reflect it. We're all so independent of each other, he realized as he gazed around aimlessly, each of us a little pocket of happiness or sadness. He didn't really notice them, and as far as the rest of the crowd in the restaurant were concerned, he was invisible.

The police detectives were waiting for him across the street when he emerged from the restaurant and headed back toward the apartment complex. They let him go a good block and a half before starting their car engine and following. After he went to his car and drove out to pick up Henry Dyce, he saw them hovering nearby.

"Right this way," he muttered and even slowed down when lights turned yellow so they could stay with him. They slowed down and waited at the corner when he went in to get Henry Dyce.

"I've developed a tail," he told Dyce.

"Figured," he said, gazing in the direction Scott had nodded.

"You wouldn't know them, would you? Lt. Parker and Dt. Fotowski?"

"Parker and Foto? Yeah, I know them. They're the original good-guy, bad-guy team. I think they based the character of Dirty Harry on Foto. Just hope that Parker's always around when he is."

"It's great," Scott said, "when everyone's your enemy."

"At least you know where you stand," Dyce said smiling.

GRANDMA BURST into Justine's room excitedly and clapped her hands together.

"Guess who's here!" she exclaimed. "Guess who's arrived."

Justine looked up from Little Bit, who lay beside her on the rug chewing on the hard rubber bone Grandma had brought earlier for Justine to give him.

"It's a toy," she had said. "Puppies can have toys, too."

Grandma stood above them, her hands clasped together, smiling as if she expected Justine would really try to guess who was here. Justine shook her head. She wanted to say Mommy, but she had been told and shown and told again and again that Mommy was up in Heaven and couldn't come back. And it couldn't be Daddy, for he had gone to some other world, a world where Daddies who leave Mommies and children go.

"Your new mommy and daddy," Grandma said. "They arrived earlier than I expected. Aren't you lucky, aren't you a lucky little girl?"

Justine felt her heart begin to pound. It was one thing to look at the pictures and be told she was going to have a new home and a new family, but for it to really happen . . . she couldn't help but be afraid. Instinctively, she reached down to scoop up her puppy and hold him close. He took the rubber bone with him and continued to chew at it while she held him.

"You've got to get up and get washed. You have to put on a fresh dress, too. And I'll help brush your hair, okay?" Grandma said.

Justine shook her head.

"I don't wanna."

"What? How silly. What a silly little thing to say," Grandma said, still smiling. Even so, Justine caught the glint of something different in Grandma's eyes. It was as if her eyes were angry, but the rest of her face was not. "Don't you want to be happy? Don't you want to be loved?" She looked down at Little Bit. "Don't you want your puppy to have his new home, too?"

Justine didn't reply. Grandma extended her hand.

"Come along, dear. Wash-up time," she said with a note of firmness in her voice, a note that carried authority and even some threat along with the firmness.

Slowly, Justine got to her feet.

"That's a good girl; that's Grandma's good little girl."

She led her into the bathroom and helped her off with her dress.

"We want to wash everywhere so we're sure to be bright and clean when we meet our new mommy and daddy, right?" Grandma said. She ran the water until it was almost too hot and then she rubbed a wash cloth with soap. Justine stood there obediently as Grandma scrubbed her face and her neck. She poked the cloth into each of her ears and turned it so hard, Justine grimaced. Then she washed behind Justine's ears.

Afterward, she helped her dry. Then she picked out a new dress and helped her put it on. When that was done, she sat

Justine down and brushed and brushed her hair, finally tying it back with a ribbon.

"Now stand up so Grandma can look at you," Grandma said. Justine did so. "Oh my, what a pretty girl. Any Mommy and Daddy would be happy to have such a girl. Come along," she said, rising. She groaned with the effort to lift her body, rubbing her lower back as she straightened up. "Grandma's getting old." She took Justine's hand. "Ready?"

"What about Little Bit?" Justine asked.

"Oh, he'll be brought along afterward. First, you have to be properly introduced and we can't have Little Bit there when we do that."

She led Justine out of the room and down the long, dark corridor to another door. When she opened it, Justine gazed in at a small living room. Seated on the sofa was the pretty woman from the pictures and standing behind her, gazing out the window with his hands on his hips, was the handsome man. They both smiled the same happy, loving smiles they had in the album.

"Oh, she's darling," the woman said. "Isn't she, Mark?"

"Far more than we anticipated," he said, nodding.

"We thought you would be pleased," someone said and Justine turned to see Doctor Goodfellow seated on the right, his legs crossed. He was sitting back and, with his right hand, holding a white meerschaum pipe in the corner of his mouth. The tiny spiral of smoke spun up and became invisible.

The pretty woman rose and approached Justine, arms out.

"Come here, precious," she said. "Let me give you some of the love I've stored up for years and years, love just waiting for someone like you."

"Call her Justine," Doctor Goodfellow advised.

"Of course," the pretty woman said. "Of course, I should call her Justine. That's your name, right honey?"

Justine nodded.

"My name's Billie. It sounds like a boy's name, doesn't it?" Justine nodded. There was a boy named Billy in her class at school . . . Billy Foggleman. "I spell my name with an "ie" at the end, the way girls do. My daddy wanted a boy when I was born so he called me Billie. Oh, I have so much to tell you!" she exclaimed. She looked like she wanted to burst with happiness: her eyes bright and wide with excitement, the corners of her mouth pulled way in and up into her cheeks, giving her a clown's smile.

Up close, her face wasn't as pretty as it was in the pictures, Justine thought. Her eyes weren't as blue and there were pock marks on her forehead, marks that didn't show up in the pictures. But she had sweet lips and a small nose and her hair was shorter than it was in the pictures. And she smelled good. She took Justine's hands into hers and squatted down.

"Can I get my first hug?" she asked.

Justine hesitated.

"Give your new mommy a hug," Grandma ordered gently. Then she gave Justine a tiny push toward Billie. "Go on, be the good girl Grandma says you are."

Slowly, Justine moved forward. Her first step was greeted with an enthusiastic tug from Billie, who then pulled her into her arms. For a long moment, longer than anyone usually held her, Billie, her new mommy, clung to her.

"Easy," Doctor Goodfellow said. "You've got to go easy at first," he warned.

"Billie," the new Daddy said, coming up behind her. She released Justine and as Justine stepped back, she saw there were tears in her new mommy's eyes.

"I'm sorry," she said, grinding away the tears with her tiny fist. "I'm just so happy."

"Doctor Goodfellow has explained how we should go along

here," the new Daddy said cautiously. He was taller than he had seemed in the pictures, and broader with long arms and legs. Justine saw that just like her real daddy, he had missed a spot under his chin when he had shaved. The tiny patch of hair looked like a stain.

"I know. I'm sorry," Billie said again and stood up.

"Hi, Justine," the new Daddy said, kneeling down and extending his hand. "I'm Mark and I'm going to be your new Daddy. I'm going to make sure you have everything you need, always, and Billie and I are always going to see to it that you're happy, okay? Can we shake hands to start?" he asked.

Justine extended her hand slowly and he took it and shook it, smiling.

"Now that's a good girl."

"Everything packed and ready?" Doctor Goodfellow asked Grandma.

"As we speak," she replied. "I'll go put it into the car."

"Can I help?" Mark asked.

"No, there's not much," Grandma said.

Billie didn't take her eyes off Justine, who was beginning to feel very self-conscious and very frightened.

"Easy," her new daddy said again, putting his hand on Billie's shoulder. He smiled at Justine.

"We're going to take a ride, not too long, and bring you to your new home," he said. "We've got everything ready for you there. On the way we can stop to have something to eat. Where do you like to eat: McDonalds, Burger King, Taco Bell . . . where?"

Justine didn't reply.

"I'm sure she would like any one of them," Grandma said. "She's a very nice little girl; she doesn't make a fuss."

"Well she can have anything she wants," her new daddy said. "We'll ride along and when you see the place you want to stop at, you can tell us, okay?"

"Remember what we've gone over concerning acclimation to a new environment," Doctor Goodfellow said. Mark nodded. "Don't try to do too much too soon and reinforce, reinforce, reinforce. If you have any problems, no matter how small you think they are, don't hesitate to contact me. I'll be here for you and for Justine, of course."

"We understand," Mark said.

Grandma opened the door.

"Everything's set," she said.

"All right. Let's move on then," Doctor Goodfellow said and stood up.

"Should I carry you out, honey, or do you want to walk with us?" Justine's new Daddy asked. She looked up at Grandma.

"She'd rather walk," Grandma said. "She's a big girl." Grandma smiled.

"Can I hold your hand?" Billie asked, reaching down. Justine nodded and joined hands. Mark moved quickly to the door and everyone started out.

"What about Little Bit?" Justine asked quickly.

"Who?" Billie replied.

"Little Bit."

"Her puppy," Grandma said.

"Oh."

"He's already in the backseat of the car, waiting for you," Doctor Goodfellow said. Justine was skeptical, but when they stepped out front and approached the car, she saw Little Bit peering out the right rear window. She ran to him.

"This is working out just fine," Doctor Goodfellow said. "Right on target."

"Thank you," Billie said.

"Yes, thank you," Mark added, shaking his hand.

"Don't thank me. Thank the Solomon Organization with your check," Doctor Goodfellow replied, smiling.

"As they say, it's in the mail," Mark said.

"Good. Have a nice trip and remember," he said, turning to Billie, "a journey of a thousand miles begins with a single step. She will come around slowly, in little ways at first, but finally, it will be as though you really gave birth to her."

Billie nodded, smiling anxiously, champing at the bit like a thoroughbred eager to gallop away. She hurried to get into the car beside Justine. Mark slipped in behind the wheel and started the engine. Someone slammed the trunk shut so hard Justine felt the whole car shake.

"Ready, honey?" Billie asked.

Justine gazed at her and then looked out the window at Grandma, who was smiling, and at Doctor Goodfellow, who was still smoking his pipe and nodding gently. The car began to move away, the strange house falling behind. Grandma raised her hand and waved. Doctor Goodfellow turned and started back into the house, but Grandma didn't turn around until the car and Justine were out of sight.

Then she sighed.

"We've saved another one," she muttered and followed Doctor Goodfellow back into the house to wait for her next little visitor.

FAYE ELLIOT WAS SEATED in her tall black leather desk chair. She kept her hands palm down on the desk, but she didn't change expression. Her gaze remained fixed. This lack of any reaction unnerved Scott. He couldn't help but fidget. Dyce, on the other hand, was shaking his head and smiling.

"What a fuckin' story," he said. Faye finally turned to look at him, her eyes wider.

"That," she said, "is an understatement."

"You've got to believe me," Scott said.

"We've got to believe you, got to believe that this mysterious Philip Dante whisked you off in a luxurious limousine blindfolded and took you somewhere downtown to face a committee of men in a room so poorly lit you couldn't see their faces, and that this committee listens to appeals of men who are about to lose custody of their children."

"That's right."

"And this committee, which you said call themselves the Solomon Organization . . ."

"Don't forget why," Dyce interjected.

"The Solomon Organization," she continued after closing and then opening her eyes, "serves as a court of final appeal and then takes some action. In this case they decided against both you and your wife and simply stole your daughter and framed you for the attack."

"Exactly."

"And you want me to take that to the district attorney," she concluded.

"So he can investigate them."

"Investigate who? Where do we begin?" she asked, leaning forward slowly. "With a man named Philip Dante who isn't really named Philip Dante, a group of men in shadows . . ."

"I realize it's going to be difficult."

"Difficult?" She smiled for the first time and looked at Dyce, who shrugged. Then she turned back to Scott, her smile fading. "You realize such a story won't win you many fans. You readily admit asking this group of modern cavemen to help you frustrate the legal system and do harm to your wife."

"I didn't ask them to do her harm. I was led to believe that they had influence with judges and . . ."

"Scott," she said leaning forward, "who the fuck, pardon my French, is going to believe that?"

He swallowed hard.

"It's true."

She stared at him for a moment.

"Now listen," she said in a calmer tone, "given the evidence they have, it would be foolish to expect the district attorney will spend a minute of police time and effort chasing down this tale. Without anything concrete to go on, I can't tell the prosecution any of this. I'd be laughed out of their offices, and frankly I'm not paid enough to deliberately make myself the object of ridicule and the laughing stock of the legal world."

"Then we'll get something concrete," Scott said. "I remember some details," he added, turning to Dyce. "I remember some things about the building they took me to. I know the general area it was in. It had an underground garage. There was maroon carpeting in the office and I saw a picture of a bridge."

"That's not much, but it's a place to start," Dyce said. Faye smirked.

"The meter ticks," she told Scott and nodded at Dyce.

"They've got my daughter," Scott said slowly. "I don't know what they've done with her, but I'm going to find out, and if it means spending every cent and losing every asset..."

"Fine. But my job is to spell out reality for you, Scott, and the reality is that some time between now and the trial date, we've got to come up with a viable defense or approach the prosecution with a plea. If not, there is no doubt you will be convicted. I'd be remiss if I didn't tell that to you."

"I know. I told you once before, and I'm telling you again. You're going to believe I'm innocent; you're going to see it's true," he said with determination.

She nodded.

"Okay. As soon as you have something concrete, call me." She stood up.

"I'm sorry we interrupted your evening," Scott said, "but I thought the faster I got the whole truth out..."

"It's all right. I have a very patient and understanding boy friend," she replied.

"Lawyer?" Dyce asked quickly.

"No. Doctor."

"Birds of a feather," Dyce said.

"I know a number of doctors involved in malpractice suits who wouldn't agree."

"Just a facade. One hand washes the other. Been that way since time began," Dyce replied. "The lawyers win the cases, get their cut; the doctors pay more insurance but charge their patients more."

"Then why didn't you become a doctor or a lawyer?" Faye responded, her eyes bright with indignation. Dyce shrugged.

"Personality flaw," he said. "Too honest."

Scott started to laugh, but stopped when he saw his attorney didn't think it was funny.

"You better get moving if you're going to uncover a secret society before the trial date," she snapped.

Dyce laughed and they started out.

They saw Faye Elliot get into a Rolls-Royce.

"Maybe he's a plastic surgeon," Dyce said. "They're richer than brain surgeons in this town."

"She didn't buy any of it," Scott said. "But I swear it's all true."

"Well, I'll bet she's one helluva advocate once she gets a case she can put her teeth into. Let's see what we can do. What do you remember about the building?"

"It was somewhere on Fourth Street."

"All right, an office building on Fourth Street that has an underground garage. Let me start with that. If I can narrow it down some, I'll call you and we'll go down there to see what else you might recall."

"Good," Scott said. He drove Dyce home, noticing that they still had Parker and Fotowski on their tail.

"They'll put you to bed tonight," Dyce told him.

"Maybe I should just invite them in for a drink. Make it easier on everyone."

"Oh, they don't mind. They love their work," Dyce said. "Talk to you tomorrow." Scott watched him saunter off and then pulled away and drove back to his apartment complex. When he checked in with his service, he found he had two messages. The first one made his blood run cold.

"Grandma called," the operator said.

"Who? Grandma?" He thought of Meg's mother. "Mrs. Turner?"

"She didn't give a name, Mr. Lester. She simply said to tell you Grandma called."

"Well what did she say? Is there a message?"

"Yes, sir. She said to tell you the little one is fine, not to worry."

"What?" The operator repeated the message. "Who was that? Where did the call come from?" he demanded.

"That's all I have, Mr. Lester."

"Oh, Christ." If the police were monitoring his service . . . surely they were. "They're framing me; they're killing me," he moaned.

"Mr. Lester?"

"I'm sorry. What about the other call?"

"Abby said to call her at 555–4343," the operator told him. He hated to do it, but he had to call Sharma's house to speak to Abby. When he asked for her, Sharma simply dropped the receiver on a table so that the sound reverberated like a gunshot in his ear. A moment later, Abby picked up.

"Meg's breathing's improved. It looks like they'll take her off the machinery very soon."

"Thank God."

"The doctor thinks she'll regain consciousness shortly afterward."

"Oh, that's wonderful, Abby. Thanks for caring enough to call me."

"I'm not calling for you, Scott. The first thing she's going to ask when she comes out of it is where's Justine. I want her to be there, Scott. I want her to be there when Meg opens her eyes."

"Abby, honest to God . . ."

"I'm sick of the lies and the stories, Scott. Just bring her back, you hear me!" she screamed. "Bring Justine back!" He heard her burst into tears before slamming the phone down. The receiver went dead in his hands. Then suddenly, he began pounding the small table with it, stopping only when he realized he had broken through the imitation wood and split the table apart.

He shuddered. They were going to win. They would either succeed in getting him convicted or they would drive him mad. What was it the man who called himself Dante had said? "They'll rectify the situation. Whatever method they choose is best."

JUSTINE STARED OUT the window of her new room. In the moonlight, she could see where the highway that ran in front of her new house turned and then disappeared behind a clump of trees. Occasionally, car headlights would send a shaft of light through the inky darkness, and then the car would follow quickly, the vehicle sailing silently into the distance.

She had come down that same road. They had brought her miles and miles in what seemed the longest ride of her life. As soon as the house had appeared, she had recognized it from the pictures Grandma had given her to study, but all during the trip, she couldn't help but gaze back periodically. She sensed she was moving farther and farther away from the life she had known, from her real mother and father.

Her new parents talked incessantly during the trip, especially her new mother. She described the house and the things they had bought in preparation for her arrival.

"The moment we knew what size clothing you wore, I went out on a mad shopping spree. Didn't I, Mark?"

"That, she did," he said and laughed. "One day she brought home so many packages I couldn't see her in the car. I don't know how she drove home or how she didn't get a ticket from a policeman."

"Everything's waiting for you, all the packages. You can spend days opening them, and if there's anything you really don't like, we'll just take it back and exchange it," Billie promised. "Oh," she said squeezing Justine's hand, "I can't wait until the two of us go shopping together . . . mother and daughter, just like . . . so many others," she added wistfully.

Justine couldn't help but be intrigued with her new mommy and daddy. Billie laughed and squealed more than any grown-up woman she had met. Her happiness was contagious; it was impossible to be sad sitting beside her. Every time there was a lingering pause, Billie would remember some other wonderful thing she had bought for her.

And then there were the promises of things to come.

"Do you like to roller skate or ice skate?" Billie asked.

"Maybe she likes to do both," Mark said.

"Oh, yes, do you?"

"I like to roller skate," Justine admitted. She had never ice skated.

"This weekend we'll go buy you the prettiest roller skates, then, won't we, Mark?"

"Maybe she uses those new 'in-line' skates," he said.

"Do you?"

Justine nodded. She had just gotten a pair recently.

"Oh, there's so much to learn," Billie said. "I watch children on television all the time, just so I wouldn't be stupid when you arrived. That's right, television. What's your favorite show? Oh, don't tell me now. Tomorrow, we'll sit together on the sofa and we'll go through the T.V. Guide and circle everything you like to watch. You have your own television set, you know."

"You don't want her to watch too much television," Mark said. "She's going to read and do homework."

"That's right. In a couple of days, we're going to enroll you in your new school where you will meet new children and make new friends. Isn't that exciting? It was exciting to me whenever I entered a new school."

"I don't want to go to a new school," Justine said. It was the first negative thing she had said since they left Grandma's. Mark looked back, concerned, but Billie didn't stop smiling.

"Sure you do, honey. You don't have to be afraid. I'll go with you and be sure you have the best teachers and the best classes. I'm going to be an active parent when it comes to my child's schooling," Billie pledged.

"Which means a pain in the you-know-what, as far as the teachers are concerned."

"I don't care. Justine's not going to be deprived of anything, especially a good education. You know how important that is, don't you, honey?"

Justine didn't reply. She looked down at Little Bit, who was still sleeping soundly in her lap.

When they had settled her in her room, they let her keep the dog there for the time being.

"Until we have his doghouse all set anyway," Mark said, winking. "I'm going to put a piece of carpet in there for a flooring tomorrow. You can help me do it, okay?"

Justine didn't like how far back behind the house the dog house had been placed.

"He's going to be scared," she complained.

"Maybe for the first night or two and then he'll get used to it," Mark said. "I had a lot of dogs in my time. Believe me, I know about dogs."

"If she wants the puppy in her room . . ."

"Billie, remember what Doctor Goodfellow said about being firm, about establishing who and what we are as soon as possible."

"I know," Billie whined, "but I don't want her to be unhappy."

"She won't be. She'll understand. She understands already. I can see it in her face. We've got ourselves a very bright young lady," Mark said, squatting down to look Justine directly in the eyes. "Don't we?"

They showed her around the house, and then Billie unpacked some of the boxes of clothing with her and they hung things up together, and organized things in drawers. Justine wanted her socks and panties in the same drawers they were in back home, but her new mother was ahead of her on that. She seemed to know.

"You like a yellow toothbrush, right? Here's a new one all ready for you. And I've got your favorite bubble bath and soap, all set up in your bathroom. Want to take a bath now? I'd love to help you take your first bath in your new home, Justine."

Before she could respond, Billie was undressing her and running the water in the tub. She was tight and nervous when this stranger who was to be her new mommy washed behind her ears and then ran the cloth all over her body. Mark came in to help Billie lift her out and stood by watching and talking as Billie dried her.

Afterward, Billie dressed her in her brand-new pajamas. Then she sat with her on the bed and talked and talked until Justine couldn't keep her eyes open. Little Bit was already asleep on his blanket in the cutdown carton Mark had provided. Billie tucked Justine in and kissed her goodnight. Very soon after, she poked her head in and looked at her. Justine squinted and waited until Billie closed the door again.

Then she sat up and stared out the window. She was still staring when Mark and Billie came by for their final time. She didn't hear them because she was thinking, hoping that Mommy or Daddy would suddenly appear on that road; one or both of them would come for her.

"Oh, she's up!" Billie exclaimed. She flipped on the light and came rushing into the room, Mark right behind her. "Justine, honey. Why are you awake?"

Justine turned slowly and looked up at the stranger who wanted to be her mommy.

"She's crying, Mark. Look. Real tears running down her cheeks."

"Easy," Mark said.

Billie embraced Justine and pulled her head to her breast. She rocked her gently and kissed her hair.

"It's all right, honey. You don't have to be afraid. We love you. We love you more than anyone else, don't we Mark?"

"Absolutely."

"I want Mommy," Justine cried softly. "I want my mommy."

"I'm here, darling," Billie said. "I'm here. You'll never have to worry ever again about losing your mommy or your daddy."

Justine swallowed her sorrow and her cries. It was as if there were two of her: one inside and one outside, and the one inside was shrinking and forgetting. The one outside enjoyed the warmth and the love this new woman was showering over her, but the one inside was dying from the loss of love.

"Come on, honey. Try to sleep," Billie said, lowering her to the bed. She tucked the blanket around her again and again, she kissed her cheek. She petted her hair and smiled. "I can't wait until morning. We have so many wonderful things to do together . . . all of us: Mommy, Daddy and Justine. Good night."

"Good night, princess," Mark said.

Her real daddy used to call her that.

The Justine inside remembered and cried out for him.

They closed the door and it was dark once more. She sobbed; she buried her face in the pillow, and then fatigue took over and she drifted off to sleep her first night in her new home, the Justine inside growing smaller and smaller with every passing moment.

# 8

A loud knocking on his door woke him. Scott groaned and scrubbed his face with his dry palms. He had fallen asleep on the sofa after drinking a third of a bottle of Scotch, and the inside of his mouth felt as if someone had been scrubbing it with a Brillo pad while he slept. The knocking got louder.

"Scott!" he heard Dyce call. "Open the fuckin' door, will ya."

He hoisted himself up from the soft cushions and waited until the room stopped spinning before he went to greet the insistent detective.

"Jesus, you look like shit, man."

"Feel worse," Scott said backing up. "Come in."

Scott saw Dyce's gaze fall on the bottle of Scotch on the coffee table.

"It's the only way I can get myself to sleep," he explained. "I keep thinking about my daughter forced to stay with strangers." Dyce nodded and looked around, smiling.

"You're getting there. Soon, you'll be a bona fide slob like me."

"Something to look forward to," Scott said. "I'll make some coffee." He headed for the kitchen.

"Sounds good. You'll be happy to know I've been up spending your money early this morning," Dyce called to him.

"Oh?" Scott popped his head around the door jamb. "And?"

"I've located your mysterious building. You were in the offices of Beezly Enterprises. They're located downtown about where you thought you were. It's an engineering firm. Builds bridges mainly, which accounts for that picture you saw."

"How'd you do it?" Scott asked amazed.

"Went back to your boss, Mr. Miller. I had a feeling he might have looked a little harder and closer at that Mercedes limousine Dante used. The old man was curious, thought you were going with another dealership. Anyway, he remembered enough of the license plate for me and my friends downtown to get a fix on the owner. I checked it out and they're located in a building on Fourth with an underground garage."

"What do we do?"

"Let's go see if it's the place, first."

Scott told him about the message from someone who called herself Grandma, and Dyce assured him the police had tapped his line and had it down in their notes.

"Maybe they know where it came from," Scott said hopefully.

"I doubt it," Dyce said. "Probably used a pay phone."

After Scott made the coffee, he and Dyce set out for East Los Angeles. They got caught in the usual freeway traffic jam.

"I read somewhere that people who do this day in and day out have enlarged spleens," Dyce said, nodding at the cars all around them. "They grind down their teeth, too. I ain't had a regular nine-to-five job for nearly twenty years and I don't miss it."

"Why did you stop being a city detective?"

"Difference of opinion concerning investigative techniques."

"Huh?"

"That was before people ran around with video cameras and recorded the Gestapo in action. I could tell you stories . . ."

"Oh."

"Seems a lot of people like to take the law into their own hands these days," Dyce said. "Some are sincerely fed up with a court system as clogged as my cholesterol-lined arteries, and some are just damn vigilantes. They like what they do. From the way you described them," he continued, "this Solomon Organization is a combination of both."

In the morning's hazy sunshine, the streets of downtown L.A. looked in desperate need of a good washing. The madness of the evening before revealed itself in the articles of clothing strewn over sidewalks, pieces of cardboard boxes used as make-shift bedrooms, and broken bottles of cheap wine glittering in alley entrances and curbside. Here and there, homeless stood or sat with their backs against buildings staring out at the traffic, their eyes glassy, their faces masks over hollow bodies. They were urban scarecrows, Scott thought, frightening off gentle folk and turning once busy boulevards and shopping areas into fallow blocks of vacuous stores with windows soaped and dark, their signs, billboards, and posters dangling like flags of defeat.

A turn here and a turn there took them into a livelier and more upbeat business district where office buildings still had washed and cared-for frontage and the homeless were waved along by security personnel. Well-dressed men and women traveled the narrow but protected corridors in this part of the city.

Dyce slowed down and then pulled to the side.

"This is it," he said, nodding. Scott gazed out at the building.

"Yes," Scott said, noting the driveway that dipped down

under the building. "This could be it. There's the underground garage."

"Okay. Let's go see what we can find out and what you remember," Dyce said, shutting the engine.

"What are we going to do? I mean, how are we going to go about investigating them?"

"Let's go into the Beezly Enterprise offices and see if it's what you remember. You might recognize the picture again and the carpeting, right?"

"Yes."

"Okay, if this is the place, we'll go head-on and see what sort of reaction we get. Sometimes, that brings things to a climax fast." He got out of the car.

"You just going to leave your car here?"

"We get a ticket, I just add that to expenses," Dyce replied smiling.

"Great." Scott got out and they walked through the front entrance and stopped to look at the directory on the lobby wall.

"Beezly Enterprises, top floor," Dyce noted. They got into the elevator.

Scott closed his eyes when the elevator began to rise, just to see if he could remember the feeling, the sense of time it took to stop. He hesitated when the doors opened again.

"We went to the right," he said.

"That's it," Dyce replied. Scott opened his eyes to confront the large wooden doors with the inscription: BEEZLY ENTERPRISES, J. BEEZLY, PRESIDENT.

They entered and stepped over the maroon rug in the lobby of the company. Scott turned and saw the picture of the bridge.

"This is definitely it, isn't it?" Dyce asked Scott.

"They took me to a conference room right down that corridor," he replied, nodding. "Yes," Scott said.

Dyce smiled and approached the receptionist.

"Can I help you?" she asked. She was a good-looking brunette with dark brown eyes. She gave Scott a little something extra when she smiled.

"Can we speak to Mr. Beezly, J. Beezly," Dyce asked.

"Who wishes to see him?" she asked, still flirting with Scott.

"My name's Henry Dyce," Dyce said, flipping out one of his cards. The secretary read it without taking it from his hand. "This here's Mr. Lester, Scott Lester, an old friend of his."

"I see. Just a moment, please." She took Dyce's card, but instead of calling J. Beezly on the phone, she rose from her seat and walked down the corridor to the first office door. She was a tall woman whose body didn't match her good facial features.

"Ain't that a shame," Dyce said as she slipped into the office. "A woman with a face like that lets herself get so hefty in the hips. Oughta be a law, a fine against doing that."

"It's probably genetic," Scott said with vague interest. His heart was pounding so hard he had trouble taking deep breaths.

"She liked what she saw when she looked at you," Dyce said and winked.

A few moments later, the receptionist returned.

"Just a moment," she said, "and he'll see you."

"Great," Dyce replied. "How many employees work here?" he asked.

"Fourteen, not counting Mr. Beezly."

"How can you not count Mr. Beezly?" Dyce teased. He looked around the lobby. On the walls were placed photos and drawings of bridges Beezly Enterprises had designed and built. "Looks like a pretty old and well-established firm," he remarked. "I've driven over some of these bridges. Ain't it amazing, the things you take for granted."

"They've been at it over fifty years," the receptionist said proudly. "And Mr. Beezly's been running the show ever since they started."

"No kiddin'," Dyce said and whistled. "Must be along in his years, eh?"

"He's seventy-six but he doesn't look or act anywhere near that," she said.

"He's not your daddy now, is he?" Dyce asked, tilting his head and smiling.

She laughed.

"No. I'm only twenty-two."

"That's nothin'. I got a granddaddy who fathered a baby when he was eighty-one."

"Really?"

"Yep. Just got drunk one night and wasn't careful," Dyce said. The secretary stared, wide-eyed. "Doesn't Mr. Beezly have any sons workin' here?"

"Oh, yes, Thomas and Kirk, both architects."

"Ain't that nice?" Dyce asked Scott. "A family business. What about Mr. Dante, is he still here?"

"Dante? There's no one named Dante working here."

"Philip's not with this firm? Thought he was," Dyce said, gazing at Scott with an impish glint in his eyes. "Maybe he was here before you started and left. How long you been with Beezly Enterprises?"

"Two years this coming December. I started as a temp and just stayed on."

"Ain't that nice," Dyce said and eyed the name plate off to the right on her desk. "Maureen. Maureen Carter. You ain't related to the ex-President, are you?"

"Oh, no," she said laughing.

There was a buzz. Maureen listened and then said, "Yes, sir." She lowered the receiver. "He'll see you now," she told them and got up to lead the way.

"Thank you kindly, Maureen," Dyce said when she opened

the door for them. She smiled and stepped back so Dyce and Scott could enter.

It was a plush office with a genuine black leather sofa and settee. Over some plaques and certificates on the right wall was hung what looked to be a Norman Rockwell illustration of a typical American family having a picnic in some lush green field under a perfect summer sky with milk-white puffs of clouds and soft blue background.

Directly in front of them J. Beezly sat behind a very large dark mahogany desk. Everything on it was neatly arranged. On each side behind Beezly, there were two large windows that looked out over the city and provided a breathtaking view. To the left was an architect's drawing table with some new project outlined on it.

The receptionist was accurate: J. Beezly didn't look his age. He had a full head of stark white thick hair with a well-tanned face, which was still rather smooth, the only lines being the ones in his forehead and at the corners of his eyes. But Scott had seen deeper wrinkles on men in their fifties. Beezly had a vigorous appearance, too. He was a firm-looking, broad-shouldered man who filled out his dark blue suit jacket, his sleeves tight around his biceps. He sat with his shoulders back, his large hands on the desk, palms down. Scott's gaze went to the ring on his pinky. He recalled the triangular diamond, and his heart began to race.

"What can I do for you, gentlemen?" Beezly asked without offering them a seat.

Dyce saw he wasn't going to get up and shake hands or go through any small talk. Everything about this man suggested a direct, no-nonsense demeanor. He was one of those business-men who really believed time was money. Scott sensed it, too, but that only raised his ire. His own shoulders and back lifted like a cat confronting an antagonist.

"I want my daughter returned," Scott snapped.

Dyce let the words settle. He was interested in the older man's reaction. Beezly didn't stir; he didn't blink, his lips didn't tremble and he didn't move in his chair, but his right hand crossed his left and his fingers began stroking that triangular shaped diamond.

"You want your daughter returned? What the hell is this?" Beezly said. Dyce forced a laugh.

"Please excuse Mr. Lester, Mr. Beezly. He is understandably anxious," Dyce said, stepping forward. "This is a very nice office. Love your view."

"Thanks, but what's he talking about? What daughter?"

Dyce looked at Scott as if he had forgotten he was there.

"Oh. I'm Henry Dyce, a private investigator. I've been hired by Mr. Lester here to investigate an attack on his wife and the kidnapping of his daughter."

"So what the hell does that have to do with me?" Beezly demanded, his voice now testy.

"Mr. Lester was brought here a few days ago to meet with a committee."

"What?" Beezly looked from Dyce to Scott. "What committee?"

"The Solomon Organization," Scott said. "I made an appeal to you and your friends and you decided to take things into your own hands."

Beezly stared for a moment and then smirked. He turned to Dyce.

"What is this, some sort of joke?"

"No, sir. It's no joke. Mr. Lester's wife is in the hospital in serious condition. She was attacked in her home, struck over the head with a statue."

"Where's Philip Dante?" Scott demanded.

"Who?"

"Whatever his real name is. Where is he and where is my daughter?"

"I don't know what the hell you two are talking about. This

is an engineering firm. Someone must have sent you to the wrong place or you have addresses mixed up."

"No one's mixed up. A meeting was held here at night, in the conference room two doors down," Scott said firmly. "This is definitely the place."

"Conference room...meeting...what the hell. Look," Beezly said finally moving, "I don't know what the hell you two are talking about, but there are no meetings of...what you call it...the Solomon Organization...held here at night, and I don't know anything about anyone's wife being attacked. If you're not out of here in thirty seconds, I'll call the police."

"I want my daughter back," Scott said firmly. He took a few steps toward the desk.

"Hold it," Beezly said, hand up in stop-traffic fashion. With his other hand, he drew a pistol out of a side drawer. "If you threaten me, I'll blow your head off."

"Why would an engineer have a pistol in his desk drawer?" Dyce asked aloud.

"For just such a contingency as this...two lunatics coming in off the street. Now turn yourselves around and march right out of here."

"Mr. Lester is positive the meeting was held here," Dyce said, coming up beside Scott. "Besides, Mr. Dante used your limousine to pick him up. I have a witness who will so testify."

"Look," Beezly said, "the only meetings we hold here are meetings about our engineering projects. We don't have anything to do with divorces. Now turn yourselves around and march out of here right now." He pulled the hammer back on his pistol. "I've used this before," he warned. "And I wouldn't hesitate to do it again if I have to."

Dyce held up his hands.

"Okay, okay." He took Scott's arm. "We're leaving, but we're going to go to the police."

"Do that. In fact, I'll do it for you," Beezly said and lifted his receiver. "Get me the police, Maureen. I want to report some sort of insane harassment."

"Let's go," Dyce said.

"He's lying. I remember him," Scott said. "I remember that head of hair and the ring." He turned back to Beezly. "Why are you doing this? Why did you decide to hurt Meg and steal Justine? Where is she? How can you put a child through such torture?"

"Let's go," Dyce repeated more firmly and pulled Scott back.

"You won't get away with this. I'll find my daughter and you'll pay for this. All of you will," Scott pledged.

"I have the police on line one, sir," the receptionist announced. Beezly pushed the button.

"Come on," Dyce said and tugged Scott hard enough to reel him in. They left the office as Beezly began explaining to the police why he had called.

The receptionist looked up with fear as they came out to the lobby.

"You were right, Maureen," Dyce said. "He doesn't look his age."

"Why are we leaving? Why don't we stay there and make him tell the truth?" Scott asked.

Dyce didn't reply. He continued to escort him out until they stood before the elevator.

"You don't believe me now, do you? Now you think I'm lying or crazy. That guy put on a great performance; he didn't crack; he didn't make a mistake. But . . ."

"Relax," Dyce said as the doors opened. He pulled Scott in. "I believe you. He did make a mistake."

"What?"

"We never said anything about any divorce," Dyce said.

"Huh?"

"The man . . . don't you remember . . . he said we don't have anything to do with divorces."

Scott relaxed.

"Yeah," he said. "That's right. He did say that, didn't he?"

Dyce smiled and hit the button marked G. The elevator took them to the parking garage. They stepped out and quickly found the Mercedes limousine.

"Look familiar?" Dyce asked.

"That's it," Scott said. "Can we go to my attorney? Can we go to the police?"

"Naw, we don't have anything really," Dyce said. "I'll have to dig into this deeper, find out all I can about Beezly and his company."

"I'll kill that son of a bitch," Scott vowed.

"Maybe, but that won't get your daughter back. And that makes you like them if you do, right?"

"What?"

"Just another vigilante, someone else makin' a decision outside the system."

Scott nodded.

"I've got to get her back," he whispered. "It's all my fault."

"We'll get her back," Dyce said. He stepped back into the elevator. "Sooner or later, we'll get her back."

Scott looked at the limousine again. Just parked there, the luxurious vehicle still seemed intimidating. It was as if it had evil power, as if it were the ferry boat that took souls from one world and delivered them to an evil, nether world. It was clean, shiny, waiting for its next assignment.

"It all makes me feel so damn helpless," Scott said, getting into the elevator. "I wish there was something else I could think of doing."

"There is somethin'," Dyce said as the doors closed. "You got your ass into trouble bein' a lady's man; now use the same shit to get yourself out of it."

"What'dya mean?" The doors opened and they stepped out and into the lobby.

"Maureen," Dyce said, pausing. "I know women. She liked what she saw when she saw you. Maybe you can charm her into tellin' you somethin'."

"I don't know," Scott said.

"It's worth a try, ain't it?"

"I guess so."

"Good. You come back here the end of the day and wait for her to come out."

"Then what?"

"Jesus, man, you're the lover boy. Follow her home, whatever, look for an opportunity to strike up a conversation. Turn on that charm."

They started out again and stopped. Through the double glass doors, they could see a meter maid placing a ticket on Dyce's windshield.

"MRS. LESTER."

She heard her name spoken, but whoever was speaking seemed so far away. It was as if she was on one end of a tunnel and the speaker was on the other.

"Mrs. Lester, I'd like you to try to remain awake a while longer," the voice said.

She felt her eyelids flutter. They wanted to stick together and keep her in darkness, but the speaker protested more vigorously, urging her to fight the fatigue. Gradually, she began to win the battle. Her eyes remained opened longer and longer and more light invaded the dark space, pushing the heavy shadows back, cleaning out the corners of her mind the way she would clean away cobwebs in the basement.

She had the peculiar feeling that she was separated from her body: her thoughts were one place, her limbs and torso another. The longer she remained conscious, the closer the parts of her came to rejoining each other. Her body was mending, the parts seizing onto each other until she was Meg Lester again.

Something beeped repeatedly beside her. She saw the machinery, the I.V. tubes and heard the muffled sounds of people moving and talking around her.

"Mrs. Lester."

She turned her head slowly and looked at the doctor, who smiled and nodded.

"Where am I?"

"In Intensive Care, Mrs. Lester. Welcome back," he said.

"Back?"

The doctor looked like he might say, 'from the dead,' but instead, widened his smile. Although he had soft blue eyes and very light brown hair, there was a firm authoritarian air about him.

"You've been unconscious; you've had an operation on your head to remove pressure, but you're doing fine now."

"Pressure?" She tried to remember.

"Mrs. Lester, I want you to answer some very simple questions, okay? What's your full name?"

"My name? Meg Lester."

"Good. How old are you, Meg?"

"I'm thirty."

He continued, asking her the simplest things. As she formed the answers, her memory began to rush back and wave after wave of recollections cascaded over the empty and dark areas—the troubles with Scott, the courtroom, Justine's subsequent depression and illnesses . . .

"My daughter," she cried.

"Yes. What's your daughter's name?" the doctor asked.

"Justine. But where is she? What happened to her? Is she all right?"

"Do you remember what happened to you, Meg?" the doctor asked instead of answering. She struggled. The most recent memories seemed the hardest to regain. "You were in your house," the doctor prompted. "In the evening . . ."

"I . . . yes." It was coming back quickly. "I went upstairs to look in on Justine. She was asleep. Then I heard something downstairs." She turned toward the doctor again, only this time, there were two other men standing beside him and neither looked like doctors.

"This is Lieutenant Parker and Detective Fotowski, Mrs. Lester. They're Los Angeles police detectives investigating what happened to you."

"Police detectives! Where's my daughter?" she cried.

"Easy, Meg," the doctor said. "You've got to recuperate if you want to help your daughter and yourself."

"Where is she?" she asked more calmly. "Tell me," she demanded of the taller policeman.

"We think she's with your husband," Lt. Parker said. "Or at least your husband knows where she is," he added.

"My husband?" She looked from one face to another. "What do you mean, you think?"

"We're here to find out what you know, what you can tell us about what happened," Lt. Parker said. The other detective just stared. Meg didn't like his eyes; they were too intent, too frightening. "Go on with what you were telling the doctor. You heard a noise . . ."

"I heard a noise downstairs . . . in the den . . . the metal louvers over the patio doors . . ."

"Uh huh. Go on," Lt. Parker coaxed.

Meg closed her eyes and then opened them fast, afraid that sleep would seize hold before she had a chance to continue.

"I went downstairs, but the noise was gone."

"What did you do then?"

"I started for the kitchen. Yes. I wanted some warm milk and then . . ."

"Then what, Mrs. Lester? Think hard and tell us everything, even the smallest details."

"I went down the corridor, but when I reached the den . . . a dark shadow . . ." She grimaced. "Someone hit me; someone hit me and something glittered," she said and started to raise her arm to touch her head, but the I.V. tube tethered her arm to the bed.

"Did you see him?" the other detective demanded. "Did you see the man who hit you?"

She shook her head and then added, "I don't even know if it was a man who hit me."

Lt. Parker almost smiled. He looked at Fotowski, who appeared annoyed with her doubt and the suggestion of an alternate possibility.

"What about a hand, an arm, a sleeve, anything before you went unconscious," he continued more forcefully.

Meg thought.

"No, I don't remember," she said, grimacing. She started to cry. "I don't remember."

"You said something glittered, Mrs. Lester? What glittered?"

"I don't know." She cried softly, but it felt horrible, like her eyes were melting and streaming down her cheeks. "I don't remember." She choked out the words once more. "I don't remember."

"All right, Mrs. Lester," the doctor said. "Take it easy."

"What about my daughter? What happened to my daughter?" she asked Lt. Parker.

"Mrs. Lester, it appears that your husband might have done this to you and kidnapped Justine. Have you any idea where he might have taken her?"

"Scott? Did this?"

"We think so, ma'am," Fotowski said firmly. "We were hoping you could make a positive I.D. on the attack and clinch it. If he knows he's finished, he might turn your daughter over faster."

"I can't believe . . ."

"You knew he was doin' coke," Lt. Parker said. "We've read the court transcript containing the accusations you've made against him in the custody hearing."

"You know he's capable of doing something like this," Fotowski said quickly.

"He called us from your house and we found him at your side quite distraught," Lt. Parker said.

"His fingerprints are all over the statue," Fotowski added.

"Statue?"

"Of cupid."

"Oh, God." She squeezed her eyes shut and shook her head hard, as if the action could throw the words out of her ears.

"I think we'd better stop for now," the doctor said. "She's done more than I wanted her to do already. Give her a chance to rest and come back," he added.

"Sure. Don't you worry, Mrs. Lester," Lt. Parker said. "We're going to straighten all this out and bring your daughter back to you."

She nodded, holding back her sobs. She couldn't keep her eyes from closing now and now she didn't want to. It was better to be unconscious, better not to hear and know these terrible things.

"Oh, Scott," she whispered, "how could you do such a thing to us?"

Hours later, she woke again, this time to find Abby seated at her side.

"Hi, honey," she said, standing and taking Meg's hand into hers. "How are you doing?"

"Oh, Abby. You came all the way . . ."

"Of course, I did. You didn't think I wouldn't, did you?"

"How's Mom?"

"I'm calling her practically every two hours, and, of course, whatever I tell her, she tells me is a lie. You know Mom. She's convinced I'm keeping the truth from her."

Meg smiled, but even that hurt.

"Where are you staying?"

"With Sharma. She's been great."

"Yes, Sharma's the one to go to when you have a crisis or any sort of an emergency. Abby, they think Scott did this to me."

"I know."

"They think he's taken Justine."

Abbey dropped her gaze.

"Have you seen him?" Meg asked.

"Yes, he was here to see you."

"He was?"

"Yes. He claims he's innocent, but he looks like a madman to me. He babbles about proving his innocence, chasing after some limousine. I think he's crazy, Meg. I think he's gone off the deep end."

"I want to see him, Abby. Tell him to come to see me. I'll know if he's lying."

Abby nodded.

"I guess everyone back home is convinced California is Sodom and Gomorrah now for sure, huh, Abby?"

She shrugged.

"People are attacked, raped, murdered, kidnapped everywhere these days. California has no monopoly on that," Abby said. Meg was surprised at her sister's tolerant attitude. She assumed it was because she didn't want to add anything more that would upset her.

"Something here ruined him," Meg insisted.

"Only because it was in him to be ruined," Abby replied. "If he's innocent," she added, "he's paying for his other sins dearly."

"If he's innocent," Meg said, her face crumbling, "then where is my baby?"

Abby bit down on her lower lip and shook her head.

"Where is my baby?" Meg cried.

THE PHONE WAS RINGING as Scott opened his apartment door. He practically lunged at the receiver.

"Meg is conscious," Abby said after he said hello. She sounded drugged. "She wants to see you."

"Thank God," Scott said.

"She knows about Justine and it's tearing her apart," Abby added, her voice venomous. "I swear Scott. If you've done this; if you have Justine . . ."

"I didn't do it, Abby. I'm on my way to the hospital," he said and cradled the phone. Without pausing, he headed out again, but when he opened the door, he was greeted by Lt. Parker and Detective Fotowski. It was as if they had crystallized out of thin air.

"Where you going, Mr. Lester?" Lt. Parker asked.

"To see my wife. She's regained consciousness. What do you want?" he demanded. They wouldn't intimidate him.

"We were sent to see you about a complaint just registered by a Mr. Beezly." He looked at his note pad. "A Jerome Beezly of Beezly Enterprises."

"You and Dyce are accused of harassment," Fotowski said. He walked past him and into the apartment. Lt. Parker followed, backing Scott up and closing the door.

"We didn't harass him. We just asked him some questions." Fotowski smiled.

"What's your scam, Mr. Lester?"

"I've got no scam."

Fotowski looked at Lt. Parker.

"Oh what a tangled web we weave . . ."

"I'm not lying."

"What's Jerome Beezly have to do with what happened to your wife and your daughter's disappearance?" Fotowski demanded.

"You wouldn't believe me."

"Probably not, but try us."

Scott thought a moment.

"I don't have anything concrete yet," he said. "But after Mr. Dyce and I . . ."

"You'll only dig yourself a deeper grave, hiring a screwball like Henry Dyce and running around making wild accusations."

"Beezly has friends, important friends in the right places," Fotowski added.

"If you have anything to say, you'd better say it to us."

"How do I know you're not his friends in high places, too?" Scott said.

Fotowski shook his head.

"You know, Mr. Lester, you might be one of those people who's had his brains scrambled doing all that coke."

"Look, if you're not here to arrest me, then get the hell out of my apartment before I call my attorney and we are the ones who charge harassment," Scott threatened.

Fotowski didn't change expression. Lt. Parker shook his head.

"Bring your daughter back, Mr. Lester, and end this thing while you still can," he said. "Come on, Foto."

Fotowski's smile metamorphosed into a smirk. Then he gazed around the small apartment.

"It just amazes me how much rent they get for these rat holes," he said and turned to follow Lt. Parker out.

Scott stood there a moment, his heart pounding. He took a deep breath and then started for the hospital again.

The doctor was leaving Meg's bedside just as Scott entered

the I.C.U. At the door, Scott introduced himself and asked
about Meg.

"She's doing well," he told him. "But she's very concerned
about her daughter," he added pointedly.

"So am I concerned. She's my daughter, too," Scott replied.
"You know what, Doc," he continued, "this principle of justice
we have: innocent until proven guilty? Don't believe it."

"I'm not looking to get involved in anyone's marital problems,
Mr. Lester, but I am worried about my patient's recovery. I
don't want her disturbed right now."

"She asked to see me," Scott said.

The doctor nodded, but his eyes were full of warning and
reprimand.

Scott left him and approached Meg's bedside slowly. Her eyes
were closed, so he just stood there for a long moment, gazing
down at her. All the anger and indignation he had felt in the
courtroom was buried in an avalanche of guilt as flashes of the
beautiful young woman he had met and romanced contrasted
with the battered woman who lay before him.

Meg's eyes fluttered open as if she finally sensed his presence.

"Hi," he said when she turned slightly and saw him. "How
are you doing?"

She bit down on her lower lip and nodded.

"I'm so sorry, Meg. God, I'm so sorry this happened to you."

"Justine," she said.

"I know. I'm working on it. I'm going to get her back, Meg.
She'll be returned to you."

"Where is she? What's happening?"

"It's a complicated mess. You'll get confused and just like
everyone else, you'll think I'm crazy if I start to explain . . ."

"Did you have something to do with this, Scott?"

"Not deliberately. I was . . . very angry and very desperate.
Someone took advantage of me."

"What someone?"

"People who think they have the right to make life and death decisions . . . fanatics, but I had no idea they would go this far. I . . ."

"I don't understand what you're saying, Scott. I'm afraid for Justine. Please . . . get her home."

"I'm going to, Meg. Trust me. I know you have no reason to have any faith in me now, but I swear, I'm devoting every waking moment, every ounce of energy . . ."

"She must be terrified, so frightened."

Scott felt the tears streaming down his face. He nodded, his throat closing. Then he took a deep breath and wiped his cheeks with his closed fists.

"Get stronger, get better, Meg. She's going to need you when I bring her back."

He turned to go.

"Scott!"

"Yes?"

"She'll need you, too," Meg said and then closed her eyes.

The rage and the sorrow married inside him and sent him rushing out, determined and capable.

They had gone to the Old Testament to get their name: Solomon. He would go to the ancient pages for his purpose, too: An Eye for an Eye.

# 9

Through the gauze-like haze of the Los Angeles late afternoon sky, the sun appeared more like a full moon.
Whenever its rays did thread themselves in and out of the layers
of thin mist, they brought a stunning sparkle to the otherwise
dull gray street in front of Beezly Enterprises. As if at the disposal
of Doctor Seuss' Grinches, a darker, heavier pocket of fog rushed
to shut off the light and return Scott's world to the dismal one
it had become.

He waited, eyes fixed on the front entrance. He wasn't sure
what he was going to do when he saw Beezly's secretary; he had
no strategy. He was here simply because Dyce had suggested
it, and in what was increasingly looking like a losing battle, it
provided him with an active and hopeful possibility of a reversal.
Up until now he was mostly on the receiving end, reacting. He
had to do something and soon or he really would go mad.

His heart began to beat harder as the flow of people out of
the tall building swelled. He studied every female, afraid she
would somehow slip by, and indeed he nearly missed her. For-

tunately, he gazed to the right just as a late model, red Honda
Civic rose out of the underground garage. Maureen Carter was
driving and she was alone. She looked in his direction before
pulling out, but he was confident she didn't notice him. As
soon as there was an opening in the traffic, she turned right
and headed toward the intersection. He started his car and
followed, remaining two vehicles behind. It occurred to him,
almost amusingly, that while he was following J. Beezly's secretary, he could very well be followed by Parker and Fotowski.
Consequently, his gaze went from Maureen's red Civic to his
rear-view mirror periodically, but he saw no sign of them.

After fifteen minutes of flowing along with the bumper-to-
bumper rush hour traffic, Maureen Carter suddenly turned into
a supermarket parking lot. Scott followed. He watched her pull
into a space and then he hurriedly parked in the nearest one
himself. Instinctively, he knew that if he approached her directly, he would frighten her. He let her enter the supermarket
and get herself a cart before he pursued. Then he went into the
market and worked it out that he would come around an aisle
just as she approached it from the other side. He pretended
interest in a jar of tomato sauce, and, as nonchalantly as possible, confronted her.

"Hi," he said. "We meet again."

She looked up from her cart. She had been pushing it along
mechanically, her eyes down almost as if she had memorized
where everything was on the basis of where she was on the floor.
Scott thought Dyce had been right: she did have a pretty face,
especially pretty sapphire eyes; but her narrow shoulders, small
bosom and wide hips worked against her.

"Oh," she said. It was apparent to Scott that she recognized
and remembered him immediately. Her right hand fluttered up
to the base of her throat where she pressed her fingers against
her collar bone.

"You're Maureen Carter, right? Mr. Beezly's secretary?" he

said, pointing at her as if he indeed were making an on-the-spot identification. "Am I right?" he added when she didn't respond.

"Yes," she said.

"You live near here?" he asked. She nodded, but quickly shifted her gaze from his face to the racks and then back to him. Shy, he thought, and vulnerable. His confidence began to grow. He smiled.

"Are you . . . following me?" she asked timidly.

"Following?" He laughed. "No." He recalled an apartment complex he had seen nearby. "I live in the Colonnades and shop here often. But it's always the case . . . you never notice someone who you've probably seen a hundred times before until you've seen them in some other setting. I bet you and I passed each other a dozen times in this very supermarket."

She nodded, a vague look on her face. She wasn't really listening to his words.

"I've got to hurry," she said. She flashed a smile and started by.

"Hold on," Scott said seizing her cart. "What's the big rush?"

"I have to make dinner and it's already after five."

"Oh, you're married," he said, releasing the cart as if it were electrified.

"No."

"Live with someone?" She shook her head vehemently.

"So? You're starving, is that it?" He laughed. His easy, relaxed manner put her at some ease.

"Matter of fact, I am," she replied with a definite note of annoyance. "I skipped lunch today."

Scott nodded as if he didn't have to have it explained. She fit the pattern of so many overweight young men and women, flitting from one guaranteed diet to another, experimenting with skipping meals, drinking supplements, exploring the entire gambit of options when, in truth, only one worked: watching your calories and exercise. He wisely pretended not to understand her motive and chose instead to get closer to the point.

"Mr. Beezly's that much a slave driver, is he?" he asked, lowering his voice and pursing his lips in grave disapproval.

"No. I've been trying to shed a few pounds."

"Oh. Who isn't?" he said and then leaned toward her to add, "especially in this town. Well, to tell you the truth, I'm tired of it," he said, pulling back indignantly, "tired of all the emphasis on youth and beauty, tired of worrying about being a few pounds overweight. They ought to call this place Neurotic Land instead of La La Land. Maybe it means the same thing," he said and she smiled. Then her smile faded and she narrowed her eyes.

"You and your friend threatened Mr. Beezly today, didn't you?"

"Naw, not really. We tried to get him to answer some questions and he pretended he didn't know anything. It's all just business posturing. Comes with the territory. Happens every day."

"But the police came to see him."

"Yeah, I know. It's all been straightened out. I'm going to call him tomorrow and apologize." She relaxed again and he looked into her cart. "Chicken breast. How do you make it?"

"In a wok with some vegetables: low fat, low calories."

"I know the greatest Chinese restaurant right near here," he said. "And they have a selection for lite diets. Tell you what . . ." He put back the jar of tomato sauce he had taken off the shelf. "Why don't we just say the hell with it and forget buying and making dinner. Let's just go have some Chinese."

Her eyes widened. Astounded by his invitation, she was speechless.

"I . . ."

"I know. You don't know me and I don't know you, but hell," he said, lifting his arms, "we shop in the same supermarket. That practically makes us relatives."

Her smile widened.

"And it's not as if I'm asking you to come up to my apartment to see my paintings or anything. We'll be in a public place. You will be in no danger except what danger comes from eating Chinese."

"Oh, I don't . . ."

"I insist. You got a very bad impression of me today and that bothers me. Really, what danger is there in my buying you some dinner?"

She shook her head.

"I hate eating alone," he added. "Don't you?" It was evident in her face that she despised it. "This restaurant is walking distance. Just a block west. We can leave our cars right where they are."

"I don't even remember your name," she said.

"Oh, I thought you did. I'm Scott Lester." He extended his hand. She took it gingerly and shook. "Well, we practically know each other's life story now," he said and she laughed again. "What'd ya say?"

She shrugged, still hesitant.

"Haven't you ever done anything impulsive, Maureen, just for the hell of it?"

She shook her head, but from the light in her eyes, he saw it was something she regretted.

"You've got to; it's good for you. Doing the same thing day in and day out can make you feel . . . insignificant. Shall we do it?"

She thought a moment and then nodded.

"Great." He laughed and took her chicken breast out of the cart. "Let's put this back then."

On the way out, he rattled on and on, moving from one subject to another as if he were afraid a moment of silence would send her fleeing back into the supermarket. He talked about Los Angeles, the people, the traffic, the movies, and the shows. He talked about the beach and about the mountains. She listened and nodded as they strolled up the sidewalk. He only hoped the Chinese restaurant he had seen on the way had a lite section on its menu. Most of the Chinese places in Los Angeles did, so he felt safe assuming so.

"Ever been here before?" he asked as he opened the door for her. She shook her head. No, he thought to himself, you haven't been around much at all.

After they were seated and given menus, he breathed with relief. It did have a lite section; he could claim he knew many of the dishes.

"So," he said sitting back after they ordered, "where are you from? The Midwest?"

"How did you know?"

"Easy," he said, "everyone here is either from the East or the Midwest. I can count on my fingers the people I know who were born and bred here."

"Mr. Beezly was," she said.

"That's right, he was," Scott said.

"Are you an engineer?" she asked.

"Engineer? No, I'm in . . . transportation. But tell me about yourself. What made you come here? How do you like it?"

He let her go on and on, barely listening to her tale, a tale similar to so many he had heard before: television and movies had made California seem like a place where dreams came true and where even if they didn't, you were better off being near people whose dreams had.

Their food was served and after her second Scotch and soda, she droned on. She ate quickly, attacking her food with a voraciousness that was quite unfeminine, he thought. He smiled at her though and continued to pretend he was enjoying himself. Get her to relax, he kept chanting, get her to relax.

Relax she did. He talked her into a third drink, but before she sipped it, she focused on him and began to demand more specific answers.

"What do you mean, you're in transportation? What is it you do exactly? Why did you come to see Mr. Beezly with a private detective? Is it something to do with his new project in Encino? Mr. Beezly says there's a lot of industrial and commercial espionage these days," she added.

"Maureen," he said, folding his hands together on the table and looking down at them, "what I came to see Mr. Beezly about today has nothing to do with Beezly Enterprises as such, nothing to do with building bridges."

He looked up at her, putting on his best look of sincerity. She was impressed and waited, holding her breath. His hesitation made her anxious.

"What was it then?" she finally asked.

"Maureen, Mr. Beezly does know a man named Philip Dante, doesn't he?" She shook her head.

"Not that I know."

He nodded and then described Dante. She thought a moment. He saw from the glint in her eye that she knew someone who fit the description, but was not sure if she should tell him.

"Why did you come to see Mr. Beezly with a private detective?" she asked again.

"Maureen," he said. "I have a confession to make. I did follow you to the supermarket. I was waiting for you to come out of work."

Her eyes widened with fear. He reached across the table quickly and put his hand over hers.

"Please, don't be afraid. Just listen to me. It's a matter of life and death, not just for me, but for my five-year-old daughter."

"What?" She shook her head. "I don't understand," she said. She looked like she was going to jump up and run out of the restaurant.

"You will. I promise," Scott said. "If you will just listen. Please," he pleaded and she sat back as he began his story, selectively telling her what would make her sympathetic, emphasizing the horror of his daughter being kidnapped. When he was finished, she looked overwhelmed. She shook her head.

"Mr. Beezly wouldn't have anything to do with something like that, I'm sure," she said.

"How do you know? You said you weren't working there that long."

"It just seems so . . . impossible to imagine him part of any organization that would harm anyone. He's the nicest, kindest . . ."

"Maybe it's not him or maybe he doesn't know he's being used this way," Scott said, deciding on another tack. "But I'm positive I was in that office. How else would I know that the room after his was a conference room?" He paused to let what he was saying sink in. "Maureen, you hesitated before when I described Philip Dante. Is there someone who fits that description?"

"Well . . ."

"Yes? Maureen, it might be the only way I can get my daughter back. My wife is devastated."

She thought a moment and then nodded.

"There is someone and he wears that same ring. It's what made me notice him, I guess."

"Who is he?"

"He's been at the office only a few times. His name is Edward Clark."

"What can you tell me about him?"

"He lives in New York. He's an attorney, or at least, that's what I've been told."

"Do you have a phone number and address?"

She thought a moment and shook her head.

"He's never left a number with me and Mr. Beezly calls him directly. I've never had to send anything to him," she added, realizing the oddity of it all herself.

"Well what is he supposed to be doing with Mr. Beezly?"

"Something to do with a project back East." She shook her head again. "Now that you bring it up, I don't know much about him and what they are doing together. It's not like other business associates. Oh, my," she muttered. "This is beginning to frighten me."

"You're in no danger, Maureen," Scott said quickly. "It's just fools like me who get themselves into one pickle after another and become victims of fanatics. Could there be something in a file, something put there before you came on board?"

"No, not in the file cabinets in the outer office. There is a file cabinet in Mr. Beezly's office, but I never go into it. It's for his personal affairs."

"Really? Well," Scott said, taking a pen out of his pocket, "if you should think of anything or if this Edward Clark should reappear, would you call me. Here's my number. I promise, no one will know you did," he added quickly. "It could provide the solution to the mystery of where my daughter is. She must be terrified every moment."

Maureen's eyes saddened and she took the phone number. Scott sat back.

"I guess I kind of lucked out with this place, huh?" he said, looking around the restaurant. Maureen smiled and nodded.

"Yes," she said. "I think I'll come back."

He nodded at her and thought, yes, but I'm sure you'll be alone. He was drained of sympathy and compassion otherwise he would have felt sorry for her. Right now, nothing seemed more insignificant than someone else's loneliness. He paid the bill and left, eager to relate to Dyce what he had learned.

*  *  *

DYCE WASN'T HOME when Scott called, so he left a message on his machine. Then he poured himself a double Scotch on the rocks and sat in his claustrophobic apartment and waited. A little over an hour later, the phone rang, but it wasn't Dyce. For a moment no one responded. Then he heard Justine's voice.

"Daddy, where are you?" she said.

"Justine!"

"When are you coming for me, Daddy?" she asked.

"Justine!" he screamed. He heard the line go dead, but he screamed again anyway.

"Justine! Oh, God, Justine," he whimpered into the mouthpiece. That was definitely her voice. He waited, hoping she would come back on. When it was clear to him that she wouldn't, he cradled the phone and fell back into his seat.

Why were they doing this? he wondered and then realized that his phone was probably tapped. The police had heard it, too. Justine's cries made it seem as if he had planted her somewhere and she was getting anxious.

They're tightening the noose around my neck, he thought. When the phone rang again, he practically flew out of his seat.

"Justine?"

"What?" Dyce asked.

"Oh, God, Dyce. They had my daughter call me just now. They're making it seem as if I put her someplace."

"Definitely her voice?"

"Yes. The bastards."

"That why you called?"

"No, I met with Maureen."

"Don't say anything," Dyce said before Scott could begin. "Go to a pay phone and call me."

Scott hurried out of his apartment and down to the corner where he knew there was a pay phone. As he punched out the number, he gazed around. All the shadows looked deeper, darker. They were watching him; he felt sure. They were always watching him. If it wasn't the police, it was the Solomon Organization.

Dyce answered on the first ring and Scott told him what he had learned by taking Maureen to dinner.

"Edward Clark, huh? Chances are that's a pseudonym, too," Dyce said, "but I'll check it out."

"What about this file cabinet in Beezly's office?"

"Yeah, my mind's took off on that one. But we get caught breaking and entering, it's all over for you," Dyce said. "Not to mention my ass being hung out to dry."

"I've got no choice. I'm nowhere, not an inch farther than I was the minute that they let me out on bail. They're tearing me apart," he moaned. "It was her; it was her on the phone. They made her ask me where I was and when I was coming for her."

"Jesus," Dyce said and then he was silent a moment. "All right," he said. "I got a friend who is familiar with most of the security systems used in this town. Let me see if he knows anything about that building."

"What have you found out about Beezly?" Scott asked.

"His wife's dead; he lives alone, but what I found out about one of his sons is more interesting."

"And that is?"

"He was recently divorced. There wasn't a custody battle, but the children were living with her."

"What do you mean, were?"

"Not a week after the divorce was final . . ."

"Yeah?"

"She was killed in a car accident: a truck ran a red light and plowed into her," Dyce said.

"That sounds like it was just an accident."

"There's more. The truck had been stolen and the driver . . . he disappeared right after plowing into her."

"Jesus."

"There's more," Dyce repeated. "His son's lawyer for the divorce..."

Scott held his breath.

"Yeah?"

"Was your lawyer too...Michael Fein. Might be just a coincidence," Dyce said quickly. "A good divorce lawyer gets a reputation and other people call him. Nothing really unusual about it."

"Except he's not a good lawyer," Scott said.

"Says you."

"But what if it wasn't a coincidence?" Scott thought a moment. "Shit, he's the one fixed me up with Faye Elliot, my brilliant attorney, who keeps mocking my story and pushing me toward a confession."

"Yeah but she fixed you up with me, so there ain't much you can make of that. Unless you're a total paranoid and think I'm bullshittin' you, too."

Scott was silent. Dyce was right, but still...

"Look, you don't have to be paranoid to know your phone's tapped for sure," Dyce said. "I'll call and tell you to meet me someplace tomorrow night. I'll mean tonight and the address won't be real. Whenever I tell you to meet me, meet me in front of Beezly Enterprises, okay?"

"Okay."

"You still got to do your best to be sure you're not followed," Dyce said.

"Right."

"And Scott."

"Yeah?"

"Watch where you park; you don't want to get no ticket." Scott started to laugh. "No, I'm serious. More burglars get caught because the cops track their cars to a street through parking tickets than anything else in this town. It's got..."

"The best parking enforcement in America. I know," Scott said. He laughed to himself and hung up. Dyce was pretty good at what he did, he thought, and he liked him, too, liked his sense of humor and his nonchalant understanding of the underbelly of life here in the City of Angels. No, there weren't many people he felt he could trust at the moment, but if there were two, one was himself, and the other was Dyce.

He hurried back to his apartment to wait for his call. Just before midnight, it came.

"All right," Dyce said, "I've got what I need. Meet me tomorrow night at one A.M. in front of the Avco Theater on Wilshire in Westwood, understand?"

"Absolutely."

Scott cradled the phone and waited a few moments. He wished there was a back way to get out of his little apartment. How was he going to be sure he wasn't followed? He turned off all the lights and peered out of his front window, searching the shadows for signs of someone watching his apartment. He saw no one but he sensed there was someone out there, waiting. He thought for a moment and came up with an idea. He went to the phone and called a taxi company, requesting a pickup in front of the laundromat at the end of the block in ten minutes. Then, as quietly as he could, he slipped out the front door.

He walked down the pathway toward the parking lot, but at the last moment, turned sharply and headed down another pathway. He heard footsteps behind him, so he broke into a run and then turned into the entryway of another building in the complex. He followed the corridor to a side exit and emerged on the west end of the street. Hovering as closely to the shadows as he could, he made his way to the corner and stepped into a dark entryway to gaze back.

A man appeared down the sidewalk, looked in both directions, and then started toward him. Scott waited until the taxi appeared. Then he shot out and got in. When he looked back, he saw the man running in frustration. They had expected him to go to his own car, Scott thought. Dyce would be proud of me.

It was an expensive taxi ride, but Scott thought it well worth it. For one thing, there was no problem with finding a place to park. He got out in front of the Beezly building and went to the side to wait for Dyce, who, he found, was already there waiting for him.

"What the hell was that all about?" Dyce asked. Scott explained his brainstorm. "Great," Dyce said. "Now all they got to do is check with the taxi company and find out where he dropped you off."

"Oh," Scott said. He suddenly felt very stupid and very helpless. This was beyond him after all.

"Let's move ass," Dyce said. He took him around the building to a rear entrance used for deliveries. There he pulled a ring of master keys out of his pocket and experimented with a few until he found the one that would open the door. He gazed back at Scott to indicate caution, and then the two of them entered the office building.

"How do you know where we should go?" Scott whispered.

"Friends. I told you . . . that's what you're paying me for, my friends," Dyce replied. They went to a service elevator and traveled up to the Beezly offices. The building was deadly quiet, but there were hall lights on. Dyce hesitated a moment and then went to the Beezly office door. Once again, he experimented with his master keys until he found the one that would let them inside. But when he opened the door, he didn't enter.

"On your knees," Dyce said.

"What?"

"Crawl."

Scott followed Dyce in on all fours, feeling rather stupid, but sweating and even trembling with anxiety. Dyce paused in the lobby and nodded toward a tiny red light.

"Laser beam security all the way to Beezly's office," he explained. "Keep low."

They continued on all fours until they reached Beezly's office. Once again, Dyce fumbled with his keys until he found the right one.

"Where'd you get those keys?" Scott asked.

"Standard equipment for us private eyes," he said, winking. The lock snapped opened, but Dyce hesitated. "My friend wasn't sure about this. Could be on an alarm." Dyce opened the door very slightly and ran his hand up the jamb. Confident it wasn't on any alarm, he opened the door enough for them to slip through. They paused inside Beezly's office and looked around. Feeling secure, Dyce turned on a desk lamp.

"You go through the desk drawers," he said. "I'll work on that file cabinet."

Scott hurried to it and began his search. It took Dyce a little longer to open the file cabinet than it took him to open the doors. He pulled a small pocket flashlight out of his jacket and started to peruse the documents. Scott paused when he located Beezly's pistol.

"I found his gun," he whispered.

"Don't touch it," Dyce commanded. "Come here," he said and Scott approached. Dyce opened a file marked S.O. and began flipping the documents. They both whistled under their breaths.

"These guys have been in business for a while," Dyce remarked. "We got enough late-night reading. Let's do it right here."

They hovered around the desk lamp and started to peruse the folders in the file.

"Looks like summaries of other divorces, other cases and their dispositions," Scott said. "Some in Los Angeles, some in other California cities."

"Uh huh. Look for something similar, something repeated in each," Dyce said. Scott nodded and went back over the documents more closely. He looked up.

"Michael Fein was the lawyer for at least a half a dozen of the Los Angeles divorces."

"I see that, too. There goes my theory of it being just co-incidence."

Scott concentrated on the summaries and dispositions.

"There are a few others that end with the same statement: delivery made to Doctor Goodfellow. The little boy in this case was just a little more than two." He handed it to Dyce, who perused it quickly. "Delivered," Scott muttered. "They kid-napped and gave away someone else's child. Dante said they do whatever they think is necessary . . . wise men," he quipped, "Solomons. We'll just go to this Doctor Goodfellow, whoever the hell he is and . . ."

"Yeah, but there's no address, no phone number. Any on those?"

"Damn," Scott said, thumbing through and not finding any. "Wait, here's a folder with canceled checks." Scott flipped through them and looked up. "They're all made out to the Goodfellow Foundation."

"Let me see those," Dyce said and turned them over quickly. "First Interstate Bank, Barstow," he read.

"That's where this Goodfellow is then, right?"

"Chances are . . ." Dyce smiled. "Easy enough to check out."

"Then this is where my daughter's been taken. "Jesus," Scott said and held up the folders with Goodfellow's name on them. "All the children involved in these divorces were . . . delivered."

"Come on. We got what we need," Dyce said. He took the

files out of Scott's hands and returned the folders to the file
cabinet.

"Wait. Shouldn't we bring those documents to Faye Elliot?
Now we have the concrete evidence, proof that I'm not making
all this up?"

"Illegally obtained proof," Dyce said. "Besides, I got to wonder about her now that we see Michael Fein's been heavily
involved here. Course, maybe she's just an innocent part of all
this and we can get her to start a real investigation. You wanna
take the chance?"

Scott thought a moment.

"No. You're right. I just want to get my daughter back and
prove my innocence. After that, we'll worry about who's doing
what and we'll have these other cases examined."

"Sounds like a very wise decision," Dyce said. He closed and
locked the cabinet.

They made their way out of the office and building quickly,
backtracking and hesitating only once on the bottom floor when
they heard the voices of two security guards down the corridor.
Once the voices died away, they exited through the delivery
entrance and hurriedly walked around the building to Dyce's
vehicle.

"What do we do now?" Scott asked as they drove up the
freeway.

"I'll get an address for this Doctor Goodfellow, and then we'll
start for Barstow. Unless you wanna get some sleep first."

"Sleep? Who the hell can sleep?"

"That's what I thought you would say. Look, we don't want
to be followed, but by now they've discovered I'm not home
and figured we were together. They'll be all over your apartment
complex, too. I'm going to drop you off at an all-night car rental
I know in Santa Monica. Get a car and pick me up at Barrington
and San Vincente in about a half hour. I'll be on the north
side, the west corner. Understand?"

"Right."

Dyce dropped him off at the car rental and Scott preceded to get a vehicle. Fifteen minutes later, he was on his way to their rendezvous.

The remarkable thing about Los Angeles was how quickly and how dramatically it quieted down after nine-thirty, ten o'clock. Streets that were routes for a continuous stream of traffic from early morning on without a moment's respite were suddenly as deserted as the streets of rural communities. Here and there, Scott saw pedestrians who had decided to take advantage of the quiet and lack of traffic to walk their dogs. An upscale section like Brentwood had no real late-night action, no discotheques, and few all-night bars. It was easy for Scott to slip through the streets quietly, unnoticed, and approach the corner where he was to meet Dyce, but Dyce wasn't there.

Scott checked his watch; it was just a half hour since they had parted. Rather than sit in a parked car waiting and possibly attracting some attention, Scott made a sweep around the block, driving slowly so it would take him a good ten minutes. When he returned to the corner, Dyce was still nowhere in sight. Now, concerned they might miss each other, Scott pulled over and parked in full view of the corner. He waited.

A little over an hour later, his heart began to race. Where was Dyce? Had he misunderstand what the detective had said? This was definitely the address, wasn't it? Barrington and San Vincente. Maybe Dyce thought he told him someplace else and was waiting on another corner. What should he do?

Finally, he got out of the car and went to a pay phone and called Dyce. His answering machine came on. Scott waited and then after the beep simply said, "Dyce?" There was no response. He returned to the car and waited another fifteen minutes. Now, nearly an hour and three quarters later, he panicked and decided the only thing to do was to drive to Dyce's apartment.

He parked about a half block away and, clinging to the protection of the shadows again, approached the old apartment building slowly. Dyce's car was parked in front. Scott watched the building for a few moments, looking for signs of someone else who might have it under surveillance. Satisfied there wasn't anyone, he hurried across the street, through the opened gate and over the courtyard. He jogged up the steps to Dyce's door. When he knocked on it, the door opened slightly.

"Dyce?"

Scott peered in. The apartment looked no different from the way it had the first time he had come here—clothes were still strewn over the furniture, coffee cups and dishes were still on the tables, and there was a newspaper spread open on the floor. He walked farther into the apartment.

"Dyce?"

He listened. Nothing. The man wasn't here. He could have been delayed and would be waiting on the corner back in Brentwood, cursing him, Scott thought. He turned to leave, but heard the distinct sound of water dripping in the bathroom. It was nothing to be surprised about, Scott thought. The faucets in this place probably all leaked. Still, he went across the room to peer into the bathroom.

At first the sight seemed so incongruous as to make no visual sense. Through the shower curtain it looked like Dyce was standing on his hands.

"Dyce?"

Scott approached the stall and slowly pulled back the curtain. The gasp that started in his throat was quickly crushed by the overwhelming urge to heave out anything and everything that had been anywhere near his stomach for the last forty-eight hours.

Dyce's feet were bound and the cord was draped over the shower head so he would dangle. His back rested against the rear of the stall and his head was turned toward the rear so that his sliced throat would drip blood in a steady stream down the drain. His large eyes were wide open and glazed with shock, and the roof of his mouth was clearly visible: pink, the tongue swelling even as Scott stared.

Scott seized his own stomach and folded over. He spun around and retreated quickly, dry heaving over the toilet until some digested matter did come up and out. When the rebellion in his stomach ended, he stumbled his way back to the living room and squatted down on the opened newspaper. He took deep breaths until he had some semblance of calmness return. Then he closed his eyes, swallowed, and lay his head back against he sofa.

After a moment he considered his own danger and struggled to stand. Without any further hesitation, he started to leave, but stopped at the door. He thought a moment. He was in danger, real danger, wasn't he? He returned to the bathroom and, holding his nose with his left hand, pulled back the curtain again. Trying not to look at Dyce's face, he reached in and lifted the pistol from the detective's holster. Then he turned and ran out of the apartment. When he reached the car, he got in quickly and pulled away, tires squealing. He drove west toward Santa Monica until he broke out on Ocean Avenue and pulled into an empty spot overlooking the ocean. There, he caught his breath again and stared at the moonlight on the water. He sat there unable to move, the image of Dyce's dangling corpse vividly returning.

Whether it was only his imagination or whether somehow through some psychic sense he was able to hear it over great distances, he didn't know, but he clearly heard Justine cry, "Daddy!" It pulled him out of the horrendous reverie and he started his car again. He backed up slowly and drove off, numb with terror, his mind scrolling through the options about what he should do next. He had no sense of time; he had only a vague sense of place. It was as if he had wandered into limbo and was stumbling through the dark and mysterious world, groping for something concrete to grasp and pull himself back to reality.

His frustration and fear metamorphosed into rage and, finally, he regained enough of his composure to choose a course of action, and direct himself toward that end.

# 10

**J**erome Beezly sat back in his leather recliner and gazed ahead with a calmness that actually infuriated Bernard Lyle. Bernard had just finished summarizing all that he had done and all that he had learned since Scott Lester and that incompetent so-called private eye had paid Mr. Beezly a visit in his office. Beezly's nose twitched and he pushed his glasses up the bridge of it as he sat forward, finally exhibiting some animation. For a few moments, Bernard was wondering if the old man hadn't finally lost it, lost his value to the organization.

"My office has been compromised," he concluded as if that were the main point, as if that were the worst thing of all. "So much for that new, elaborate laser beam alarm you suggested I install, Bernard."

"Nothing works if someone knows about it in advance, Mr. Beezly," Bernard said dryly. He shifted his weight from one foot to the other like a school boy, impatient to be dismissed for recess. "But more importantly," he pointed out sharply, "Doctor

Goodfellow has been, as you say, compromised. No telling when this man will set out for Barstow and find him."

"Yes," Beezly said, nodding. "That's very annoying."

"Annoying?" Bernard almost laughed. "If he gets into that house, finds those records or in any way gets the old lady or Doctor Goodfellow to talk . . ."

"Yes, yes," Beezly said, waving his hand as if he were driving away Bernard's bad breath instead of his bad news. "I understand." He sighed and shook his head. "It was working so well for us in Barstow. Perfect point from which to ship our deliveries. My idea, you know," he added, raising his bushy white eyebrows. "I never liked Sherman Oaks. Too damn close to the action."

Lyle didn't speak. It hadn't been Beezly who had thought of moving the operation out of Sherman Oaks; it had been he, but Beezly had a habit of forgetting to give him proper credit. He stared, glaring, his patience just about depleted. He was considering offing Beezly and taking charge himself. The others wouldn't approve, of course; but once he explained the crisis and Beezly's slowness to react . . .

"I think you had better make a phone call, Mr. Beezly," he said without disguising his impatience. "We don't have that much time to waste."

"Yes, yes, all right," Beezly said, reaching for the telephone. He punched out the numbers slowly and then sat back, his glasses sliding down his nose again. Dressed in a ruby silk robe and matching silk pajamas, the old man looked too comfortable to be in any sort of crisis. He looked like he was making just any social call. Without a greeting of any sort, he went right to the heart of the situation as soon as the call connected.

"We have some problems," he muttered into the receiver and then added, "Bernard's here," as if that were the problem. "As you know, he's been keeping an eye on our latest client. Things haven't worked out exactly as I had planned."

"What's happening?" the man alternately known as Philip Dante and Edward Clark demanded.

"That black detective Michael Fein suggested to Faye Elliot was better than he was supposed to be. I knew he'd be trouble as soon as I set eyes on him in my office . . . too cocky to be incompetent. I called Michael and let him know, but Michael assured me the man was ineffective. Even so I had Lyle watching him and I'm glad I did. Now Bernard tells me my office was compromised."

"Compromised? What do you mean, compromised?"

"They broke into the building and got into my files. They know about Goodfellow and they know he's in Barstow. Bernard seems to think that Mr. Lester will be heading that way soon, if he's not on his way already."

There was a silence. Beezly continued to gaze up at Lyle, whose eyes widened with interest. Beezly shrugged and waited.

"What about the detective?" Dante asked.

"He's dead, but not before Bernard persuaded him to reveal what they had learned," Beezly reported. "I thought it had all been set up rather well, but apparently . . ."

"You say Bernard is there now?"

"Right here, standing right in front of me."

"Let me speak to him."

Beezly held out the receiver and Bernard took it.

"Yes, sir?" He listened and nodded. "I understand. Yes, sir, my thoughts exactly," Lyle added after listening for nearly a minute without speaking. He handed the receiver back to Jerome Beezly who put it to his ear.

"Listen," he began, but immediately sensed the line was dead. "Hello?" He looked at Bernard. "Did he hang up?"

"Yes," Bernard said.

"Well, what does he want us to do first?" Beezly asked, cradling the receiver.

"First," Bernard said, "he wants me to do this." He took out

Scott Lester's nine-millimeter pistol and shot Jerome Beezly in the forehead. The force of the bullet snapped his head back and sent his glasses flying off his nose. It looked like he was pulling himself back to let out a terrific sneeze. His back did slap the rear of the seat and then his body folded forward, sagging as it did so. The blood dripped profusely onto his lap. Lyle regretted ruining the silk robe.

"Another thing for Lester to be accused of doing," Lyle casually remarked. He returned the pistol to the inside of his jacket.

"Second, I've got to go up to your office and make sure no one finds nothin'. After that," he continued, "I've got to go to Barstow and make sure of the same thing.

"Then I got to decide about the girl, decide if it's necessary to wipe away all traces of this one and chalk it up to what we have to do to keep the Solomon Organization protected. Are you satisfied that you know everything now, Mr. Beezly?" he asked and actually stood there waiting as if he expected the dead man to sit back, smile, and thank him for the information.

"I'm glad you approve," Bernard said. He turned around and walked slowly out of the house, stopping only once in the corridor to dip his hand into the bowl of mints Mr. Beezly always had placed there on a table.

Reminds me of a restaurant, Bernard thought and left to complete his assignment.

SCOTT PARKED HIS CAR on Seventh Street in Santa Monica and got out slowly. He waited for a moment, scrutinizing the automobiles that went by and then checked to be sure that none had pulled up somewhere behind him. He felt confident that he hadn't been followed. The rental car's thrown them off, he thought. It was Dyce's last meaningful contribution to the investigation.

Satisfied he was alone, Scott turned his attention to the small gray beach house. Quaint, he thought, but not what he would have guessed was Faye Elliot's residence. She looked more like a half-million dollar condominium on Wilshire Boulevard in Westwood with marble entryways, plush carpets, and imported Italian furniture purchased on Robertson Boulevard in Beverly Hills than she did an old beach house. He checked the address that Dyce had given him. He had written it on the back of an old business card. There was no mistake. He crossed the street casually and paused at the gate. There were lights on in the house, but dim and only in a few rooms. He started up the narrow walk that curved and turned with the small incline. In fact, the house itself looked like it had shifted and stretched. It was built on uneven ground, jacked up with stone and constructed so as to conform with the natural rise and fall of the earth.

From the entry way, he heard the sharp, short barking of either a poodle or terrier. He hated small dogs; they always gave him the impression they would nip at his ankles and they were always the most belligerent. Perhaps they were overcompensating for their diminutive size. The dog was right at the door, scratching and barking. At least it served as an alarm system, Scott thought. Just as he raised his hand to press the inconspicuous door buzzer button, the door itself was thrust open.

Faye Elliot, dressed in a pair of dungarees and a flannel shirt tied, stood facing him. She held her poodle in her arms. Her hair was down; she wore no makeup and she looked totally pissed off.

"How'd you get my address?"

"Dyce had gotten it for me. He was good; he was worth every penny. You were right about that. Something you probably didn't count on, huh?" he asked her.

She twitched her nose out of annoyance and confusion.

"I see my clients in the office or at a restaurant or in prison," she declared. "Never in my home."

"Tonight you'll make an exception," Scott said and took

Dyce's pistol out of his pocket. Her eyes went wide and bright. The poodle growled. "Dyce is dead," Scott added and walked into the house. He turned when she didn't move. "Close the door and put that dog someplace, please," he commanded. "Now," he added sharply when she still hadn't moved.

She closed the door and strutted past him. He followed in admiration of the way her tight rear end shifted against her jeans. She put the dog in a room off right, a small den, and then closed the door.

"What do you mean, Dyce is dead?" she asked turning to him.

"They killed him. He was supposed to meet me on a corner. When he didn't show, I went to his apartment and found him hanging upside down in his shower, his throat cut."

Faye grimaced.

"You got a drink . . . straight Scotch? I've had a helluva lousy day."

She nodded and he followed her into a small living room furnished with antique pieces, most of light maple and oak. There was a curio case loaded with Dresden figurines. The walls were peppered with dark oils, landscapes, and scenes at sea. A pole lamp next to the easy chair and a Tiffany table lamp provided all the warm, subdued light. Scott thought the room had a comfortable, lived-in feeling about it. He wished he were here under other circumstances and able to enjoy the pleasure of relaxing in such a room, drink in hand, and maybe a fire in the small brick fireplace. He sat on the settee and watched Faye Elliot pour his drink into a tumbler.

"Thanks," he said, taking the drink. He took a quick, long gulp. She stood staring down at him, her eyes a mixture of fear and anger now, her face flushed.

"Who killed Dyce?" she asked softly.

"The Solomon Organization. Beezly's people, I suppose," he added. She simply stared. "Maybe your people, too, eh?"

"My people?"

"Dyce and I broke into Beezly's office earlier tonight. We rifled through a private file cabinet and found evidence of past cases, other divorced people and other children, many of whom they delivered, as they like to put it." He drank some more of his Scotch. It warmed his stomach and strengthened his resolve. When he looked back at Faye Elliot, he saw she looked more than skeptical; she looked like she was confronting someone in the midst of a hallucination.

"Delivered? Delivered where?" she asked.

"Somewhere in Barstow. That's where my daughter is, I'm sure." He lifted the pistol and cocked back the hammer. "I want to know exactly where."

Faye shook her head.

"I don't understand. Why would you think I had anything to do with this?"

Scott smiled.

"We saw the name of the attorney who was involved with many of the cases—my divorce attorney, Michael Fein, who brought you to me so you could defend me by working your ass off to get me to plead guilty."

Faye simply stared a moment. Then she turned around and went to the liquor cabinet and poured herself a straight Scotch. Scott watched her sip the drink and think. She was either the coolest woman he had ever met or . . .

"Let me understand what you're saying and what you think," she began. "I confess I put most of what you told me before out of mind; it seemed that incredible at the time. You said you were brought to some clandestine organization that was supposed to help you with your custody battle. It turned out they had you framed for the attack on your wife and now you've discovered they kidnapped your daughter to be delivered . . . some place in Barstow?"

"To a Doctor Goodfellow."

"For what purpose?"

"I imagine to farm her out, give her to some acceptable family or sell her. You tell me," Scott said. She took another swig of her Scotch and moved to the arm chair.

"You and Dyce broke into this office and got this information?"

"And then we were to meet and head out to Barstow, but the Solomon Organization got to him first."

"And you think Michael Fein is part of this and because he recommended me, I'm part of it?"

"Yes."

She nodded.

"If what you're saying is true, I don't blame you for having the suspicion, but I'm not part of it and what irks me even more is that if you're telling the truth, they probably assigned you to me because of my inexperience. They thought I wouldn't do much of a job defending you."

"I'm sorry your ego's been bruised," Scott said. "But my daughter's still missing."

She looked at him as if she hadn't heard.

"And they told me to hire Dyce because they thought he was a fuck-up. Is that it?"

"Probably. But he wasn't. Unless you call getting killed fucking up." Scott downed his Scotch. "What do you know about Doctor Goodfellow?"

She shook her head.

"I never heard the name mentioned. Look," she said, "Michael Fein's office called me and told me about you. They asked me to take over the case and I did. I've met Michael a few times at professional meetings, maybe at a cocktail party, too. I don't remember. But he's not a close acquaintance."

"Didn't you think it odd that he called you then?"

"No. It's the way we work . . . we refer clients to each other when they need specialties. My firm's directed some business toward his and vice versa."

"I don't want to go driving off in the night blindly. I've got to know where to go to get my daughter back," he said firmly.

"I really don't know where your daughter is."

"But Michael Fein knows. He's part of it. If you're not part of it, will you help me get him to tell us?"

"Why don't we just call the police?"

"And tell them what? I broke into Beezly's office and got this information?"

"They'll see that Dyce is dead and . . ."

"And they'll probably blame it on me. First, I want to get my daughter home. Then I'll go to the police. These people reach into every aspect of our world, it seems . . . doctors, lawyers, judges. Police too, I'm sure." He pointed to the phone with the barrel of his pistol. "Get Michael Fein on the phone. Arrange some sort of meeting without telling him I'm involved."

"This time of night?"

"You can do it. You're better than they think you are," he said. She smirked.

"I don't need to be stroked."

"Pity," Scott said.

She stood up and started out of the room.

"Where are you going?"

"My den. You don't think I have Michael Fein's home number committed to memory, do you?" she retorted. He followed close on her heels. When she opened the den door, her poodle began a low growl.

"Quiet, Pebbles."

"Pebbles . . . logical name for a dog that lives near the beach, I guess." He kept an eye on the dog and an eye on her as she rifled through her desk and came up with a small address book. She found the number and looked up.

"What am I supposed to tell him?"

"Just tell him something very serious has come up with my case. Tell him you have reason to believe there is some validity to my story and you want him to know what I'm saying. Tell him you can't talk on the phone. Sound scared and he'll agree to meet you, I'm sure."

"Sound scared?"

"I know it's beyond you, but try. If you want, I'll help you by putting this pistol against your temple and keeping my finger on the trigger."

She smirked and dialed.

"Hello," she said. "May I speak to Michael please. Tell him it's Faye Elliot, Scott Lester's attorney." She waited, staring at him.

"Michael, hi," she said. "I'm sorry to bother you at this hour, but I've got to speak with you right away. No, something's come up with Scott Lester's case . . . something that leads me to believe his story about a secret organization being responsible for the attack on his wife and the whereabouts of his missing daughter." She paused and focused on Scott as she listened. Her face turned a bit white as she continued to listen. Scott tilted his head and widened his eyes, curious.

"No, I don't know where he is right now," she finally said in a more subdued tone of voice. Scott flashed his pistol as a reminder of the call's purpose. She nodded at him. "Well, can we meet for just a few minutes? Un huh." She listened. "I understand. Yes. All right." She wrote something down quickly. "Thank you," she said and cradled the phone slowly.

"What?"

"I've got to drive over to his house, but he doesn't want me to come in. He'll come out and meet me in my car."

"See?" Scott said quickly. "Isn't that weird?"

"No. He says his wife is very upset because they just heard a good friend of theirs has been murdered tonight."

"A good friend? Who?"

"Jerome Beezly," she said. "He was shot with a nine-millimeter pistol. Do you own a nine-millimeter pistol?"

"Christ."

"You do, don't you?"

"It wasn't in my house when I went to look for it. This is Dyce's pistol," he said.

"Did you kill Beezly?"

"Hell no. I wanted to, but I didn't."

"Did you threaten him earlier in his office, you and Dyce?" she cross-examined.

"Shit."

"You did, didn't you?"

"We didn't threaten him, but he made a formal complaint and the police came to see me. Now they'll think I killed him for sure. Christ, I'm sinking like a lead balloon. Why did they kill Beezly?"

"Yes, why would they kill their leader?" she asked, folding her arms under her breasts and glaring at him.

"I don't know, but it's obvious they're trying to frame me for this, too. We have to talk to Michael. Get up," he demanded. "If we drive up in your car, he'll come out. Get up!"

"Scott, listen to me. You've got to turn yourself in."

"That's exactly what they want me to do, I'm sure. Move," he said. She started around the desk. "Wait a minute," he said. She hesitated. "If the police know Beezly's been shot and they know he was shot with a gun like mine and they know I had a confrontation with him earlier, why haven't they called you to see if you know my whereabouts? Why would they call Michael Fein? They know you're my attorney now, not him."

She stared at him.

"Well?" he demanded.

"I don't know."

"I do. The police don't know Beezly's dead yet. Fein does

because they killed him. I'm not lying, Faye. Honest to God, I'm not lying."

She nodded and led him out of the room.

BERNARD LYLE SHOVED a couple of pieces of sugarless gum into his mouth and turned up the Carl Sacks Talk Show. Sacks, an outspoken radical right commentator was berating a caller who had tried to defend Affirmative Action.

"I didn't own slaves; I didn't whip and rape and oppress black people. Why the hell are you punishing me?"

"Social responsibility," the caller began.

"That's a pile of buffalo chips, and a convenient buzz word for the bleeding heart liberal establishment. What about my responsibility to my wife and children? I, who am just as qualified, even more qualified than the minority applicant, should step aside out of social responsibility? Thanks, but no thanks."

"Right on, brother," Lyle muttered. He turned off the San Bernadino Freeway and headed toward Barstow, accelerating up to eighty miles an hour. He could risk a speeding ticket. There was always someone who would take care of it as long as he got it while on the job.

It felt good having that sort of clout behind him all the time. Ever since he had begun with the organization, he had felt more important, more significant. He hadn't gone to college as did most of the members of the board, nor was he born with any sort of silver spoon in his mouth, but here he was hob-nobbing with blue bloods. He had plenty of money, a beautiful apartment in Brentwood, an expensive car, and an impressive wardrobe. The maitre d's at the best restaurants knew him and kowtowed to him. He impressed any and all women he escorted. Life was good and he felt comfortable and justified about everything he did. It was, after all, for a higher cause—the stability of society, a return to the well-adjusted family.

The liberals had brought this all about—this ease with which people entered into and absolved their sacred marital relationships. They might as well skip the marriage ceremonies, civil or religious. Neither had much significance once the two parties became bored with each other or their lifestyle. Forget the children. The children were expendable, easily sacrificed to the gods and goddesses of hedonism. Well not as far as the Solomon Organization was concerned. No, sir. They were doing something to put a stop to it and he, Bernard Lyle, had a major responsibility toward that end. He loved his job, his responsibilities, his contributions to the cause.

Nothing was more important than the organization now. It must be protected at all costs and those who were in it, who had volunteered their services and benefited in some way from their work, had to accept all the consequences and be willing to make the sacrifices, if indeed sacrifices were required. He would. The organization demanded that kind of devotion if it were to succeed and continue.

Buoyed by his purpose, he rushed through the night and arrived in Barstow in record time. The lateness of the hour made the surroundings seem ethereal. He was like a man traveling through a dream, passing images, floating through the imagination. He shut off his radio, spit his gum out the window, and turned off the main drag to head north for two miles. As he approached the quaint old house, he saw the porch light had been left on. Goodfellow's car was in the driveway, but the house itself was dark.

Pity, he thought as he slowed down to turn in. He had been right about this place: it had been a perfect location, a wonderful hub from which deliveries could be easily made, their activities barely noticeable. But if Lester had gotten here first, or had somehow convinced the authorities to investigate, the entire network could fall and with it all the good work they had done not only in California but throughout the country. Everyone would be in jeopardy.

He turned off the lights, shut off the engine, and got out of the car. He had to stretch a bit. He hated the long ride, even in the BMW 750. He was far too muscular to remain in one position for so many hours. A man like me's got to move, turn, stretch, lift, he thought and felt his biceps flex and the muscles in his thighs jump as he strolled up to the front door.

He pushed the buzzer and waited. After a moment, he heard the sounds of someone moving about within. He pressed his forehead against the panel window on the door and peered through the dark entry way. Toward the rear a light had gone on and a moment later, the old lady appeared. She looked enormous in her house coat, her heavy bosom lifting the garment. She had her gray hair down and when she drew closer, he could see she wore a very annoyed expression.

She peered through the window and saw it was he. Then she put on the hall light.

"Where's Goodfellow?" Lyle demanded the moment she opened the door.

"Asleep, of course. What's going on?"

"We need to evacuate," he muttered and walked into the house.

"Evacuate?" She closed the door. "What do you mean, evacuate?"

"Evacuate means evacuate. Leave the premises," he responded sharply.

"Leave . . . the house?"

"Now you're getting it, Grandma. Wake up Goodfellow," he added and went to Goodfellow's office. Grandma hesitated, her hand at the base of her throat, her heart pounding. Grandmothers don't evacuate their homes, she thought. And what about the children who were coming? Who would be here to welcome them?

Instead of going to wake Doctor Goodfellow, she followed Bernard Lyle. He was already rifling through the files, taking them out, and throwing them into the garbage can beside the desk.

"What are you doing? Doctor Goodfellow needs those papers."

"Didn't I tell you to go wake him up?" Lyle snapped. "How the hell can he stay asleep anyway?" he wondered aloud.

Grandma straightened up and folded her arms over her bulging bosom. She grimaced. She had handled naughty boys before.

"You stop that immediately. Put those papers back in those drawers this instant."

Lyle paused and looked at her. She was scowling at him so intensely, he couldn't help but smile.

"Who do you think you are? My grandma?" he asked and laughed.

"Yes," she said firmly. "I am Grandma. I'm Grandma to all those children and I won't let you destroy their records and disturb the good work. Now you put those papers back this instant, Bernard. Go on."

"Bernard, eh? Okay, Grandma," he said. "I'll be a good little boy. And Grandma will give me cookies and milk?"

"We'll see," Grandma said, her arms still folded over her bosom. Bernard smiled.

"Yes, Grandma," he said and reached into the garbage can to pick up a file. At the same time, he slipped his pistol out of his jacket so that when he stood up he held the file in one hand and the pistol in the other. Grandma didn't seem to notice or care.

"Oh," Bernard said. "I've changed my mind, Grandma. I don't want cookies and milk," he said and he shot her, the bullet entering the base of her throat.

Grandma gasped, brought her hands to her wound, and then

folded quickly to the floor, sprawling out as she descended, her house coat spreading and spreading so that she looked like she had been turned into Grandma jelly.

Bernard went back to the files and continued to empty them. A few moments later, Doctor Goodfellow came charging into the office. He wore his bathrobe and wool-lined black leather slippers.

"What the hell..." He gazed down at Grandma. "What happened?"

"Grandma was ready for the funny farm," Bernard said. He knelt down and pulled out his cigarette lighter.

"What are you doing?" Doctor Goodfellow asked.

"Closing holes, plugging gaps, erasing traceable lines, covering ass," Bernard said as he lit the edges of the papers. A small fire began quickly. He stood up and watched the files burn.

"Those are... our files. Are you crazy?" Doctor Goodfellow cried and charged forward. As soon as he drew close enough, Bernard spun around and punched him sharply and smoothly in the mouth. The blow lifted Doctor Goodfellow off his feet and he fell smack on his back, his head slapping the floor. For a moment he was in a daze and could only groan. Bernard continued to feed files to the fire. The smoke was building. He worked faster and faster.

Goodfellow turned and sat up, feeling his mouth and looking at his fingers, which were bright red with his blood.

"I don't understand," he said, gazing up at Bernard.

"We've got to evacuate this location. As Mr. Beezly said before retiring, we've been compromised. You understand, don't you?"

"No," Goodfellow replied. He got to his feet. "I like to keep track of my wards, check on their welfare from time to time. That was understood. That was the agreement I made. This is a professional operation. It requires follow-up."

"We can't take that chance; it's not worth it. They've all been placed in proper homes. No need for any traces."

Goodfellow began to cough from the smoke.

"You're going to have the fire department out here. Open that window," he commanded.

"The fire department," Bernard thought aloud. "Good idea. Why didn't I think of it? I'm getting too soft, too complacent. Thanks, Doc."

Bernard walked over to the window, but instead of opening it, he set fire to the curtains. The flames shot up to the ceiling. Goodfellow screamed and charged at the windows to pull the curtains down. As he did so, Bernard struck him in the back of his head with the pistol. Doctor Goodfellow fell forward against the wall and slid down into a sitting position, unconscious. Bernard shook his head and laughed. He watched the flames spread for a moment. Doctor Goodfellow groaned, but he didn't open his eyes. Bernard considered putting a bullet in his forehead, but decided the good doctor should go down with his ship instead. In moments the smoke would asphyxiate him. Bernard already had to cover his own mouth with his handkerchief. Shortly, the old house would explode like a firecracker.

Satisfied he had done what had to be done, Bernard casually strolled out, even taking the time to close the door behind him. Inside, the flames had reached the bookcases and had begun to crawl over the volumes. The old walls accepted the fire willingly, surrendering their surfaces, crackling, exposing their beams. Electric wires snapped.

Bernard got into this car and sat there for a moment watching the flames brighten until every room in the house looked lit. It appeared psychedelic to him because of the way the fire licked at the ceilings and made colors dance over the window panes.

"Beautiful," Bernard muttered and sighed with appreciation.

He started his engine and backed out of the driveway. Then he turned down the highway, his tires squealing.

He wasn't sure about Scott Lester's daughter, but in his gut he thought he had better give it serious consideration. He would go to her new location and he would make a decision on the spot. He trusted his impulses and his instinct. He had been the one, and not Beezly, to suggest following Dyce, even though Beezly had tried to take the credit. And hadn't he thought Beezly had outlived his use to the organization? The phone conversation simply confirmed what he already knew had to be done. Now this fire . . . wasn't it a great idea? he thought. Funny, how the doctor had inadvertently suggested it. Must have been Providence speaking. After all, the Solomon Organization had its roots in the Bible, didn't it?

He laughed top himself, shoved some fresh gum into his mouth, and accelerated, cutting through the darkness, unstoppable, moving like Destiny. And very proud of it.

# 11

Faye Elliot's narrow driveway ran alongside the house to an unattached garage in the rear, the structure of which looked to be the same vintage as the house. She took Scott through a side entrance off the cozy, immaculate kitchen, pausing to scoop up a chocolate-brown leather pilot's jacket hanging on a hook next to the door. When they stepped outside, Faye produced a transmitter from her jacket pocket and pressed it to open the garage door. It went up to reveal a late model, pearl black Porche 928.

"All right," Scott remarked. "This is more like it. For a while back there I was worried you weren't making a living as a lawyer."

"The house is old, but practically everything in it is a valuable antique," she said caustically. "It belongs to my parents; the car's mine," she said, slipping in behind the wheel. He got in quickly and watched her put on her black leather driving gloves. She inserted the key into the ignition and the car growled into life. Then she paused and turned to him.

"It's not too late to change your mind," she said.

"Get going," he ordered. "We don't want to keep Mr. Fein waiting. A lawyer's time is money."

She shifted quickly to back out with precision down the narrow driveway to the street.

"Where does Michael Fein live?" he asked after she turned up Seventh and headed for San Vincente Boulevard.

"Camden Drive, Beverly Hills."

"Why doesn't that surprise me."

She glanced at him and sped up.

"Tell me about this meeting you had with these people who call themselves the Solomon Organization. What did they tell you? What did they ask you?"

He described how they had sent a limousine to pick him up, how he had been searched by Bernard Lyle first, and how he had been brought to the conference room. She listened quietly as he related the details of the inquiry.

"So there was no question they had access to your court proceeding," she concluded.

"Michael Fein had apparently turned everything over to them. It just didn't occur to me at the time. I was so confused and angry, I wasn't thinking straight anyway. Dante had convinced me this was my last chance to hold onto Justine."

"And when you left, you had no idea what they were up to?" she asked, her voice dripping with incredulity.

"I really thought . . . hoped, I suppose, that they had influence with the court. Violence simply wasn't an option in my way of thinking. These men were described to me as being doctors, lawyers, judges, psychologists . . . not mobsters." She smirked as if to say, tell me another one. "Look, I was given the distinct impression they were doing something about the inequities of the system when it came to divorces and custody hearings, that's all."

"Inequities?"

"Most of the considerations are weighted in favor of the woman. And the woman is not necessarily the better parent all the time."

She looked at him and shook her head.

"So you're telling me these people see themselves as a kind of privately operated child welfare agency?"

"Sort of. In a distorted way, I suppose."

"From what you're telling me of what you think's happened, they apparently weren't very impressed with you. In their eyes you weren't a fit parent, either."

"Maybe I wasn't, but they had no right to do what they've done." After a beat he added, "Meg's not a bad mother. I exaggerated in an effort to get them to help me. But they had no right to play God with our lives like this."

"Of course not. Look," she said in a calmer tone of voice, "what you're doing now is just making this all more complicated and getting yourself deeper and deeper into a situation from which you can't hope to escape blame. If we take what you've learned to the police . . ."

"No," he said sharply. He glared at her. "And it doesn't do you any good to keep suggesting that course of action. It keeps me questioning your innocence."

She shook her head and drove on in silence. When they reached Beverly Hills, she slowed down and told him the address to look for. The Porche purred up the avenue, hovering to the side. Finally, they spotted the Spanish-style two-story house with a circular tile driveway in front. The front of the house was well lit up, but there were pockets of shadows in the entry way and atrium.

"Slowly," he commanded just before she started to turn in. "Very slowly."

She drove in and came to a stop.

"The keys . . . quickly," he said. She pulled them out of the ignition and gave them to him. He got out quickly and stepped back in the shadows. Then he nodded and she hit the horn twice. A few moments later, Michael Fein emerged from his house. He wore a sports jacket and a pair of jeans and new white sneakers. He looked very relaxed and casual and certainly not a man involved in some deadly conspiracy.

"Hi," he said approaching the car. "What's Scott been telling you? What is this all about?"

"It's about my wife and child," Scott said, coming up behind him. He shoved the pistol barrel into Michael's ribs.

"What the . . ." Michael Fein looked down and saw the gun in his side.

"Get in the car," Scott ordered. "Go on. Get around and get into the car."

"Scott, you're crazy. You can't . . ."

"If you don't think I'll use this, you're the one who's crazy. At this moment I don't have much to lose. I'm already suspected of attempting to kill my wife and now I'm surely going to be accused of killing Jerome Beezly. I don't mind adding another death to the list, if I can really commit the murder myself this time."

Michael Fein moved around the car. Scott opened the door.

"Get in the rear."

"What rear?" Michael Fein whined.

"You'll manage. Get in," Scott snapped and poked Fein with the gun again, this time sharply enough under his ribs to bruise. He groaned but moved quickly to squeeze himself into the small rear seat. Then Scott got in.

"Now what?" Faye asked when he handed her keys back to her.

"Just drive. Head up to Sunset and go west toward the 405 Freeway," he ordered.

"What's going on, Scott? Why are you doing this?" Fein asked.

Scott turned, holding the pistol in clear view between the two front seats, the barrel pointed at Michael, who glanced at it fearfully.

"Here's what I know and I know you know I know," Scott said. "You're part of the Solomon Organization. You've been involved in a number of their, shall we say, 'special cases.' You even helped Mr. Beezly's son with his divorce and custody hearing, which resulted in the death of his wife, a death that was made to look accidental."

"It was accidental."

"Save it. I know now that you gave the panel my case history and you've been actively involved in framing me for the attack on my wife and the kidnapping of my child."

"What . . . now look, Scott . . ."

"There's no sense in wasting time claiming you're innocent or telling me I don't know what I'm talking about . . . whatever bullshit you come up with will go in one ear and out the other. Before Dyce was killed, he and I broke into Beezly's office and we saw the documents and your involvement. Now we're heading toward the freeway. We have a long drive ahead of us, at the end of which we will find my daughter. Whether you live or die depends entirely on how cooperative you are. Am I making myself clear?"

Fein didn't respond.

"Where do we find Doctor Goodfellow in Barstow?" Scott asked softly.

"Faye," Michael said, "are you listening to this and believing it?"

"Frankly, Michael, I don't know what to believe anymore. Why didn't the police call me about Beezly's murder? If they're looking for Scott, why did they call you?"

"I don't know. What's that have to do with anything?"

"You knew Beezly was dead before the police did, if they do know now," Scott said.

"That's ridiculous. Look..."

Scott pulled back the hammer on the pistol.

"It's going to make a lot of noise, I know. If she hits a bump too hard..."

"Faye," Michael appealed. "He's out of his mind. Don't listen to him."

"There's no sense trying to convince her, Michael. I'm prepared to shoot her, too, and she knows it. Look," Scott added, raising his voice so that the note of hysteria began to ring clearly, "my daughter has been living in some horrible terror for days and you, you son of a bitch, are part of the reason why. When I think of that act you put on in the police station just before they booked me... pretending to believe I had attacked Meg, pretending to be disgusted while all the while you were plotting and planning. Who the hell made you people into gods, huh? Who told you to decide people's lives? You fucking..."

Scott reached over and pommeled Michael Fein on the side of his head with his left fist. Fein howled with pain and Faye jerked the car to the right and then to the left, the tires squealing.

"Stop!" she screamed. "Stop or I'll deliberately drive off the road."

Scott stopped striking Fein, but rose in his seat and pointed the pistol at him, taking aim at his skull.

"We'll find her without your help," he threatened in a throaty voice.

"All right, all right, for Christ sakes," Fein cried. "I'll show you where Doctor Goodfellow lives."

"And you don't deny being involved?"

"No."

Scott lowered himself to his seat slowly and then gazed at

Faye Elliot. Finally she wore an expression of utter terror. They turned into the entrance to the freeway.

"Okay," Scott said in a much calmer tone of voice, "let's see if the Porche can live up to its reputation."

She shifted down and entered the freeway, quickly pulling away from nearby vehicles. In the rear, Michael Fein sunk down, his head still throbbing. Scott glared at him for a moment and then made himself comfortable. Faye relaxed, too.

"How many people have such things been done to?" she asked after a while.

"Michael?" Scott said. "You've been asked a question and the court directs you to reply."

"A dozen or so in Los Angeles," he muttered.

"You mean, this is going on in other cities?" she asked.

"Michael?"

"Yes," he said. "And what you're doing now is not going to stop it. There are people in very high places committed to our purposes," he added proudly.

"Which is what?" Faye asked.

"To stabilize the American family, to ensure our children grow up in an emotionally and psychologically well-balanced environment."

"Well balanced . . . by killing people?"

"We do what has to be done. Sometimes, sacrifices are made," he said coldly.

"Yeah, well if this doesn't go well," Scott said, "you can be sure you'll be the next one to be sacrificed."

"Scott," Faye said. "It's not too late. Let's take him to the police and present his testimony."

"For what? You heard him. They have friends in high places. No," Scott said, settling back again. "I put myself and my family into this mess. I've got to get us out. With or without your help," he added.

Faye glanced at him and saw the cold determination in his eyes.

"Do you understand?" he asked.

"Yes," she said softly and pressed down on the accelerator, one part of her numb and the other part terrified.

BERNARD LYLE TOOK the next exit off the freeway to look for a place to have a cup of coffee and make a phone call. Although there was a definite sense of urgency to everything that he had to do, Bernard believed one should always have a clear mind and as much of a rested body as possible before taking action. Those who acted abruptly, who pushed the envelope, usually made mistakes. He wanted to remain calm, clear thinking, totally in charge of events.

He spotted an all-night diner and drove into the parking lot. He could see there were only a few other customers. The one waitress and the counterman were talking casually. It was a good place to stop—the fewer people to remember him, the better. The waitress smiled when he entered. She was a stout woman with bad teeth, but warm, friendly eyes.

"Sit anywhere you want," she said.

He took the first booth. He hadn't intended on having anything to eat, but the pies looked great in the pie case and all this activity had indeed stimulated his appetite.

"Give me a cup of coffee and . . . which is the freshest pie?"

"The apple," she said, shifting her eyes conspiratorially, as if she was supposed to push the least fresh one first.

"I know fresh apple pie when I taste it," he warned. She laughed. Only someone who knew him well would realize he was making a serious threat. He was quite capable of seriously harming someone for less.

"It's fresh. A la mode?"

"No. Got to watch the figure," he said. The waitress laughed.

"Tell me about it," she said, running her hand over her wide hip. Bernard nodded in full agreement, which was something she didn't expect. Her eyebrows went up and she turned away quickly.

Bernard sat back and gazed out the window. At this moment he felt very powerful, very successful. The organization had been protected. There were higher-ups who were going to appreciate him and surely reward him. He had seen the possibility of a bad hemorrhage and he had stopped the bleeding before it had had any real chance to start.

Of course, the question remained how much had Scott Lester learned and how far would he go before he was stopped. Bernard felt he had done his part, more than his part. Now it was up to them to contribute, to use their influence with the police, the judges, whoever to get this man off their trail.

The waitress served the coffee and pie without comment this time. Bernard ate and drank quietly, pleased that the pie was fresh. When the waitress returned to give him a refill, he asked her how much farther it was to Ludlow.

"Less than a half hour," she said.

"I'm that close? Great. Thanks."

She returned to her conversation with the counterman. After Bernard had sipped half of his second cup, he got up and went to the pay phone in the rear. It was time to check in. He used his calling card and waited.

"Yes," Dante said after only one ring.

"The Barstow problem has been solved . . . completely solved," he said.

"Good. Where are you?"

"Half hour out of Ludlow. I thought I would head in this direction in case more had to be done. Ready and prepared, that's my motto," he said pedantically.

"Good thinking. As it turns out, we do have a new problem.

Michael Fein stepped out of his house to meet with Faye Elliot, Mr. Lester's attorney. She had called, claiming there was reason to believe in the validity of his tale. Michael was supposed to call in as soon as he discovered what she knew."

"He hasn't phoned in?"

"No and it's been some time. His wife doesn't know what happened to him. His car is still in his garage and he had no other appointments. She's on the verge of calling the police."

"I don't like it."

"Me neither. They could be on their way to Barstow."

"They won't find anything."

"Nevertheless, you had better complete the mop up. Everyone agrees it's not worth the risk."

"Understood," Bernard said.

"Do it cleanly," Dante warned.

"Have I ever been sloppy? You're going to appreciate the way I handled Barstow."

"Bernard," Dante said. "We already appreciate you. I assure you, we will make that clear when this is over."

"Thank you," Bernard said. "I'm off to see the Wizard . . ."

"The wonderful Wizard of Oz."

Bernard cradled the phone and returned to his booth. He left a very good tip. He was feeling generous; his heart was full. He could be nice to almost anyone, and no one would annoy him while he was in this state of mind. All the way to Ludlow, he sang along with the radio and beat out rhythms on the dash board. When he pulled into the sleepy town, he checked the address he had and drove directly to the pretty little house with the picket fence, the immaculate lawn, and well-pruned hedges. He parked across the street and turned off his lights.

The occupants of the house were long asleep. There was just a small night light on above the front door. Bernard thought about waking them, but then reconsidered. That might cause suspicion and commotion at such a late hour. No, this had to be done right, done smoothly. Everyone was depending on him to be perfect. Besides, they weren't going anywhere.

Despite the coffee and the pie, he was drowsy. After all, he had had a big day. In fact, it only just occurred to him that he had killed four people today: Dyce, Beezly, Grandma, and Doctor Goodfellow. That's more than a day's work for any good mechanic, he thought and chuckled. Boy, they sure got their money's worth out of me today.

If he lowered the seat and relaxed, he could catch a few hours of sleep before morning. Parked in front of the house like this and cloaked in the dark shadows of this sidestreet that had no street lights, he could watch over the house as well and be alert should Scott Lester somehow appear before the work was done. Confident that wouldn't happen anyway, and comfy, he closed his eyes and leaned back. In moments, he was asleep. He never had trouble falling asleep, no pangs of conscience, no stress to keep him tossing and turning. He was a well-adjusted man and his loud snoring quickly confirmed it. Fortunately, there was no one around to hear him, nothing but a few hungry bats who had circled the front of the house and then soared off for better pickings.

The moon sunk behind some clouds and the glow of warm illumination that had washed over Bernard Lyle's car slipped away. The expression, It's always darkest before the dawn, seemed to be reaffirmed.

Inside the house Justine moaned and turned. She was having another nightmare, but unlike the others, she wasn't waking up to scream. Instead, she was trapped in her own unrelentingly morbid imagination. Mommy was being pulled upwards toward Heaven, but Mommy didn't want to go and Mommy was crying for her, but all Justine could do was look up and watch her disappear into the dark clouds until she was nothing but a point of darkness herself. Then Daddy went by in his car, the windows all rolled up. She screamed and screamed for him, but he didn't hear her nor did he look at her. In moments he was gone, too, and she was all alone until Grandma emerged from the shadows with Little Bit in her arms. Only when she drew closer did Justine see that the puppy was dead.

She whimpered in her sleep and tugged the blanket up to her lips. Finally, the nightmare dissipated. It thinned out and disappeared leaving her in a strange, dark void, eager for the sun to rise and the day to begin.

Bernard Lyle was eager too; eager to do what had to be done and go home.

THE MOMENT FAYE, Scott, and Michael Fein entered Barstow, they knew something unusual was happening. A town that should be relatively quiet and asleep at this hour was buzzing. There was considerable traffic and an unexpected number of pedestrians moving about excitedly. A column of silver and gray smoke spiraling and dissipating over the west side of town drew Faye's attention.

"What's that ahead?" she asked.

"Looks like a bad fire," Scott said.

Michael Fein sat up. He had been asleep for the past two hours.

"So we're in Barstow, Michael. Which way now?" Scott demanded.

"You make a right here and then a quick left," he said, his voice filled with concern. As they drew closer to Doctor Goodfellow's house, the traffic became more congested until, finally, a policeman blocked any farther progress. People lined the street and fire hoses crisscrossed like thick, brown snakes over the pavement. Horns blared. An ambulance wove its way through the traffic and then shot away.

Faye rolled down her window. Scott did the same and tried
to look behind the trucks and cars ahead. Then he turned to
Faye as they reached the policeman.

"Careful what you say," Scott warned.

"What's happening, officer?" she asked.

"House fire. Pretty bad one," he said. "It's just smoldering
now, but we'd like to keep any traffic away from the scene.
There are electrical problems right now and the area is not
secured."

"Whose house was it?" Michael Fein asked, shifting in his
seat to see.

"Marvin Goodfellow."

"Goodfellow! Is he all right?"

"Are you related?" the policeman responded.

"No, but I know him and his mother. Are they all right?"
Michael asked again.

"There are no survivors, sir. Please pull over to the right or
turn back," the policeman said and started to wave at another
car.

"Wait a minute," Scott screamed. "Wait!"

The patrolman turned back, annoyed.

"Look, Mister, we've got . . ."

"How many bodies were found?"

"Two bodies, Doctor Goodfellow and his mother."

"Any children hurt?"

"Not as far as I know, no."

"Well, who knows for sure?" Scott demanded. "It's very important," he added when the policeman hesitated.

The patrolman tipped back his cap and then stretched out
his arm to point.

"See that fireman over to the right, just behind the pick-up.
He's the chief. Pull over into that space ahead, but don't go
any farther."

"Thanks. Drive," Scott ordered.

"Jesus," Michael muttered.

"This fire is rather convenient, don't you think?" Scott said.

"Convenient?"

"What Scott means is your people knew he was aware of Goodfellow and that he might be coming out to see him and see if his daughter's here," Faye said.

"So we burned down his house and had our own psychological expert killed?"

"Why not?" Scott said turning on him. "You don't hesitate to kill other people when it's convenient. Just think, Michael," he added, "it's probably going to be convenient for them to kill you now, too."

Faye pulled the car over to the curb behind the pick-up truck.

"I'll go myself. Give me your keys again," Scott demanded, holding out his palm.

"You don't have to worry about me," she responded. "I'm not running off and neither is he," she said, glaring back at Michael Fein. Scott hesitated, still holding his hand out. "Scott, you've got to trust someone. Your lawyer isn't a bad place to start."

"My lawyer?"

"Yes, your lawyer," she said firmly. "I don't like the way I was being used, either."

Scott held her gaze for a moment and then pulled back his hand.

"All right. If he gives you any problem, just scream." He looked at Michael. "After I kill him, we'll explain why."

"Mr. Fein isn't going to give me any problems," Faye said and reached under her seat to come up with a snub-nose 38. Scott smiled.

"You had that under there all this time?"

"Call it feminine paranoia. On the other hand, with an

organization like the Solomon Organization at work, it might not be so much paranoia as good preparation."

Scott nodded and got out of the car.

"Excuse me," he said, approaching the fire chief. He looked up from his clip board. He was a tall, lean man with graying dark brown hair. Right now his face was streaked with soot and ash, and his eyes revealed his fatigue. "The policeman back there told me you were the man to ask."

"Ask what?"

"Were there . . . any children killed or hurt in the fire?"

"Children? No, sir. Only two bodies have been found, both adults."

Scott looked toward the smoldering ruins. Most of the house was down to its foundation. Some of the firemen were chopping away at the pieces of charred walls that remained.

"Are you positive? I had reason to believe my daughter might have been in that house tonight."

"We've combed through that place pretty good, sir. There are no other victims but the owner and his mother."

Scott released a long-held breath.

"Thank you."

"You might want to speak with those police detectives from Los Angeles, though," the fire chief added and nodded toward the opposite end of the street. "They were asking after possible child victims, too."

"Detectives?"

Scott focused his eyes on the two men talking to a local policeman. When they turned and looked in his direction, he quickly backed away.

"Thank you," he said and retreated to the car.

"Well?" Faye asked as he got back in.

"No other victims."

"Thank God," Faye said.

"They're here," he said.

"Huh? Who's here?"

"They're here, too," he said and spun around to seize Michael's collar at the throat. He squeezed hard. Fein's face turned red as he struggled to free himself. "Are those two with you? Were they the ones sent to shut up Goodfellow? Talk, you son of a bitch."

"What, two, Scott?" Faye asked.

"The policemen who first arrested me and who came to my apartment to warn me to stay away from Beezly . . . Detectives Parker and Fotowski. Well?" he demanded from Fein again.

Fein shook his head vigorously.

"You don't even know who's in your organization and who isn't, do you? Do you, you bastard?"

"As far as I know, they're not with us."

"Maybe he's not lying, Scott. We should go to them and ask for help."

"Why would they be here? They're out of their jurisdiction. And how would they know to come?"

"Where are we going to go from here, if we don't go to the police now, Scott?" Faye asked quietly. Scott thought a moment and then spun on Michael Fein again, this time pressing his pistol to the man's temple and pulling back the hammer.

"Where is she, damn you? Where have they taken her? Tell me or so help me God . . ."

"I don't know. I don't have anything to do with this end of it. Honest."

"He could be telling the truth, Scott," Faye said. "Killing him isn't going to get him to talk anyway, is it?"

"She's right, Mr. Lester," Foto said. He had come up beside the car and now leaned in through the open window. Scott felt the barrel of Foto's pistol on the back of his head. In the mean-time, Lt. Parker opened Faye's door.

"Why don't you all get out, real slowly now," he said. He had his pistol drawn, too, only much less conspicuously.

"I'll shoot him," Scott promised. "I swear I will."

"So what?" Foto said. "Shoot him. What the fuck do we care?"

Faye looked at him and shook her head.

"Don't do it, Scott. If you do, you'll be no better than they are."

"I'm not any better," he replied. The hysteria and frustration had him close to tears. Faye put her hand on his wrist.

"Yes you are, Scott. You have remorse; you care."

He hesitated and then he lowered the gun.

In the quiet moment that followed, everyone became aware of the stench. Michael Fein had lost control of himself in a state of utter fear.

"Give me the gun," Foto said. "Quickly. I can't take the stink."

Scott handed it over.

"Step out," Foto ordered. He and Faye did so. Michael started to move.

"Not you, Mr. Fein," Lt. Parker said. "Just remain where you are for the moment, sir. Step to the side, please," he ordered Faye. "We'll precede this way toward my car," he added and pointed with his pistol. "Mr. Lester."

Scott and Faye started down the street, walking in front of Lt. Parker. When Scott looked back, he saw Foto lean into the Porche with a pair of handcuffs.

"What the hell are you going to do?" Scott demanded. Lt. Parker paused. He had placed his pistol back in its holster.

"Well," he began. He looked at his watch. "In about twenty minutes or so, it will be morning. I figure we'll all get some breakfast. There's an all-night flap jack place in town I've been to before."

"Breakfast?"

"And then what?" Faye demanded.

"Then we'll help Mr. Lester here get his daughter back," Lt. Parker said.

# 12

Billie Madison straightened up so abruptly she frightened Justine. Justine's new mommy's eyes were bright with fear as she turned sharply toward the front entrance of the house. Billie had just helped Justine wash and dress and had brought her out to the breakfast nook where the table had already been set and where Justine's glass of fresh orange juice waited. Her new mommy had even remembered to put out a dish of milk for Little Bit, who lapped contentedly at her feet.

The door bell sounded again.

Mark entered the room, tightening his tie.

"Awful early for a visitor," he remarked.

"Mark," Billie said, seizing his wrist quickly as he turned toward the front of the house. Justine's eyes widened. Billie looked like she wanted to keep Mark from answering the door.

"It's all right. I'm sure it's nothing," he assured her. He kissed her on the cheek and then smiled at Justine. "How's the little princess this morning? Did you sleep well?" Justine nodded.

"No more nightmares?" She thought about telling him and decided against it. She shook her head. Mark smiled at Billie and then at her. The bell was rung again. "I'd better go see who that is. Probably the newspaper boy. Did we forget to pay our last few months' charges?" he called back as he headed toward the front of the house.

"No. We're up to date," Billie replied. Unable to control her nervousness, she made herself busy by going to the cabinet and getting the variety pack of cereal. Then she started to take them out to place them before Justine.

"Choose whichever one you want, honey," she said, her attention half tuned in on the sounds coming from the front door.

"Good morning," Bernard Lyle said and smiled when Mark opened it.

"Morning."

Without introducing himself first, Bernard turned in the doorway to pan the surroundings.

"When I arrived last night, I didn't get a chance to appreciate how pretty it is here," he said. "So quiet, so stressless . . . suburban paradise, huh?" he asked. His face beamed. He looked fresh and awake, despite the creases in his clothing and the untidy way the strands of his hair crossed and flopped over his forehead and temples.

"We think so. What can I do for you, Mr . . ."

"Lyle," Bernard said, extending his thick fingers. They wrapped firmly around Mark's soft, graceful hand, clamping down as though Bernard had no intention of ever letting go. "Bernard Lyle," he said.

"How can I help you, Mr. Lyle?" Mark asked, aware that the man was still clinging to his hand. Bernard smiled again and released him.

"Doctor Goodfellow sent me," he said.

"Oh." Mark instinctively looked back toward the kitchen and Billie. "Something wrong?"

"Oh, no, no," Bernard said, nearly laughing. "Everything's perfect. In fact, things couldn't be better."

"That's good," Mark said, relaxing his shoulders. "Well then . . . oh, I'm sorry. Come in, please."

"Thank you," Bernard said. He stepped into the house and gazed around the entry way and through the doorway that opened on the cozy living room. "Very nice. I love what you've done with the front. It's picture perfect. Belongs on the cover of Suburban Living or something," he added. The way he pronounced suburban, it almost sounded like a pejorative.

"Thanks, but that's mostly my wife's doing. A house might be a man's castle, but his wife designs it," Mark quipped. Bernard laughed.

"Mark?" Billie said, coming to the doorway of the kitchen. "Anything wrong?"

"No, honey. This is Mr. Lyle."

"Bernard, please."

"Bernard Lyle. He's come from Doctor Goodfellow, but there's no problem," Mark added quickly.

"No. I'm just here to make sure there's no problem," Bernard explained with a grin. "I didn't mean to come so early, but . . ."

"No, no, that's fine. Matter of fact, we're just about to have some breakfast. Can we offer you something?"

"Oh, thank you. Cup of coffee?"

"You need more than coffee, Mr. Lyle," Billie said with a motherly tone. "How about scrambled eggs, toast . . ."

"You're too kind, Mrs. Madison. Thank you." Bernard leaned toward Mark and whispered, "How's the little one doing?"

"Just great. Wait until you see her. Come on," Mark urged

and led Bernard into the breakfast nook where Justine was eating her cereal. She looked up curiously at the stout man who smiled down at her.

"Hello there," Bernard said. "I bet your name is Justine. Am I right?"

Justine nodded. Bernard's gaze went to the puppy that had curled at her feet and was chewing on an artificial bone.

"And who's that?"

"Little Bit," Justine replied.

"He certainly is," Bernard said. He laughed and turned to the Madisons. "She looks good, looks happy," he confirmed. Billie's eyes brightened. "Doctor Goodfellow is going to be pleased. It's a lot harder than you think to find good homes today."

"Oh, we can imagine," Mark said. "Have a seat, Bernard. Please."

"Thank you." He sat across from Justine and winked at her. She continued to scrutinize him. There was something vaguely familiar about him. As if she were turning the pages of a photo album, she reviewed the faces of people she knew, for she had the distinct feeling this man was somehow involved with her real mommy and daddy. Was he one of their friends? One of Daddy's customers?

Thinking about cars brought back an image—she was in the backseat of a big car and there was that horrible woman and . . . yes . . . this was the man who was sitting in the front. She felt sure and that certainty made her stomach feel as if she had just swallowed an ice cube. The chill exploded down her legs and made her shudder, but no one noticed, no one but Bernard perhaps, for his eyes narrowed and his smile turned cold.

"Doctor Goodfellow didn't mention any follow-up taking place so soon," Mark said after he had sat down. Billie poured the coffee.

"Well . . ." Bernard began and then looked up at Billie. "It's our way to drop in unannounced. Doctor Goodfellow feels we'll get a much more accurate picture of things. Not that we mean to spy on you from here on in, mind you," he added quickly. Billie nodded, happy to hear that. "We've just found that spontaneity produces the most reliable results. But once you're over the initial period, visits by me or anyone else become very infrequent. Unless there is a problem, of course.

"But," he continued, looking around the nook as if its neatness and cleanliness were proof enough, "it's clear that's not the case here. Nor will it be," he added, his voice deepening with just the hint of an ominous tone.

"We couldn't be happier," Mark said. He leaned forward. "I have to admit that when the proposition was first made to us in that clandestine manner, we hesitated. We're not the sort who like to do anything underhanded. Hell," he added with a smile, "I don't even cheat on my income taxes."

Bernard laughed and sipped his coffee. Billie began scrambling the eggs.

"But when it was explained to us . . . how unfortunate things were for a little girl like Justine and how we could change it for her practically over night . . ."

"Exactly," Bernard said. "Sometimes, people who have the power and the skills have to take action and bypass the bureaucratic system. The arteries of our government are clogged with the cholesterol of inefficiency. Oh, sorry," he said. "I don't mean to preach. It's just that I can get carried away whenever I espouse the benefits of our organization."

"We understand," Mark said. He looked at Billie, who nodded.

"How do you like your eggs?" Billie asked.

"Oh, practically raw, Mrs. Madison."

Billie nodded and then dumped the batter into the pan. As

she watched it take form, out of the corner of her eye, she noticed Justine's body had begun to tremble. She turned with surprise. Tears had begun to trickle down her cheeks, but she didn't utter a sound.

"Mark," Billie said softly, but with a distinct tone of anxiety. Mark Madison, still holding a smile, looked up at his wife. He saw how she was clutching her hands.

"Billie? What's the matter, honey?"

"Justine," she said and he turned. Justine's shoulders began to shake.

"What is it, Princess?" Mark said rising. "What's wrong?"

Justine's response was to cry harder. Mark scooped her out of the chair and held her in his arms.

"What's wrong with her?" Billie cried.

"Justine, honey. What's wrong? You can tell us. Come on, honey. Don't be afraid. Do you have a pain someplace?" Justine shook her head, glancing quickly at Bernard who was leaning over the table now and gaping up at her, his arms and hands completely hidden. "Then what is it, honey?"

"Justine?" Billie said, touching her arm. "Something frighten you?"

Justine nodded.

"What, honey? What's making you afraid?" Mark asked. Justine hesitated and then looked at Bernard. "Mr. Lyle? He's frightening you?" Justine nodded. "Oh, you shouldn't be afraid of Mr. Lyle. He's a nice man who just came here to see that you're okay." Justine remained skeptical, her tears continuing to flow freely, her body still trembling.

"Why is she afraid of you, Mr. Lyle?" Billie asked. Bernard smiled.

"I think," he said nodding softly, "that she remembers me. Is that it, Justine? You remember me?"

Justine nodded.

"I don't understand," Billie said. "Remembers you from where? Doctor Goodfellow's house?"

"No. She remembers me from her own house and the car ride, don't you, Justine?" Bernard asked. His tone of voice was still quite soft, pleasant. Justine had no compunction about replying truthfully and no reason to think she should lie. She nodded again.

"What does that mean, Bernard?" Mark asked with more concern. "Her house? Why would she remember you from her house?"

"We had to go get her," Bernard explained.

"Go get her? But I thought . . ." Mark looked at Billie. Her hands were pressed against her bosom, her face crimson with fear. "We thought . . . her parents were dead and she was in a temporary home."

"They are dead, in a sense," Bernard said.

"In a sense? Now wait a minute," Mark said. He lowered Justine to the floor. Instantly, she turned and ran out of the room.

"Justine!" Billie cried.

"Let her go," Bernard said.

"What?" Mark said.

The eggs began to sizzle in the pan.

"There's no point in her being here for this," Bernard said and brought his hand up from under the table. Clutched in it was his 357 Magnum.

"What the hell is this?" Mark demanded. He put his arm around Billie, who gasped and brought her small right fist to her mouth.

"Mop up," Bernard replied. He stood up.

"You're not from Doctor Goodfellow, are you?"

"I came from Doctor Goodfellow's house," Bernard said, "but Doctor Goodfellow didn't send me."

"Who the hell are you? What do you want?"

"I'm rapidly becoming an executive type," Bernard explained. "And I told you, I want to mop up."

"Mop up? What is that supposed to mean? What do you want?" Mark demanded more forcefully.

"Let go of her and turn around," Bernard ordered. "Do it quickly," he said, raising the pistol and pointing it at Billie.

"Jesus."

Billie started to cry.

"Do it!" Bernard ordered. He pulled back the hammer on the pistol and the click reverberated like thunder in Mark's ears. Reluctantly, he released Billie and turned around.

"Face the wall. Go on, put your nose up against that wall and be quick about it."

"What is this?" Mark asked. "Why are you doing this?"

"Against the wall," Bernard ordered and jabbed him in the back. Mark moved forward. Billie, clutching herself, was sobbing as quietly as she could. Bernard stepped back and poked her in the shoulder. She gasped.

"Don't hurt her," Mark cried and turned around.

"Against that wall or you'll see her brains splattered," Bernard threatened and brought the barrel of the gun to Billie's head. She closed her eyes and bit down on her lip. Mark swallowed and then turned around again. Bernard lifted Billie's chin and held it firmly between his stubby thumb and forefinger so she would be unable to turn away.

"Take that bread knife out of the holder there," he ordered and nodded toward the dark oak knife caddie that held bread knives, fruit knives, and steak knives. Gingerly, she lifted the bread knife. As soon as she had, Bernard Lyle placed his right hand over hers and squeezed hard, clamping her fingers around the knife handle firmly. Then he shoved her toward Mark and, before Mark could react, jerked her hand forward, driving the knife into Mark's side, slicing up effectively while pressing the blade deeply.

Billie screamed and Mark screamed and started to turn. Blood spurted over Billie's hand and wrist, as well as Bernard's. She tried to pull back, but Bernard's hold was unbreakable and his body was pressed firmly against hers, preventing any sort of retreat.

Mark finally pulled forward and spun around, but Bernard, still holding his hand around Billie's, drove the knife into his stomach. This time, he released his hold and permitted Billie to fall back. She fell to her knees, sobbing, hysterical. Mark clutched the knife in his stomach, looked up at Bernard, and then sunk to his knees. His eyelids fluttered and then he fell back on his right side. Like a fish out of water, his mouth opened and closed without producing any sound and then stopped. His eyes remained opened, glaring up, locked in position by death.

Billie screamed and screamed until Bernard clutched her face in his big hand and muffled her. He leaned over her, forcing her to bend toward the floor and gaze closely at Mark's corpse.

"You're a murderer, Mrs. Madison. You've killed your husband," Bernard said. "How can you live with yourself after doing something like this?" He slid his hand down her arm and over her hand again. Then he dropped his left arm around her waist and lifted her enough to drag her right beside Mark's body. "Look at what you've done," he said.

Billie shook her head and started to scream again. Her eyes went back in her head and, suddenly, she fainted.

"Well," Bernard said. "How cooperative. Do it cleanly, I was told, and here you are helping. Everyone helps. It's so nice."

He took Billie's right hand, his hand over it, and squeezed the fingers closed over the handle of the bread knife once more.

Then he tugged it out of Mark's body. Dripping blood, the knife hovered for a moment between Billie and Mark.

"So looking at what you've done, you've decided you can't live with yourself anymore," Bernard recited and turned her wrist until the knife pointed at her own heart. Then, fixing his grip securely, he shoved it forward, again with a professional expertise, and sliced into her heart.

"I DON'T UNDERSTAND why you didn't act sooner," Scott said angrily. He and Faye Elliot sat in the rear of the police car. After Foto had seen to Michael Fein, and they had grabbed some coffee and buns, they drove out of Barstow and headed east on Route 40.

"We weren't sure how involved you were with the Solomon Organization, Mr. Lester. Despite what was happening to you, you didn't come forward with any information about it. My partner here," Lt. Parker said, nodding toward Foto, "was convinced you weren't going to ever say anything about it. He thought you were just going to come up with some defense or you had been promised a fix in court by these people. We've seen it happen before. Your wife would be out of the way and you would retrieve your daughter and live happily ever after."

"But your wife survived the attack," Foto said.

"Which complicated things. We assumed you were caught between a rock and a hard place and you were expecting the organization to get you off the hook."

"Initially, you did go to them for help, didn't you?" Foto demanded.

"I got sucked in, yes, but I never intended any physical harm to Meg. I know how stupid I sound," he said, glancing at Faye Elliot, "but . . . I guess I was doing a lot of stupid things then."

"You guess right," Foto said.

"So you've been investigating this clandestine organization for a while?" Faye asked.

"Yes, but they've been very sharp, very good, very efficient, and they do have friends in high places. This was our first opportunity to cash in on mistakes, so we kept a close eye on Mr. Lester and after you guys hired Henry Dyce, we went to see him and . . . if you'll pardon my corniness . . . made him an offer he couldn't refuse."

"Dyce was working with you?" Scott asked incredulously.

"Who do you think his so-called friends in important places were? We filled him in on the alarm system at Beezly Enterprises. He called in his information to us just before he was killed," Foto said.

"We were set to take action when we received the call about Jerome Beezly," Parker added. "A preliminary investigation led us to suspect you might have done it. You were running around like a loose cannon at this point. You hadn't returned to your apartment. We thought you might screw up the investigation."

"Why did you call Michael Fein if you were looking for him? Why didn't you call me?" Faye asked.

Foto turned around.

"To be truthful, Miss Elliot, we weren't sure you weren't part of this operation."

"But why call Fein?"

"We didn't. His own people did and led him to believe Scott committed the murder. The truth about what was done was on a need-to-know basis, I guess, and Michael Fein wasn't as high up in the organization as he assumed. He still doesn't believe the organization killed Beezly and tried to erase all the evidence in Goodfellow's office. But in their sick minds, everyone's replaceable and everyone outlives his use, I suppose," Foto said.

"Anyway, we left the A.P.B. on Scott in L.A. and headed out to Barstow. We almost got here too late," Parker said.

"What do you mean, almost? Weren't you here after the fire had gotten underway?" Scott asked.

"Yes. And after the killer shot the old lady. Apparently, he didn't shoot Goodfellow. He left him for dead, and out of some devotion to his work or whatever he rescued some of the files and nearly made it out of the house."

"The smoke got him and he died near the rear door. His body was found over the files, some of which was still legible," Foto said.

"And either out of pure luck or his desire to keep track of your daughter, her file was one of them," Parker explained. "And that's how we know where she is."

"Thank God," Scott said.

"Yeah, maybe," Foto said nodding. "Who's to say why you have a guardian angel watching over you and your family right now?"

Scott nodded and buried his face in his hands for a moment. He thought about Meg and how small and fragile she looked in that hospital bed. He remembered how beautiful she looked in a different hospital bed at a different time—Justine's birth, and how happy they had been then. It seemed we live more than one life, he thought. One life dies or we destroy it and another starts. And no matter how much you wanted to go back, you couldn't. It was all . . . all a downward motion, a descent into the grave.

He didn't deserve a guardian angel, but maybe the angel wasn't there for him; maybe the angel was there for Justine and Meg only.

"How much longer?" he asked.

"Not much. Relax. There's nothing left to do but collect her and take her home," Parker said.

Scott sat back. Faye Elliot put her hand on his and smiled.

"Just think about holding her in your arms and bringing her back to your wife."

"And then crawling away," Foto said. He shoved a piece of

gum into his mouth. Forgiveness wasn't a part of the job. He left that for social workers and bleeding hearts.

Scott swallowed hard. He had no grounds on which to build a defense. Foto was right. Afterward, he would crawl away.

BERNARD LYLE STOOD UP and surveyed his work. Mark Madison lay on his back and Billie lay on her stomach, her torso over her husband's legs. He didn't like the way her rear end jutted up, so he pulled her legs out and brushed down her skirt. He thought a moment and then placed her right arm over his legs and turned her hand in so that it looked like she was trying to embrace him.

"Like Romeo and Juliet," Bernard muttered. In his distorted mind, where thoughts were twisted and tangled like so much loose wire, he felt a sense of pride in what lay before him. It was artistic; he had sculptured his own version of death and imbued it with his own particular sense of drama. He wished he had brought along a camera so he could record it and paste it in an album entitled, THE WORKS OF BERNARD LYLE.

After another moment, he sighed and then remembered the job was only half completed.

"Justine," he called. "Where are you, sweetheart?"

The puppy had either fled or followed Justine out of the kitchen and down the corridor toward her room. Bernard Lyle saw it sniffing the carpeting. It paused and then spread its legs to tinkle.

"Now look at that," Bernard muttered. "Why anyone would want an animal is beyond me. Go on with you," he snapped and kicked the dog out of his way. It yelped and hurried down the hallway to the safety of another room. Bernard turned into Justine's room and gazed around. She wasn't in sight.

"Justine?" He smiled and knelt down to look under the bed, but she wasn't there either. "Come on, sweetheart. We have to go. I can't leave you here. I'm taking you home. You'd like that, wouldn't you?" He stood up, and with his hands on his hips, gazed at the bed and dresser and then focused on the closet. The door was slightly ajar and through the crack, he could see the child sitting under her hanging garments. He smiled.

"I wonder where Justine's gone," he said. "If she doesn't come out soon, I'm going to have to leave without her and she won't see her real mommy and daddy ever again."

He waited. The child didn't move, didn't make a sound. It brought a chuckle to his lips. Then he grew serious and considered the best way to go about this. The child's body certainly couldn't be left here. The operative word was cleanly, and that was the way he intended to complete the job: cleanly. Fortunately, he always came prepared. That's why he was so good at his work; that's why he was appreciated, and that was why he would be promoted and rewarded handsomely.

She wasn't going anywhere, he thought and walked out of the room, through the kitchen, whistling as he passed the bodies and went to a door that he imagined opened to the garage. He imagined correctly. Just inside the door was the button to lift the garage door. He pressed it and watched it go up. Then he went out the garage to open the trunk of his car to get the body bag in which to put Justine's corpse.

Back in her room, Justine heard Little Bit whimper. She had heard the bad man kick the puppy, but she had been too terrified to rescue her dog. Now that the man had left, she thought she could do something. She opened the closet door wider, saw he was completely gone, and hurried out to get Little Bit. She found the puppy sitting and whimpering in the hallway. After she lifted the dog into her arms, she gazed through the kitchen entrance and saw her new mommy and daddy sprawled on the floor.

What were they doing? she wondered and inched forward.

It took just one glance at Billie's face, her eyes closed, but her mouth twisted and ugly, to send the coldest chill through her small body. It was as if she had fallen into a puddle of ice water. Almost too numb to move, she backed up a few inches. Then she heard the door to the garage open. Without hesitation, she spun around and ran through the house, toward the rear door. Still clutching Little Bit, she opened the door and slipped out as quickly and as quietly as she could. She skipped down the small steps and ran frantically into the back yard. Then she stopped and spun around, wondering where to go, where to hide.

Her eyes settled on Little Bit's dog house. She glanced behind herself once and saw that the bad man had not come after her yet. She ran to the house, and, holding her puppy as closely to her chest as she could, crept through the opening and folded her body as tightly as possible within the small confines. It was uncomfortable and she felt horrid spider webs over her neck and arms, but she swallowed down her fear and drowned her screams deep inside herself.

There, in the dog house, she waited, afraid that the sound of her own breathing would give her away. She held her breath for as long as she could and then had to gasp for air. Little Bit struggled to get more motion, but she kept the puppy tightly against her body. It whimpered and even yelped once before she clamped its mouth shut and pleaded with it, whispering and begging the dog to understand the danger they were in. Its eyes widened as it struggled against such restraint. Finally, Justine was forced to put it down and just keep it from leaving the safety of the dog house. For the moment it seemed contented and for the moment, she felt safe.

LT. PARKER SLOWED DOWN and pulled up to the corner where two elderly gentlemen were having a conversation. They both turned with interest.

"Excuse us," Parker said. "We're looking for Western Avenue."

"What number?" the taller of the two asked. Parker checked his notes.

"1240 South Western."

The two gazed at each other for a moment.

"The numbers go that high on Western?" the shorter man asked the taller. He shrugged.

"Those numbers make no sense. I don't know who the hell decides on street numbers. My number's 213 and the house directly across from me is 276."

Parker laughed.

"Maybe the post office decides," he suggested. The two senior citizens liked that.

"That's why it takes as long as it took the Pony Express to get my mail anywhere," the taller man said.

"He looks like he might really remember the Pony Express," Foto quipped. Parker nodded.

"Anyway, Western Ave?"

"Western . . . Western . . . you go up three blocks to the hardware store on the corner and make a left."

"A right," the shorter man corrected. "He said South Western. Didn't you?"

"Yes, I did."

"Well, then that's a right."

"So it's a right," the taller man said. "Western's still three blocks up."

"Thanks," Parker said. He pulled away. "I wonder if we'll be like that when we're their age."

"Who says we'll be their age? Neither looked a day under ninety," Foto remarked. Parker made the right turn and they headed south on Western. The numbers jumped quickly and, then suddenly, there were no houses for almost a quarter of a mile. When the next house appeared, it was 1100 South Western.

"Getting close, I suppose," Parker said.

Scott's stomach churned nervously. How would Justine greet him? Would she be angry? Did she blame him for all that happened? Deep in his heart he felt that somehow the child would sense he was at fault, the child would understand that his behavior had brought all this misery to the family and she would resent him, maybe even hate him. How devastating it would be to have come all this way, go through all this, only to have his own daughter glare wrathfully at him. The first words out of her mouth were sure to be, "I want Mommy."

Well, he couldn't blame her.

Faye Elliot sensed his anxiety. She took his hand into hers and squeezed it reassuringly.

"It's going to be all right," she promised. "It will be all over soon."

He nodded, but he felt as if somehow his stomach had been removed and in its place had been inserted a vacuum cleaner, the hose of which was directed at his heart. It sucked every beat down into his guts.

"That's it," Foto announced.

A whip of fire lashed across Scott's chest and he leaned forward to look at the house.

"Looks like someone's preparing to go somewhere or is bringing something inside," Parker said, seeing Bernard Lyle's car backed in with the trunk open.

"Unloading groceries, I bet," Foto said. Parker nodded and they turned into the driveway.

"Now just stay calm, Mr. Lester," Parker advised. "Foto and I will do all the talking. We're not sure about these people and there still might be some danger. Keep back, understand?"

Scott nodded.

"Here we go," Foto said and opened his door. Scott, Faye, and Lt. Parker did the same and everyone stepped out.

"Finally, the end of a nightmare," Scott muttered as Faye came up beside him. She smiled.

"Front door?" Lt Parker asked.

"Let's go through the garage. Can't hurt to have a little surprise on our side," Foto replied. Parker liked it and nodded. Then the four started toward the open garage door.

INSIDE THE HOUSE, Bernard Lyle was fuming. The child had been smart enough to leave her room. She could be anywhere in the house, hiding. It would take him longer than he intended and he hated it when something interfered with or in anyway complicated his plans. With the body bag folded under his arm, he turned to leave Justine's room, but instead, through the window, caught a glimpse of the puppy waddling out the door of the dog house and Justine reaching out quickly to pull him back in.

Bernard laughed.

"Kids," he muttered.

He quickly found the rear door and went out, the body bag still under his arm.

Inside the garage, Lt. Parker rapped on the door. There was no response so he rapped again, harder. Again, there was no response. Foto slipped his pistol out of its holster and then they turned to Scott and Faye.

"Stay back," Lt. Parker ordered. Faye and Scott retreated a few steps. Then Lt. Parker nodded at Foto and he opened the door. Scott and Faye watched them charge in, guns drawn. There were no sounds, no gunshots, no words. Scott and Faye took a few steps closer to the door, but Lt. Parker stepped in the doorway and gazed back.

"Stay right here," he commanded. "Don't move, don't make a sound."

"Wha . . ."

"Not a sound," Lt. Parker repeated and went back into the house.

BERNARD LYLE STROLLED casually to the dog house. Memories of his own childhood returned. He had been brought up in a semi-rural region, not so unlike this one. He remembered when his next door neighbor, Howard Taylor, had his cousin visiting from Philadelphia. His cousin was a few years older than they were, but not too old to play with cap guns. They staged a cowboys and Indians scenario in which Howard's dog, Homer, had been harnessed with a clothesline and tied to the front of its dog house. Then he and Howard straddled the dog house and pretended it was a wagon and Homer was a horse. Howard's cousin was the Indian laying in ambush.

Howard's cousin sent a rubber arrow their way and they began firing their cap guns. Homer, excited by the noise, began to bark. Bernard grabbed the thin branch Howard had as a make-believe whip and began smacking Homer on the back until the dog's barking turned into yelps and Howard's mother came running out of the house to chastise them for torturing the poor animal. He recalled feeling like turning the whip on her.

Those memories put him into a playful mood, however, and he straddled the dog house as if he were straddling a horse.

"Giddy up," he cried.

Inside, Justine had fallen into the deepest pit of terror imaginable. Why would a grown man, an adult, crawl onto the dog house and make these sounds? Her little heart pounded and she began to sob. Above her and behind her, Bernard Lyle began to kick and pound on the dog house. Each rap sent a clap of thunder through her body and she began to scream. She lost her hold on Little Bit and the puppy charged out of the house, terrified itself. She reached after it too late and recoiled in horror. Its small, warm body had given her some comfort and now that was gone, too. Bernard Lyle pounded harder. It sounded as if he were coming through the sides of the dog house.

Above it, Bernard moved forward the moment he saw the puppy emerge. He reached inside his coat pocket and brought out the old-fashioned, straight-edge razor in a pearl handle. It was an antique; it had been his father's, but Bernard had kept it in good shape, shiny and sharp. The blade unfolded swiftly. He put the body bag aside and positioned himself so he was leaning over the front. Then he kicked and kicked at the sides of the dog house. Finally, Justine's head appeared. He let her get just far enough out so he could get a good grasp on her hair, and then he reached down, grasped a handful of strands at the top and front and tugged upward. Her sweet little neck was fully exposed. She screamed and he started to bring the razor down to make one swift slice when the bullet crashed into his right temple.

For a moment he did look like a rodeo cowboy straddled on a bucking bronco. His body jerked back and forward, he released his hold on Justine and his arms flailed wildly. Then he fell forward and to the side as if thrown from his wild horse. Justine, freed, crawled ahead, scampering quickly away from the dog house. She paused when she saw Foto at the back door rise slowly from a crouched position from which he had taken aim.

She turned to look back and saw the bad man all twisted and scrunched beside the dog house, a line of blood streaming down his cheek. She seemed out of sound. Nothing came when she opened and closed her mouth, but she was sure she was screaming. Her whole body shook with the effort, yet her ears heard nothing. The man with the gun was moving very, very slowly toward her and another man with a gun emerged from behind him, also moving in slow motion.

Then, like a miracle, like the dollar that was under her pillow the morning after she had lost her first tooth, like "The World of Disney" magic on television, her daddy appeared. His body filled the back door of the house. She lifted her body from the grass and at last, when she screamed, she heard her own voice.

"Daddy!"

It seemed he could fly, for that was how fast he had her in his arms and held her to him. That was how fast his lips were smothering her with kisses and that was how fast she felt safe and warm again. He held her so tightly she could hardly move, but she didn't complain. She didn't want him to ever let go and she didn't want him to stop kissing her, either.

"Take her to the car," Lt. Parker ordered. "Don't go through the house. Go around the side there."

Scott nodded and started away, but Justine turned in his arms and reached out for the little black and white puppy that squatted fearfully in the grass.

"Little Bit," she cried. Faye Elliot came around quickly and picked up the dog. She brought him to Justine, who immediately embraced him. Then Scott continued to carry them both away.

Afterward, he would say he couldn't feel his legs. He felt he was floating. In a true sense, he had lost contact with his body and with everything that surrounded him. He didn't remember much about the return trip either, except for when they stopped to feed Justine.

In Barstow, they got into Faye Elliot's car and then drove back to Los Angeles. Late in the afternoon, they pulled into the parking lot at the hospital. Scott had done his best to explain why Meg was there and had tried to prepare Justine for the sight of her mother in a hospital bed with all the equipment, I.V. tubes, etc. around her. He assured her Meg would soon be better and be home with her. But the child had gone from one terrifying experience to another. This one, because it promised her mother would be part of it, seemed the most manageable.

Justine saw her Aunt Abby waiting in the corridor outside the ICU. She broke down in tears at the sight of Justine and hugged her dearly until Scott tapped her gently on the shoulder and nodded toward the door of the ICU. Abby rose and took Justine's hand.

"Abby," Scott said softly. "I'd like to be the one who takes her in. Please."

His sister-in-law nodded and wiped away her tears. Then she released Justine's hand. Scott took it into his and walked his daughter in to see her mother.

If he had ever felt guilty before, if he had ever felt remorse, it was nothing compared to what he felt when Justine was once again in Meg's arms. Tears of joy were no lighter than tears of pain. All of the nurses stopped their work and watched, their eyes as wet.

"My baby, my baby," Meg chanted. Scott waited, his head down. When he lifted his eyes, he saw Meg had closed hers. He knew she was thanking God for answering her prayers. She opened her eyes and looked at him and then at Justine, who clung to her desperately.

"She's been through hell and back," Scott said. "But she's okay physically."

"Thank God," Meg said.

"Abby's going to look after her until you're well enough," he said. "I've got to go back and talk to the police and get as much of that straightened out as I can."

Meg nodded.

"It doesn't do any good to keep saying I'm sorry. In fact, it sounds stupid after a while," he said.

"Not to me," she replied. He smiled.

"Thanks. Well, I'll . . . I'll stop by every day just in case there's something I can do for you. I wish . . ." He choked on his words.

"It's going to take time, Scott," Meg said. "There's a lot of healing to be done." He nodded. "Afterward, let's see if we can understand why and where it went wrong."

He smiled through his tears.

"All right." He started to turn away.

"Where are you going, Daddy?" Justine cried.

"Not far," he said. "I won't be far away from you again. That's a promise."

Justine smiled.

"Mommy," she said excitedly. "I've got a puppy and his name's Little Bit."

"Really?" Meg looked at Scott.

"We brought another victim home with us."

Meg laughed. To Scott it was the most beautiful sound he had ever heard. He took a deep breath and walked out of the ICU. His steps grew stronger and more determined as his slumping shoulders rose.

He felt reborn.

# Epilogue

Sam Williams had his head down so long he looked like he had fallen asleep. The truth was he couldn't stand watching and listening to the way his wife's attorney described him and promised to substantiate every claim, every damning fact. His own attorney looked bored, distracted, and certainly not very involved.

Whenever Sam did lift his head and then gaze at his wife across the way, he found her glaring at him with such hate and loathing, he couldn't look at her long. He felt like he had withered in his seat anyway. The things his wife's attorney were saying about him shrunk him. How he wished the man was talking about someone else, for he would condemn such a man himself if he had heard these allegations.

"That's a lie," he muttered once, but his attorney shook his head and indicated he should keep himself contained and quiet. Contained and quiet? How do you do that? he wanted to ask. It's easy for you to say keep your mouth shut. He ain't talking about you; he's talking about me.

They weren't just going to win custody of the children; they were going to destroy him, ruin his reputation and make it impossible for him to keep his job, the respect of his friends, and certainly the esteem of his superiors.

"This is a lynching," he groaned. His wife's attorney had solicited the testimony of psychologists; he had dug up people from the past whom Sam had forgotten; he had acquired Sam's medical records. His bouts with alcohol would be exposed, all his indiscretions would be openly paraded. He felt like a man who had lost his pants and was wearing underwear with holes in it. There wasn't anything thought sacred, nothing too private.

His wife's attorney completed his remarks and sat down. Why was it her attorney looked more involved, more determined, and more dedicated to her position than his attorney looked dedicated to his position? His attorney wasn't some cut-rate hack; he had been recommended as one of the top divorce attorneys in Manhattan. The lawyers would drain them both before this was over, but his wife would come out on top. He felt it in his heart and it made him sink in his seat, shrivel in his clothes, and sweat profusely.

"What? What's happening?" Sam asked quickly when he heard the judge's gavel.

"We're taking a recess. Lunch," his lawyer responded. "I gotta go make some phone calls," he added and got up quickly to hurry away.

"Huh?" Sam looked about stupidly. His wife looked so cheerful, actually invigorated by all this. Was he going mad?

He rose from his seat slowly; the effort seeming to take all his strength. He looked after his attorney disdainfully.

Lunch, he thought. His lawyer could eat, but how could he eat? He had been eating his heart out all morning. He turned anyway and started up the aisle, not noticing the handsome gentleman step out in his path until he was practically on top of him.

"Oh, sorry," Sam said stepping back.

"Not at all. I was waiting to talk to you."

Sam looked up at the nearly six-feet-tall, distinguished-looking man in a dark blue pin-striped suit. His gray eyes sparkled.

"Oh?"

"I was passing through the courthouse and just had to stop in to see another poor fish get gutted."

"That's it; that's the way I feel exactly." Sam said, nodding and then realized all he had said. "What'dya mean, another? You here for a divorce, too?"

"I was, and like you, I was crucified on a cross of exaggerations, accusations constructed by my wife's skillful and, I must confess, very talented attorney."

"Tell me about it," Sam said.

"The women always get the better lawyers because everything's weighted on their side and the lawyers would rather back winners. Makes them look better."

"I bet." Sam nodded again. The guy made sense.

"One hand feeds the other. You look like you could use a drink. Care to join me for a cocktail and some lunch? I know a great little Italian place just a block from the courthouse."

"Don't mind if I do," Sam said. It was the first time all morning that he felt any enthusiasm for anything, but this man seemed very sharp and very clever, as well as very sympathetic to his position. "I'm Sam Williams," he said extending his hand.

"Philip Dante," the distinguished gentleman said. "Pleased to meet you, Sam. Relax," Dante added, putting his arm around him. "Things aren't as bad as they seem."

"Oh, no?"

"No," Dante said and smiled with such confidence and self-assurance, Sam Williams had to question his own despondency.

Maybe there was some hope after all.